A Country Called Home

A Country Called Home

KIM BARNES

ALFRED A. KNOPF NEW YORK 2008

THIS IS A BORZOI BOOK
PUBLISHED BY ALFRED A. KNOPF

Published in the United States by Alfred A. Knopf,
a division of Random House, Inc., New York, and in Canada by
Random House of Canada Limited, Toronto.

www.aaknopf.com

Library of Congress Cataloging-in-Publication Data
Barnes, Kim.
A country called home : a novel / by Kim Barnes.—1st ed.
p. cm.
ISBN 978-0-307-26895-2
1. Married people—Fiction. 2. Country life—Fiction.
3. Idaho—Fiction. I. Title.
PS3552.A6815C68 2008
813'.54—dc22 20080022200

Manufactured in the United States of America
First edition

for my father—
believer in dreams—
your vision yet guides me

If a man could pass through Paradise in a dream, and have a flower presented to him as a pledge that his soul had really been there, and if he found that flower in his hand when he awake—Aye, what then?

—SAMUEL TAYLOR COLERIDGE

A Country Called Home

Prologue

1977

First, the river.

Mountain wash of snowmelt through granite, past fir, larch, red cedar, and pine. The canyon where the water widens, runs deeper, eddies in against rimrock, gullets the bank's soft pallet.

And then the car, sun-bit to ruddy red, following the highway that parallels the river, matching it curve for curve.

Late morning. The rain is nearly done, already a remembered thing. Swallows rest in their cool fists of mud. Trout do not rise but hold in the submerged roots of cottonwood. Rattlesnakes thick with summer vole find fissures in stone, stretch themselves thin.

The farmers have taken to their houses to nap. Or they sit at the tables of their wives, drinking iced tea, creamed coffee, thinking their silence nothing more than what is wise, their women, wind-scalded, planning cold cuts for dinner. Stock lean into shadow, ear flick of fly, twitch of hide and tail. All nearly motionless except the river and the car beside it, one channeling west toward the ocean, the other marking east.

The driver is young, clean of face, frankly beautiful. Her mouth is simple, contained, her eyes noticeably gray. Chestnut hair, layers of lighter gold and darker brown, long lengths of it rising and falling in the wind coming in through the window.

The steering wheel is loose in her hands. Fingers gently curled, wrists relaxed. When she guides the car left, she leans her head left. When the road swings right, she moves with it, as though to a slow music.

A simple cotton skirt, a quiet floral print. Hem hiked to mid-thigh. Her ankles are swollen. The heat.

The air wings in, the feel of it at the hollow of her throat, lifting the fine hairs at her neck, along her legs, mineral and silt, musky alder.

The old dog rises to a sit, rests its muzzle on her arm, eyes clouded white, the silver of its ruff faded gray.

There are no cars ahead, none behind. Still, she remembers to signal left at the one-lane bridge condemned by the county, seldom used except by the locals, who, as they always have, weigh risk against utility. Wooden planks clack and rattle beneath her. Right at the crossroad, then up and over Angel Ridge.

Miles of river below her now, edged by fields of mown wheat, floodplains of stubbled alfalfa. She stops at the first side road leading back down the canyon face, considers, drives on.

The skin of her legs is blushed with sun. Sweat beneath her breasts, in the bends of her arms. She spreads her knees, brings them together again, feels the moisture there.

The second dirt road she forgoes, and then the third. At the fourth, she shifts into low, descends into the shelter of locust. A few months earlier, the grove would have been heady with sugar blossom, a vast black drone of foraging bees. She feels a small regret: perhaps she should have come sooner. Still, there is the comfort, the respite from sharp light.

The road narrows to a rutted path. The car's undercarriage

catches dirt, then granite. She holds the wheel harder, hears the scree of metal against stone, the clatter of something torn loose. The dog tries to stand, to balance itself, but falls forward against the dash.

The canopy grows dense with sumac, cottonwood, vine maple, the air through the window damp, like the inside of a cave, walls seeping. Birds flit and trill from their cover. A grouse beats up; quail sally from behind a mossy stump, take wing, disappear into a tangle of wild rose. Somewhere just ahead is the railroad track running its spine of land, and then the river. Before her, an ancient bramble of blackberry, the small, bitter fruit still pale, no sun to ripen.

She noses forward against the shriek of canes raking the doors. The car groans and she pushes harder until the tires spin, the smell of sap and berry pulp mixing with the sweat of rubber. She presses in until the canes have bent and broken, let down their wounded limbs behind her, pushed up over the top. When the engine dies, she clicks off the key, imagines she hears the river, its constant thrum like the sound of sleep. She slides back the seat to give herself more room. It is easier to breathe, the jab of the steering wheel gone from her belly.

She'll have to walk to the river now. There is no other way. She pulls the handle, pushes the door open, but the vines hold tight. An inch of space, no more. She resists the urge to roll the glass shut against the bramble. She has seen how quickly the canes snake and grow. Like the kudzu her father once spoke of, how it wreathed the telephone poles, covered entire houses in a matter of days, alive with intent.

She leans across the seat, thumbs open the glove box, and finds her father's straight razor, mother-of-pearl, blade newly honed. It is the tool she has known all her life, seventeen years, memories of early mornings. She thinks she might cut her way out, but the blade only bleeds the vines. There is a flutter of movement in the cradle of her hips, a tightness low in her groin, like a fist squeezing from the inside, then letting go. An exhaustion so complete that she must let her head loll back against the seat. I need to rest, she thinks. And then I'll go to the river. The dog pants, whines, sniffs the breeze through the open window.

She closes her eyes, hears the sawbugs cutting the air, the whisper of branches, the ravens overhead. She is held in that pleasant lull between waking and dreams. She hears her father talking in the gray tones of a serious man, his voice growing faint as she drifts closer to sleep. He is bidding her back, insisting that she stay in this place he has made for her. This paradise.

She is cold. She wishes for her father's arms to lift her, to carry her to the house with its smells of cold bacon and laundry. To lay her in her bed, cup her head like a blessing. Like the moment of her birth, when he pulled her from her mother, that river of water and blood, and guided her into another world.

Part One

The fall from grace is endless.

—JOHN GARDNER

Chapter One

1960

The druggist waited, whistling, looking out the window, nodding to each person who passed along the Main Street of Fife. It was early, the bank not yet open. The warming September wind wafted through the door seams. On the north hill, he could see the sun just hitting the flat metal roof of the Clearwater Mental Hospital and, across the shared parking lot, the high school. Dr. K often joked that the children of Fife could look out their windows and see their future before them.

"How much?" Manny asked again. The boy was tall enough to meet the older man eye to eye, but he kept his gaze on the faded counter as though some miracle might transpire there.

"Same as last time."

The cola sat between them, dripping condensation. Manny laid out three pennies, pretended to search for more.

"Don't got it, do you?" The druggist was not an unfriendly

man but brusque and burly, built more like a butcher than a purveyor of medicine. Dr. K, the locals called him, his full name, Kalinosky, too much to mess with. His role in the town went beyond the filling of prescriptions and the dispensing of antiseptics: he diagnosed strep throat, checked children for lice, scoured the wounds caused by pitched rocks, chain saw slips, bicycle wrecks.

"No, sir." Manny freed his hands, let them drop to his sides. He peered at his shoes, the seams stretched and frayed.

Dr. K sighed, shook his head, pointed toward the door. "Broom's just outside. Make yourself useful for an hour."

Like others in Fife, Dr. K knew the details of Manny's life: his parents' move from California to the isolated Idaho land they believed a more honest place; the strange little canvas hut that inspired the town's curiosity and contempt. His father's insistence on learning the dying art of horse-logging from an old man who stank of sweat and juniper berries. Manny's birth just a few miles up Itsy Creek, and the death of his mother twelve years later when his little sister, born already dead, was followed by the blood they could not stop flowing. The father, once admired for his native ingenuity and his matched team of Percheron geldings, had headed south to find work and never came back. The good women of Fife had proceeded with a kind of communal adoption, passing the responsibility for Manny's care from one to the other, each week a different mother, father, cast of siblings, and then the cycle repeating. Dr. K remembered the morning he'd opened the drugstore to find Mrs. Keasling wringing her hands, repeating again and again that *der boy, der boy* was missing. Dr. K had found Manny where he thought he would, asleep in the fair barn, his father's auctioned draft horses snuffling his hair, placing their great hooves gently beside him.

Manny stepped outside with the broom, scattering the cats that had gathered for their morning meal. Too many toms, Dr. K thought. Too many litters, but he couldn't turn away a single one of them. He watched as Manny worked the windows clean of cobwebs, pleased with the care he took with the corners. Despite everything, or maybe because of it, he'd grown into a fine young man: tall and strong-shouldered, more handsome than he needed to be. Thick dark hair, dark eyes, skin like an Italian, Dr. K thought. He looked like he might be broody, but wasn't. When Manny ran the broom a final time along each crack of the sidewalk and knocked the bristles clean before stepping back into the store, Dr. K opened the cash register and pulled out a dollar bill.

"Here. Buy yourself some *real* food." Dr. K slipped the pencil behind his ear, wiped a hand the length of his face. "Listen. You need to get out there and do something. Ray Coon's logging outfit might need a swamper. Or what about the railroad? Didn't I hear that they were hiring?"

Manny shrugged. "Guess I'm okay."

"Okay? What's that mean? There's just no reason for you to be living like a hobo. It's one thing when you're a boy to be spending your days piddling around at the river, but you're about past that now. Pretty soon, if you're not doing nothing, you'll be good for nothing."

Manny nodded, agreeable as always. "You got more work you'd like me to do?"

Dr. K sat down on the high stool he kept for resting his feet. "Another few months, I might use you for delivery. Bad weather sets in, business picks up. Which reminds me—how many jars of VapoRub you see on the shelf?"

Manny counted three, one large, two small. The druggist grunted, made a note on a piece of paper. "Better order more. Those Carter kids *eat* that stuff. Mother thinks it does them more good from the inside."

Dr. K was tallying his laxative inventory when a man stepped in. Dress shirt and shoes, pants still holding a crease. Sharp nose and chin. Hair just past a good cut. Outside, a faded red Volkswagen sat at the curb, a young woman in the passenger seat, holding her hair away from her neck, fanning herself with a map.

Dr. K moved to rest his meaty palms on the counter. "Yes, sir. What can I help you with?"

"I'm looking for Bag Balm." The man's voice had a strange cadence.

"Bag Balm we got." Dr. K pointed around Manny. "Grab that green tin, Manny. Large size?"

The man nodded his head and pulled a money clip from his pocket.

Not many people came in who weren't known by the pharmacist in some intimate way. He'd sold the boys their first condoms, seen most of the town's women through menstruation, childbirth, and menopause. He prescribed headache cures and hangover remedies, administered narcotics to the suffering and sedation to those stricken by grief. If this new man had settled himself within the county, Dr. K would soon make him familiar; if he were only passing through, Dr. K would extract some anecdote to amuse or enlighten the next customer who came in.

Dr. K extended a thick hand. "Burt Kalinosky."

"Thomas Deracotte." The stranger shook quickly. He seemed less nervous than efficient. Knew his business and wanted to get on with it.

"Just traveling through, then?"

"We're here from Connecticut. My wife and I have purchased the Bateman place."

"Sure, I know the place. Knew Olie, too." Dr. K dealt out the man's change and followed him to the door. "Bateman place, huh? Last I heard, it'd gotten pretty lean."

The man took a moment to examine his shoes, looked out the window to Main Street before turning his attention back to the pharmacist. "You might let people know that we'll be looking for a few laborers. We'll be able to offer room and board, once our buildings are complete."

"Well, then," Dr. K said, "you should meet this young man. He could use some work."

"How old is he?"

"Manny? Hell, I'm not sure exactly. How old are you, Manny?"

Manny cleared his throat. "Near eighteen."

"He's got a good head on him. Only fault that I can see is that he'd rather fish than break a sweat. That and read books."

Deracotte's face relaxed. His eyes were stone gray, the color of river rock. "What are you reading these days?"

The boy flushed with the sudden attention. "*Great Gatsby,* sir."

Deracotte gave a slight nod of approval. "Are you a fan of Fitzgerald?"

"Guess I'm not sure yet."

The man smiled. "How about Monday morning to start? Do you have transportation?"

"Yes, sir."

"And you know the place?"

"Yes, sir."

"Good. I'll see you then."

Dr. K watched through the window as Deracotte ducked into the little car and said something to the woman, who nodded and laughed.

"You better be grateful. I might decide I want that job myself." He walked to the cash register, began counting change into the till.

"Bet he's that doctor we heard might be coming," Manny said.

Dr. K stopped counting his money long enough to gaze toward the door, process the possibility. "You think?"

"I do."

The druggist stacked the quarters, then the dimes, scratched numbers on the back of a receipt. "Wonder what that would mean." He touched the nickels, looked up at Manny blankly. "I can't remember how many goddamn five-cent pieces there are in a dollar."

"Twenty," Manny said.

"Yeah," Dr. K said. "Twenty." He let them drop back into the till one at a time. "Guess a doctor might mean more business. More prescriptions to fill."

"That's true."

"Injured wouldn't have to travel so far."

"You've always been good to come to."

Dr. K let his fingers rest in the drawer. "I think I saved your life once."

"You did. When I swallowed all the baby aspirin."

"Yeah, that's it." The druggist's eyes focused, took on more light. "You'd crawled up on the counter, got into Lily Wendle's medicine cabinet. Whole bottle. Ate them like candy."

"I remember you holding my head over the sink."

"Made you drink raw eggs and vinegar." The pharmacist snorted. "*Nothing* stayed down. Taught you a lesson, too." He rolled the bank bag snug. "Think you can work for that man?"

"Guess I might see." Manny pulled his pants higher. "Think I'll be going."

Dr. K nodded and turned to his shelves of pills and syrups. "Thought that rickety-ass salesman was supposed to drag in here today. I'm about out of thyroid."

He waited for the door to open and close before sitting back down on his stool and pulling out the pack of cigarettes he carried in his breast pocket. The smoke would help take his mind off of the truth laid out before him: a month's worth of bills and not enough money to pay.

He tapped the ash of his cigarette and considered the man who'd come in for Bag Balm. Myrta, the city clerk, had chippered away at anyone who would listen about the call she'd gotten from some man wanting to know about farm property for sale. "Sight unseen," she said. "Didn't even care to look at the place." Buying without first walking the lay, weighing the dirt in your hand, seeing with your own eyes the well and tasting the water—beyond comprehension to anyone who made his living off the land. Dr. K couldn't imagine what a physician might want with the Bateman place, but sometimes these people coming in from outside had funny ideas, had to find out things for themselves. With enough money and a little luck, you could make about anything work.

He lifted the bank bag and weighed it in his hand. If the new doctor took away more than he gave, the store would be in trouble. It might have been enough for his father, who had tended the sick with next to nothing and still made something of himself, but lately Dr. K had been thinking less about his father's life and death and more about his widowed mother, who had moved to Kansas for reasons she couldn't explain, except that in all the years she'd lived in the river canyon she hadn't witnessed her share of sky. She was a ninety-year-old woman living two thousand miles away when she'd called him to say that her head hurt. The neighbor found her the next morning, dead of a massive stroke. Maybe he could have saved her, given her a few more years of life, had she stayed near. An aspirin, or a shot of whiskey at bedtime—sometimes it takes so little. What was left in Fife to keep him? His name on the glass and the need he felt to mend and minister to the townsfolk he'd known all his life.

He began to whistle to fill the silence. A few more hours and he could make his way up the stairs to his apartment and turn on the stereo. Maybe he'd choose Verdi, or maybe Puccini. *Madame Butterfly.* How many times had he listened to the death song of Cio-Cio-San and cried as though it were a new sadness just visited upon him? He'd have some whiskey, and then some dinner. Maybe some of the venison Lyle McNutt had traded for his wife's medicine. The druggist figured he'd eaten his own weight in deer roasts and sausage over the course of the year it had taken Tally McNutt to die. But it was good and tender and an easy trade for the drugs that erased some part of the woman's pain.

He'd have offered to feed Manny but the boy had always been shy of charity. Dr. K halfway envied such a life, unencumbered by anything more than the simplest of needs. Maybe working for Deracotte would change all that. A little money always begged for more. He hoped Manny would stop in, let him know how the job was going. Bring him a little news. Want another soda and stay long enough to drink it down.

"You're a lonely sack of shit," he said aloud and nodded because there was no arguing with someone as stubborn as he was.

Chapter Two

The air was cooler than Manny had expected. He'd need to split some wood before dark, maybe find another blanket. He tucked his hands into his pockets and headed south down Main Street. It had been some time since he'd made his way to the houses of families not his own. At first, both parents gone, he'd slept on sofas and floors, found himself in beds already crowded with boys who would never call him brother. He carried the smells of each family with him—the womanly perfumes, the odor of tobacco and turpentine, the oily residue of fried venison, the steamy evaporation of turnip stews. The musk of unwashed feet, of boys packed tight into windowless rooms, of older sisters trailing their mysterious incense from bathroom to bed. He wondered if the neighborhood dogs were confused when they snuffled his pant legs, or if in their way they still remembered the people to whom he'd once belonged.

At sixteen, he'd quit school, relieved when no one seemed surprised and folks left him be, and moved inside an abandoned shack—perhaps an old boathouse—nestled in a depression between the railroad tracks and the river. He caught fish and set noose traps for rabbit and grouse. He gathered blackberries from the draws and watercress from the mouths of springs. He worked odd jobs when he had to—mowed lawns, picked rocks from the fields, delivered groceries. He thought he might be a hermit, call himself Manny the Loner, let his already moppish hair grow longer still, be happy with his place at the water's edge and the few books he'd borrowed from the library and never returned.

But there were times when the boy in him got the better, and he yearned for a walk down Main Street, past the Jet Club with its neon spaceship blasting into a helix of five-point stars, the Blue Ox Café, a rough carving of Paul Bunyan guarding the door, just to see what dogs lay where and how much farther Baxter's fence had leaned into the alley. He craved chocolate malts, bubblegum, white cake. He hoped that Miss Richter, the young blond-haired librarian, wouldn't remember his trespass and would allow him another armload of novels that he could read through the night, the pages illuminated by one candle and then another, each lit off the other in succession, so that by morning, the melted wax had pooled, run down the sides of the apple crate that served as his nightstand, and spread to the floor. He believed that the smell of wick and wax, of wool and the dry paste of book spines, was the smell he might be known by.

As he walked, breathing in the sharp air, he thought of the Carter family and their taste for VapoRub. He'd been in line for a spoonful the winter every child in the household came down with the croup. He'd taken his medicine, felt it slide warm and slick into his belly. Later, he'd watched the youngest Carter boy, the one they called Happy, crawl from bed and find the jar, dip two fingers full, suck it down, then two more. Manny imagined he could see the boy's breath wafting out like heat ribbons off boiling tar. Three days later, Happy was dead, killed, they said, by a ruptured appendix. Manny still believed it was the VapoRub that had inflated the appendix like a balloon and that what they found when they cut the boy open was a gelatinous pool redolent of eucalyptus.

He followed the pavement until it gave way to rough dirt, to rock then sand then shallows, where dragonflies dimpled the pools. As he followed the narrowing path, winged insects rose like smoke around him, caught in the momentary current of his passing. They were the last of the season's hatch. He scooped a fat grasshopper from a blade of rye and felt it clutch at his finger. It would bring a trout to the surface—enough for dinner and maybe for breakfast too.

Work was probably good, he thought, but he was glad it wasn't yet Monday. He wanted a few more days of late summer and did not want to think about how many dollars he had in his pocket or what kind of jobber he might be. Just the sun revving up and the hopper in his hand. He sniffed his fist and smelled the sharp odor of tobacco. He always felt a little bad when the hook pierced the thorax and the bug grabbed on to the very thing that was killing it.

He cast to where the current rimmed against stone. The tug came on the first drift, and he hauled in a twelve-inch rainbow. He squatted and cleaned the fish at the water's edge, leaving the entrails to the crawdads, and fried the fish over a small campfire. He ate, throwing the bones to the shallows, scrubbed the skillet with sand, then found a few flat rocks he hadn't already pillaged and skipped them across the current. Fifteen skips was his record. He began pitching bigger stones for the far bank. Some part of him believed that if he made the other side, good things might come.

He rested in the grass and closed his eyes against the sun's slant through the limbs of black locust. Maybe luck would bring him a girlfriend, though he couldn't imagine how that might happen. Sometimes he saw the girls from school at the library, but they whispered and giggled behind their long hair. Better to keep to the river, where things were familiar, made sense.

When he woke, it was dark, the ground chill beneath his back. He lay for a few minutes, letting the sleep leave his head, and then he heard what had roused him: the dry rustle of snake-grass, the snuffling of an animal nosing the air for scent. He sat up and peered into the blackness of the dense undergrowth. He raised his face to the upriver breeze. He might know bear by its odor of carrion, elk by the musk it would carry into rut.

He rose slowly, remembering news of a big cougar crisscrossing the canyon. It had taken Mr. Belieu's prize peacock in a flurry of iridescent feathers and dragged down the goat that Earl Ziwisky had kept staked, moving it a few feet each day so that it grazed the weeds in concentric circles. Earl had found the billy still hitched, the tender underside gone, except for the stomach full of grass, which the cat had neatly eviscerated and pawed aside.

Manny knew better than to run, knew a mountain lion would have him on the ground before he ever reached his door. He pulled his knife from his pocket, thumbed it open, and took several slow steps backward. The animal moved with him, and Manny believed he could see the tall grass parting in the moonlight. He was almost inside, could feel the door at his back, when he saw the eyes, then the snout. Heard a whine, a pant. Another whine.

He let his shoulders drop, gave a light whistle. The dog came out of the grass and belly-crawled its way forward a few feet, gave two short barks.

Manny folded the blade, took a deep breath, felt the quaver in his lungs. The dog rolled to its back. Some kind of dingo, he thought, but then he saw that the hair was too long, the face too narrow. He knelt, ran his hand down her side, felt the ribs beneath skin, the narrowness of her hips. She was young, little more than a pup.

"You're hungry, aren't you, girl?"

She rose to the sound of his voice, licked his chin, and tucked herself against his knees, shivering. When he opened the shack's door, the dog looked from his face to the room and back.

"Don't be so damn polite. Mosquitoes are getting in."

He lit several candles while the dog watched, intent on his every move, as though she were learning something. In the soft light, she resembled a small collie, but he had never seen one of her color or conformation. Her back and sides were a silvery blue, mottled black. Feathered legs and jowls a deep copper, feet the same white as her thick ruff, the blaze of her face.

"You're sure a pretty thing," he said. The dog opened her mouth in a full pant, and it seemed to him she was smiling. "I've got three saltines," he said and held out one of the crackers. The dog sniffed, took a corner between her front teeth, looking to his eyes to make sure she had permission.

Manny sat in the single wooden chair, admiring the way she held the cracker between her paws and ate it in small bites. Her dainty mannerisms reminded him of a cat. When the same ritual had been repeated with each of the two remaining crackers, she didn't beg for more, as though she understood numbers. She began cleaning herself, paying elaborate attention to each white paw, licking and taking little nips with her teeth until all the dirt and burs were gone and her feet shone sleek in the candlelight.

Manny stretched his legs out in front of him and folded his hands across his stomach. The dog grunted as she settled, tucking her nose. He thought that she was too pretty to be a working dog, but she had the appearance of a herder. Tomorrow he'd take her into town, ask around.

When the dog whimpered in her sleep and began paddling her feet, Manny roused himself long enough to blow out the candles, move to the bed, and kick off his boots. Nighthawks called, rising, falling, rising again. He lay in the dark and imagined all the animals that were moving across the land, lipping browse, sifting the water, uprooting stone. He was glad that he had felt his fear and not run from it.

Deracotte and the woman in the car—there was something different about them, something foreign yet familiar. He thought about how the Bateman place sat at the edge of a bluff overlooking the river—tough land to get to, tougher to farm. Manny tried to remember what structures stood on the property. A shipwrecked barn. A few collapsing outbuildings. A broken-backed house. He wondered what it might mean to trade labor for room and board. Food he could use, but he had this bed, this place. He wondered if they had a radio they might barter.

From the tall cottonwood outside his window, an owl took up its query. With every *who,* Manny added the remaining W's his English teacher had taught him: *why? what? where? when?* Three times he chorused along, a whispered exhalation sailing him into sleep.

Chapter Three

Ravens lifted from the trees in a clatter, black opals against the hardpan sky. Guttural, cacophonous, query and response—there was no other way to say what they were saying. They were talking. *Talking.*

Deracotte repeated the word, *talking talking,* as he finished his morning shave outside the tent, dried the straight razor, and laid it in its case. He found it a minor miracle that the razor had passed into his possession and not been lost or pawned for whiskey. It was an early memory that stayed true even after his father's disappearance from their home in New Haven: the larger hand steady atop his own, guiding the blade along the strop, testing its sharpness against the hair of their forearms—the boy's nearly invisible and falling away like down, the man's dark and coarse, lifting and dropping like fur.

To talk. To tell. What made up the language of ravens? Deracotte remembered his Bible stories—the flood, the dove that returned with the olive leaf, the covenant that was the rainbow. But what had always intrigued him was how, before the dove, Noah had set loose a raven that crossed back and forth over the world until the land was dry. There was no mention of the raven's return, but his kind remained extant, which could only mean that at some point the bird had rejoined his mate. Contained in the raven's untold tale was some knowledge, some wisdom the bird had gathered in his flight. Secret even from God. Perhaps the birds were telling it still, and no ears to hear.

The china bowl came up heavy in his hands—a ridiculous luxury inherited from her grandmother that Helen had insisted they carry with them from Connecticut to Idaho, cushioned between her winter sweaters. It always seemed that the heft of water alone might be enough to shatter the dish, and he was careful as he dumped the foam into the ditch. Below him, the canyon bent and bowed into the shape of a horseshoe. The river flashed with sun, a long, undulant fish, a different animal than the New Haven harbor that had lain fat and indolent, lipping the sailboats. What Deracotte wanted more than anything was to step into the river's current, cast his line to those places where the light prismed and the insects opened their wings. As a boy, he'd spent hours reading *Field and Stream,* making flies from found feathers and bits of yarn from his grandmother's knitting basket, then taught himself to cast with a bamboo rod he'd found leaned into the corner of the cellar, threading the dark street with his line while the neighbors slept. He'd read the journals of the mountain men, Hemingway's stories, Izaak Walton's *The Compleat Angler.* He saved enough from his paper route to mail-order a compass from Vermont and carried it with him as he walked, checking all ways west. He'd always dreamed of living along the banks of a wild river, and now he did.

Trout for breakfast. Reason enough. But Dewey and Stubb, the two men he'd hired, would arrive soon. He hung the towel on a stob of pine. Work before pleasure, he thought, a motto his father had failed to observe.

There must have been a time before. The only thing he knew

for certain was that his father, a printer's apprentice, had lost his job to new machinery, and that was when the bottles began to appear: between rafters in the garage, behind the coal bin, beneath the bed. Even as the fifths sprouted as though seeded, the kitchen cupboards grew bare. He remembered how his father's appetite for food diminished, then disappeared, as though the only thing that kept his spirit alive was this other spirit, clear and smelling of pine. Soon the house held no food at all, and in Deracotte's memory they subsisted on nothing more than liquid and smoke and air. At night, his stomach roiled, and he imagined he was being eaten from the inside out, the way his history teacher told them prisoners of war died, the body digesting itself for food.

The last time his family had sat together at the kitchen table, it was over a meal of blood sausage donated by the widow next door, whose dead husband had left her with a freezer full of meat. She appeared each Saturday afternoon toting a paper sack filled with heavy white packages. Deracotte came to read the neatly marked abbreviations—RND STK, LVR, PRK RST—as a grim reminder of his mother's anger as she fried the meat black, the taste of charcoal in his mouth.

Deracotte remembered his mother's resolve to change her husband, to save them all with her soft evening prayers. She was a believer, a member of the little congregation that met in the basement of the VFW hall. Deracotte was there with her when the preacher announced from the pulpit that it was her own lack of faith that had failed, that if she called upon the name of God without sin in her heart, he would not turn away. Deracotte had despised the preacher's smug authority, the way he shamed his mother into tears. As his father slipped more surely into the advanced stages of alcoholism, she prayed harder, her bare knees taking on the hue and texture of the wooden floor upon which she knelt. Finally, when the prayers failed to save her husband, she resolved to save herself: grocery money gone to buy a new dress, cigarettes in a silver case, a hat that shadowed her eyes. *Backslider,* the preacher pronounced. *O ye of little faith.* Both mother and son had been shunned from the church, and Deracotte was glad to have Sundays at home, quiet mornings with nothing to do but read. It took some time for him to realize that his father's final bender was not just an extended drunk but a disappearance: he was gone for good.

And then his once pious mother had mounted her own form of escape: first with the insurance salesman, who sent the boy on lunchtime errands to the other end of town, and then the banker, who parked in the alley at dusk before sneaking like a thief through the back door. The men who followed, some more, some less sober than his father, came with flowers and boxes of candy that clotted his mother's mouth with caramel; they left with something that Deracotte believed belonged to him: his mother's affection, her attention, her care. The stinking ashtrays and lipstick-smeared glasses that littered the kitchen made him nauseous. The sight of wing-tipped shoes outside his mother's bedroom door filled him with rage. Deracotte came to hate the pitying looks of the townspeople. When the grocer proffered him a horehound candy, he shook his head. When the mortician's wife pretended to drop a nickel as she stepped from the beauty parlor to the car, he left it as it lay. Their small offerings did nothing to fill the emptiness in his gut.

Finally, like his father, his mother had felt the need to disappear. Deracotte had waved good-bye as she tripped in her new heels toward the waiting car, leaving him at the door of his father's boyhood home with his widowed grandmother, who had never traveled outside New Haven and never would. His mother blew him an awkward kiss, a gesture she was still learning. His grandmother's fingers fluttered around his head and guided him inside. They ate a simple but filling meal of toasted bread and warm milk; they slept together that night and many nights after on the same ancient horsehair mattress, between them a tether of air.

The simplicity of that life provided the fondest memories. In the oysterman's shanty that she'd lived in since her wedding night, his grandmother filled her days with household chores, while Deracotte sequestered himself amid the books piled on the overstuffed couch, where he could sit and feel their weighty promise at his elbows. As he read his way through the *Encyclopedia Britannica* and its accompanying *Illustrated New World Dictionary*, bought on time from the traveling salesman, his grandmother kept the radio low so as not to disturb him. It wasn't until he was in his teens that he realized she was illiterate: his ability to decipher the marked pages was a miracle that kept her reverently silent. Instead of writing a check for the few monthly bills, she carefully counted ones and fives into an envelope. She steadfastly refused to fill out the forms that might have provided them with government assistance. The Bible she cherished, the cobbled leather worn smooth by her hands, was a stone she worried to a shine.

No matter his love affair with words, it was his superior marks in the sciences that prompted the scholarships and led him to medical school. He was a little amazed each time he found himself before a Bunsen burner or filleting the muscles of an already shredded cadaver. While the other residents smoked their cigarettes and drank cup after cup of black coffee, he ate the lunch his grandmother had prepared for him: a single cold biscuit smeared with lard and two graham crackers—a menu that never varied in all the years of his education. Evenings, he would study his lessons and listen to the jazz recordings he had found in his father's old trunk. Coleman Hawkins and Thelonious Monk filled the room even as his grandmother worried that the soul of the music might somehow take the place of his own, just as it had his father's, bringing with it the whiskey and smoke.

Deracotte checked the sun's rise over Angel Ridge before stepping into the tent, where he and Helen had chosen to sleep rather than in the old house with its curling linoleum tufted with mouse nests. He hadn't expected the buildings to be in such disrepair, the windows gone, the door hinges broken. No electricity, no phone line, the only water a meager spring laced with blackberry canes and poison ivy. The only answer was a clean, deep well. Perhaps they could borrow the money now, but Deracotte preferred waiting until his medical practice was stable. He despised indebtedness of any kind. They'd paid for the land with the proceeds of his grandmother's house and the gifts of money they'd received from Helen's family and friends. They'd make do with what they had until their savings grew. The truth was that Deracotte thought he might prefer sleeping beneath the stars, shaving in the open air. He sometimes wondered if he wouldn't be happiest living just this way, like the mountain men he had read about as a boy.

Though one part of him wished Helen up and around, he was careful not to wake her. He loved to watch her sleep, her eyes closed so that she couldn't see him examining the perfect lines of her eyebrows, the lips lightly parted, the hair spread across the pillow like an auburn wing. Her hair had entranced him from the moment of their first meeting. She'd been an undergraduate, younger than he was by several years, and Deracotte thought she might be one of the crowd that he sometimes spied laughing and drinking wine near the campus pond, their bright blankets spread out around them. But she was different from the other girls, her long dark hair sometimes held back by a red handkerchief, other times falling around her shoulders. No lipstick or eyeliner. Plain skirts and flat shoes. A slow, casual stride that made Deracotte wonder what she was so sure of.

One late spring evening, he was surprised to find her alone as he left the library. She held a book in her right hand, a cigarette in her left. The flame of her hair beneath the streetlamp was dappled with moths.

"Why do you do that?" he'd asked.

She was taller up close, her hips more rounded, her eyes brown and half-lidded, as though she were loose in some dream.

"Read?"

"No. Smoke."

"Why do you care?"

"It's not becoming."

She'd laughed, high and girlish. Then lowered her voice. "What *do* you find becoming?"

He had stood silent for a moment, aware of how he must appear to her: hair badly cut, shoulders still slumping with unaccustomed height.

"Health, I guess. I'm studying to be a physician." He was suddenly aware of the word's currency, a gold coin in his pocket. He straightened and waited to see its effect on her.

"My mother would slap me for saying so, but doctors don't interest me much." She closed her book. He'd wanted to say that doctors didn't interest him much either, that it was an opportunity he couldn't turn away from rather than a calling he'd heeded, but instead he had followed the ember of her cigarette pointed toward the night sky.

"Tell me what you see," she said.

He'd taken in Cassiopeia as he worked to slow his heart. Her forwardness was startling. She smelled like crushed clover.

"There," he said, lifting his palm toward the tip of the Big Dipper. "The polestar, always to the north." He had a dim memory of following his father's finger as it traced the bail and handle. He remembered the smells of aftershave and whiskey, the pleasant roughness of his father's hands as he lifted him toward the sky.

"If you can see that," Deracotte said, "you can always find your way."

She tilted her head and smiled. "I don't plan on getting lost anytime soon."

There was something unexpected about her, a willfulness that made him bold, and he asked if they could meet again. He made reservations at the Bangkok Garden, where Helen ordered garlic soft-shelled crabs and a bottle of Gewürztraminer. By the time he had finished his plate of mild cashew chicken, she had eaten each crab whole, and he watched as she ran one finger around the moon of her plate, stuck it into her mouth and sucked, an action so lewd he felt his pulse quicken. The total of the bill had fallen from his memory but not the humiliation of having to ask Helen for money to cover it, and he'd determined that their next date would be a picnic in the park. Helen seemed as content with the wedge of sharp

Cheddar and single pear he offered as she had the expensive meal. When she leaned to kiss him, her lips were sweet with fruit.

Near the end of that spring semester, they layered two blankets on the grass, named the constellations, and Thomas found that the lisp of sounds in Helen's mouth—*Cygnus, Delphinus, Pegasus*—made her seem more vulnerable somehow. She invited him to move between her legs, and then it was the only place he wanted to be. That night and the nights after had been a wonder to him. They talked about politics, religion, music, books, his dream of moving west. She confessed that she'd been watching him on campus, the way he always carried a paperback in his pants pocket. It was when she'd spied Ayn Rand riding his ass, she said, that she'd been charmed.

Still, they were different, and Deracotte sometimes marveled that they had found each other at all. He remembered his first meal with Helen's family at their home in Southport. Even as he sat at the long table, eating from her mother's Havilland, fielding questions from her father—no, Deracotte answered, he hadn't known Dr. Chapin but had met Dr. Endicott; certainly, the research being done on long-chain polysaccharides showed enormous promise—he'd kept his eyes on Helen's hands, mimicking their movement: the shorter fork for the salad, the thin cut of butter applied not to the bread but to the edge of the smallest plate; the strange little china boats into which he, like Helen, placed the bones pulled from his flounder. Soups alternating between hot and cold, the wine red and white, the cleansing sorbets and tidbits meant to excite the palate—Deracotte had lost count of the courses. He had been queasy with nervousness when he first sat down, but as the food continued to appear, he feared he might be ill, regurgitate their largesse right back onto the enormous and valuable platters. He watched Helen's mother, her collarbone as sharp as the beef chine, select the smallest servings, even as Helen's father, a third-generation Yale man whose shoulders still held the stance of a linebacker, bellowed at Deracotte between his own monstrous mouthfuls: "*Mangia, mangia!* You eat like a girl!"

After the meal, when they'd retired to the den, Helen's father passed around port and Cuban cigars, both of which Deracotte at first declined before acquiescing, fearing that another failure to partake would provoke suspicion. Watching the languid movement of Helen's arms, her straight back and delicately rounded hips as she played an étude by Chopin, he was transported into a British novel, a contained and knowable world in which the women entertained while the men chatted amiably about matters of global importance. Nothing was expected of him except a mild attendance to his host and an exhibition of an intelligent and pleasant demeanor. A gentleman's pose. The tawny port helped him act the part, to believe that he was believable in his role, and when the talk had turned to a recent fishing trip to Michigan, he'd allowed himself to become overly animated, blustering over the merits of dry flies versus wet, denying the virtues of nymphing with a spurious conviction born of too much reading and not enough time spent thigh-deep in water. Helen's father had seemed delighted to debate casting techniques and leader weights, but though she didn't say so directly (knowing too well that, of all her daughters, Helen couldn't care less), Helen's mother disapproved, not only of Deracotte's lack of dinner decorum but of what she referred to as his unfortunate life. When Deracotte woke the next morning, it seemed fitting that his head was sore and his mouth tasted of ash. Yet, in the days after, Helen had made love to him with such gusto he feared they'd break the backseat of her father's car. In a household manicured to its very foundations, Helen seemed wildly misplaced. He saw what pleasure she took in denying her mother's expectations even as she manipulated her father's affections. Deracotte often wondered if part of her attraction to him wasn't a kind of perversion. She seemed to care little for what her family's money could buy, preferring thrift shops to Macy's. Easy enough, Deracotte thought, to live so by choice rather than necessity, but her impulses seemed haphazard. One day, she was sipping soda at the five-and-dime, the next it was champagne. Her mercurial nature unsettled Deracotte, a state he found both uncomfortable and arousing. Why had she chosen him? If a different man had walked by with Ayn Rand in his pocket, would she have been just as easily charmed?

He might not have had the courage to ask for her hand in marriage if she hadn't suggested it first. He'd been reading *Living the Good Life,* which detailed the beginnings of the back-to-the-land movement, and had told her how fascinated he was by the philosophy that promoted a primitive existence with little dependence upon the exchange of money. She'd surprised him with her response, as she so often did.

"Why not choose our own simple life?" she asked.

"Do you think you could do that?"

"Why not? You don't think that I want my mother's life, do you?"

His hesitation caused her to tilt her head and peer at him with something like bemusement. He was sure that he knew what he could live without, but he wondered if her aversion to her inheritance had less to do with social conscience and more to do with ennui. She worked her hands beneath his shirt, lifted her face to his.

"Let's make our own grand adventure," she said, and all his doubts vanished. It was just the plan he'd been hoping for.

That spring, when his grandmother died suddenly of an aneurysm, he put the little house up for sale and, together, he and Helen had scoured the maps, drawn to Idaho by its promise of cheap land and free-flowing rivers. How far from her family was she willing to travel? Thomas asked. A long way, Helen replied. It was like a treasure hunt, searching the almanacs, inquiring about farms for sale, sending out letters to medical offices, reading up on root cellars and food preservation. When he discovered the little town of Fife along the banks of the Idaho river known for its depleted gold mines and plentiful trout, he wrote the city clerk, asking what parcels of land might be for sale. "Olie Bateman died just last week," the clerk wrote back. "His daughter's wanting to rid herself of the place and needs money since her son had the rheumatic fever that went to his brain. I don't know of any other land for sale of the size you need, and I don't know anyone else who is interested."

They broke the news to Helen's family that, when Thomas had completed his residency, he would open a practice where doctors were few and much needed. It was an honorable mission, one that her parents could hardly denigrate. Even as plans were being made for a formal June wedding, Helen discovered that she was pregnant.

Deracotte knew that Helen had had other lovers before him, but any doubts he had concerning the child's paternity disappeared when Helen pressed his palm to her stomach. "Feel," she said. "Inside is a life we made together." They found a judge who performed the ceremony in the five minutes between his lunch hour and his haircut appointment, then told Helen's outraged mother that they were too much in love to wait. Instead of an extravagant church affair, they endured a magnificent reception in the family's courtyard, where a quartet played Vivaldi (even though Thomas had requested Coltrane's ballads) and the fountain sprayed water tinted lavender to match Helen's dress. They dismissed her parents' offer of a weekend in Barbados and spent their honeymoon night on his grandmother's old couch, entwined so tightly that Deracotte believed they shared the same breath. They bought the little red Volkswagen from a friend who had joined the army, set Thomas's compass on the dashboard, and headed for Idaho, their map marked by small towns circled and x-ed out, except for Fife, ringed by blue ink, like a planet in a diminishing galaxy.

Deracotte thought he knew the meteorological definition of aridity, but since arriving in the Idaho canyonland, he'd had to revise his understanding: he woke each morning, his eyes scratchy, throat and nostrils raw. Helen had asked that the next time he drove into Fife he pick up more Bag Balm from the drugstore. She'd taken to slathering her elbows and feet with the last of their cooking oil and slept in her socks even as she shunned her nightgown in favor of nakedness. She loved the musky redolence of sheets gone too long without washing, the tent piled with a banquette of pillows. He thought he might wake Helen now, just to hear her voice husky with sleep, touch her breasts grown round and firm, but when the cough came from outside the tent, he drew back quickly and peeked outside. Dewey and Stubb stood at the fire pit. They'd be sweating by noon, but the cold morning air kept their hands pocketed, their shoulders hunched.

Stubb was a larger man than his name gave him credit for. Suspenders strapped his gut; his graying hair was shorn down to skin. Dewey was the one they called the Little Giant. His hair, dark and burred, reminded Deracotte of a hedgehog. Shorter than Stubb by a foot but solid as hickory, except for the one milky eye that rolled outward. A top-notch hand before he'd reached beneath a load of logs to snag the choke chain and had the whole thing give way. From what Deracotte had gathered, it was a miracle that Dewey had lived at all, his head swelled to the size of a melon, his scalp splitting down the sides. They'd hauled him in the bed of a pickup to the hospital in Folgate, the druggist sitting with his back against the cab, holding the ruptured head steady between his thighs. Dewey had lived, but his walk was more of a stagger, his sentences slowed by the run of his tongue along his toothless gums.

It seemed important to Deracotte that they build the barn before the house, and in a matter of days the two men had brought their tools, poured the footings, and framed. The barn was what would anchor them, big enough to hold all the promise of their new life.

"Build a fire?" Dewey peered hopefully at the ashes.

"No need for a fire." Deracotte rolled his sleeves. "We'll warm ourselves with work."

"What about the missus?"

"Helen will make do." Deracotte saw the men glance at each other, then look away. He motioned toward the outbuildings and began walking.

The ribs of the barn glistened with frost. As the men climbed their way up the ladder, Deracotte pretended to inspect the previous day's work. At first he'd believed he could bluff his way into a knowledge of the skills needed to pound two boards together, but he'd been wrong. Even with Dewey's guidance, he'd been unable to hammer a straight nail. Finally, it was less the men's teasing that drove him from the work site than his own disgust. What good would it do to tell them that though he could wield a hemostat, he had never touched a pair of pliers? If his father had ever owned a wood saw, Deracotte never laid eyes on it. Finally, it seemed easier to simply disappear once the work got started, and he sensed that Dewey and Stubb found this arrangement as much of a relief as he did.

Deracotte waited until the hammers were pounding out a steady beat, then wandered from the building site to walk the perimeter of the property. By the time he had paced off the land's boundaries, stopping now and again to watch the pheasants he'd flushed take wing, loitering at the high end of the draw where Bedrock Creek purled beneath elderberry and began its steep descent to the river, the sun had worked its way toward noon. He squatted next to the spring that fed into the creek, dipped his hand, and remembered he'd eaten no breakfast. He gathered watercress and chewed the peppery leaves, then folded more into the tail of his shirt, a surprise for Helen. He was nearly at the barn when he heard a shout.

"Doc!" Stubb was motioning frantically. "Dewey's down!"

Deracotte saw Stubb scrambling from his perch, dropping like a chimp. He began running, the watercress falling from his shirttail like wedding flowers. By the time he reached the barn, Dewey was blue.

"Get his head back!" Deracotte knelt, reached one finger into the man's mouth, felt the hardened gums, the tongue slumped back into the throat. He probed farther, touched something slick and round.

"It's a Lemonhead, ain't it?" Stubb stood behind him, breathing hard.

"Help me turn him over." The man was small, hardly larger than a child. As Stubb lifted him beneath his armpits, Deracotte hit him hard between the shoulder blades. The third whack, a yellow piece of candy popped from Dewey's mouth; a strangled sigh rose from his throat.

"Lay him down," Deracotte ordered. He began breathing into Dewey, inflating the narrow chest, feeling the nubby flesh where teeth should have been, like the mouth of a baby.

"Come on, Dewey," Stubb said. "Come on, you sonofabitch."

A wet rag of breath, then another, and Dewey was coughing, his face gone from blue to bright red.

Deracotte sat back on his heels and wiped his mouth with the back of his hand. He wanted water to rinse the stickiness away, but he had left the canteens at the tent, unfilled. He looked to the rafters dripping frost melt where the sun hit. He should check for broken bones, concussion. He wondered how he might evaluate a man already so damaged.

"Started hacking up on top," Stubb said. "Saw him keel off, clutching his throat. Thought for sure he was dying."

"He was." Deracotte took the hand that Stubb extended, aware of his palm sticky with spit. "Maybe you should stop for the day."

Stubb found Dewey's hammer and pointed it at the little man, who was still gasping for air. "We keep at it, we'll have this thing knocked together before dark. Ain't that right, partner?"

Dewey nodded and sheepishly rubbed his knuckles against his lips. "Never had another man's mouth on me before."

"You little shit." Stubb laughed. "I catch you sucking on them damn things again, I'm going to kill you myself." He reached out and pulled Dewey to a stand. "Get your sorry ass back up there."

Deracotte watched as the two men joked their way to the ladder. He waited for his heart to slow, for the familiar fear to dissipate. It had been with him since the beginning, that foreboding sense of having somehow mistaken his own fate. All through his internship and residency he'd sheltered himself from his growing self-doubt. But then the pediatric ward, the twelve-year-old girl, pallid and shivering with fever. She'd cried as he examined her, covering her eyes with both hands like a child playing hide-and-seek. He remembered how hot and dry her skin felt beneath his fingers, how the organs bulged and rolled away from his prodding, as though desirous to keep their contagion a secret. Finally, the girl's muffled sobs, the pain his hands invoked, had been too much for him to bear, and he had moved to the next room, where a boy lay whose prognosis was definite: he would die, not because they didn't know the disease but because they did—neuroblastoma, the tumor virulent inside his skull. Deracotte remembered the comfort of this. The cool projection of what the future held, for one of them at least. But as he stepped from the boy's bed, the attending surgeon, a tall, balding man who smelled of furniture polish, had stopped him. "Dr. Deracotte," he'd said, "you're not finished."

Deracotte knew that the surgeon meant the girl. But what could he say? That he didn't know what might be causing her illness? That, finally, he couldn't bring himself to spend another second in the face of her suffering? He'd dutifully followed the surgeon back to the girl's bedside. He couldn't remember what conclusions he'd drawn, if they were right or wrong, if he saved the girl or doomed her, but the surgeon's words remained with him still: "You can't turn away from any of it, Dr. Deracotte. Not the body, not the disease, not the pain. You must absorb it all. You must *desire* to be in its presence."

He'd realized then that the patients were the very thing he wanted to avoid: their weeping and lament; their grimaces of agony; the awful way they took news of their impending demise with pitiful resignation or, worse, a cheerful nod of gratitude, as though instead of a death sentence he had just delivered them a basket of holiday fruit. But in the face of his family's poverty, how could he walk away from a future of prosperity and recognition? And how could he deny what the medical degree had already earned him? He had Helen. He had this land, this place where the river ran as true as any promise he had ever known.

He looked toward the canyon and saw the sun's tilt toward the western horizon. His grandmother often said that if his father could have waited until quitting time to drink, he might have made it. "Only so much liquor a man can put down between closing and sleep," she said, but Deracotte wondered. He'd seen fifths go from full to empty in an hour. What he knew for sure was that fishing was like whiskey to him. He couldn't get enough. Dawn to dusk was too short a time to tipple each cutbank, to meet the cast of first light with a cast of his own. Not quite quitting time, but he'd performed his work well. A little fishing couldn't hurt.

He felt his heart lighten as he made his way back to camp. Helen was reading inside the tent, propped upright by a levee of duffels and pillows. Her shoulders glistened in the filtered light.

"What time is it?" She stretched her arms above her head, and the blankets fell from her breasts.

"Long past time to be up and around." Any amorous affection he might have felt had been replaced by a sense of urgent efficiency as he gathered his wool long johns. He sniffed a pair of socks and threw them into the corner.

"You're not working on the barn?"

"I've just saved a man's life and am on my way to celebrate with a couple of hours of fishing."

"What man?"

"Dewey. He choked on a piece of hard candy."

Helen bent her knees, took several deep breaths, and stretched her neck left and right. "I hope you won't stay gone long. I'm starving."

Deracotte remembered the watercress, ruined now. But there would always be more, free for the taking.

"Let's share a can of sardines before I go," he said. "Some crackers."

Helen shook her head. "I'm sick to death of sardines. What else is there?"

"I'll bring you a fat trout, fry it up with potatoes and onions."

Helen leaned toward him, her breasts swaying heavily. "Kiss me, you fishing fool."

Deracotte grazed her lips, remembering his mouth sticky with lemon. "An hour, maybe two. Then dinner."

"What about breakfast and lunch?" She was fully uncovered now, blooming into the sun-warmed tent like a tropical flower.

"All rolled into one. I'll drive into Fife in the morning, get more groceries. Manny will be here first thing Monday. We'll need to feed him."

"You need to feed *me.*"

"That's what I'm about to do."

He'd choose a fly once he got to the river. Perhaps the sun had provided a last hatch he could emulate. Or maybe a single grasshopper had survived the frost and he could match its color. He told himself he'd search the banks for more watercress, perhaps a few mussels that could be rinsed free of silt. Who knew what pleasures he might find?

Chapter Four

Helen stepped out of the tent and marveled at the canyon topping out onto farmland that dipped and swelled, dusty greens giving way to the amber stubble of harvested fields. An osprey sailed past at eye level, brought itself to hold above water, then plummeted. So much drama, she thought. As though everything could fall away at any moment.

She watched as Thomas pulled on his waders. She'd taken great pleasure in his body from the start, lean and finely muscled. The thin line of his face and gray eyes had seemed to her a profile of intelligence. Aquiline, she often whispered as she traced the slope of his nose. Classic.

She spread a blanket on the ground and rested back on her elbows as Thomas tested the rod her father had given him as an early wedding gift. It pleased her that Thomas had become the extension of her father's wishes. She was the youngest of five daughters, the last desperate try for the son her parents had wanted but never had. Her sisters were all older by a decade or more, married and staid. They might as well have been aunties, disapproving of her from afar. While they rolled their hair into chignons or sported fashionable bobs, Helen let her own hair grow long and thick. Instead of a closet full of A-line skirts and cashmere, she had boys' jeans and wrinkled shirts draping her bedstead. Yet, even as her mother fussed over pilled sweaters, her father kept his eye less on his youngest daughter's appearance than he did on the men with whom she appeared. Each son-in-law in succession had proven a failure, capable of market talk and a respectable handicap, but none had shared his passion for fishing. Until Thomas.

" 'As no man is born an artist, so no man is born an angler,' " her father noted, quoting Izaak Walton. "Anyone with the noble aspirations of a fisherman can aspire to great heights and succeed." Whatever misgivings her father might have had about the marriage seemed to fade as he bantered with Thomas about hackle patterns and stonefly hatches. Boisterous, possessed of a hardiness of spirit that often overwhelmed all lesser souls in proximity, Helen's father too often deferred to his wife's sharp insistence, but on the subject of Helen he held steady. She had a mind of her own, he proudly noted, her willfulness an attribute that he claimed was part of her patriarchal lineage. But where Helen's father saw self-direction, her mother saw a desire to shame the family with low ideas and unseemly behavior.

Helen remembered a time when she was ten and at the beach with her family. She'd found a small piece of driftwood onto which she'd carefully engraved her mantra: I JUST WANT TO BE FREE.

"Free from *what*?" her mother had demanded. "What could you possibly want that you don't already have?"

Could she say, even now, what it was she was meaning to escape? Sometimes she believed she was driven by nothing more onerous than her own boredom. There was little she despised more than familiarity. Waking every morning to the same bed, the same window, the same faces, she felt all the air being pressed from her lungs. More than anything, she longed for each day to be new, to surprise her with possibility. To drown out her mother's voice suggesting that perhaps a girdle would wear well under that skirt, paired with the black shell, which made Helen look thin and who couldn't stand to lose a few pounds anyway? Certainly not her mother, whose place at the table was purely pretense. A sip of water, a single strand of capellini threading her fork.

"Hold your shoulders back," her mother warned, prodding with her pencil-sharp fingers, "or you'll have a dowager's hump before you're married." And married was what her mother wanted her to be. "You need a man," she asserted, "to keep you respectable. The *right* man." By which she meant someone whose family name was familiar, perhaps a name etched in granite above one of the Ivy League halls. But instead of extending dinner invitations to clean-cut polo players dressed in argyle, Helen had found men at the wharf who looked like they might appreciate a good meal: a rugby player just in from New Zealand who emptied a bottle of her father's thirty-six-year-old Dalwhinnie and insisted that they sing along as he led them in a chorus of "God Save the Queen"; a Kenyan sailor who ignored Helen and focused his amorous attention on her mother, who blushed and forgot herself until dessert was served and she realized halfway through her crème brûlée all that she'd eaten. "That man," she accused the next morning, damp tea bags covering her eyes. "That *man* made me *ill*."

Like her clothes and hair, Helen liked her sex loose and undone. She'd never held to her mother's warnings about bad reputations. If some promising beau thought her ruined, he wasn't the man for her. But then she'd found Thomas. A doctor—the very profession her parents most revered—yet the antithesis of every blue-blooded construct they held dear. "You want to have your cake and eat it too," her mother had scolded. And here was the truth of it: she had her doctor, and he was delicious.

When she'd discovered that Thomas was a virgin, she'd laughed aloud before realizing the shame it caused him. But then she'd been even more surprised: the tenderness of his touch made her shy. Thomas had explored her body with such wonder that she forgot she was the one with things to teach him. She hadn't understood that her usual galumphing lovemaking style had protected her from her own need. The other boys had taken her roughly in the back-seats of cars or approached her with such formality that she wondered what desire moved them. But Thomas took his time, each of the flaws her mother had so faithfully pointed out—her rounded chin, the small fold of flesh at her waistline—precious to him.

But how could she say this to her mother, who distrusted her daughter's judgment as much as she did her future son-in-law's motivations? "Water finds its own level," she warned Helen. "Be ready to sink or swim."

Helen felt a spasm, an elbow or a knee. She sat up and inhaled deeply, then cupped her stomach, lifted the bundle of herself and the baby, and breathed through her nose. She'd been having contractions for the past week, but Thomas had assured her it was nothing more than false labor. She massaged with her fingertips until the tension eased. Helen was sure that she knew the moment of conception. They'd been at one of her parents' lavish gatherings—a *soiree,* her mother called them. While Thomas felt charged with the responsibility to socialize, she had done what she'd learned early on would stave off the mindless boredom of such functions and found the buffet table laden with food: oysters Rockefeller, foie gras with apple brandy, wild boar in black truffle sauce. Thomas caught up with her as she tipped her fifth flute of Veuve Clicquot.

"Where have you been?" He gripped her arm like a rudder and ferried her through the crowd to the veranda.

"What do you mean? I've been right here." She gave him a crooked smile and leaned in for a kiss.

"You're embarrassing me," he hissed. "You need to control yourself. You smell like a distillery."

She'd pulled away and looked at him in his rented tuxedo and cockeyed bow tie. "And you," she said, "smell like you've had your nose up someone's ass."

They'd left the party in stony silence and gone to his grandmother's house. Helen was sure that the child was conceived that night, in that unprotected place between the harshness of their words and the forgiveness of their bodies. And though some part of her resented his patronizing intrusion, another part welcomed his correction. Maybe her mother was right: maybe she did need a man to keep her in line. Always, she felt caught between her desire to act autonomously, giving no mind to her mother's *tsk-tsking* tongue, and her need for affection. With Thomas, she found both. There was something endearing about his overweening nature, his need to control every minute detail of her life. She understood that his insistence that she take her vitamin each morning precisely at nine was an act of affection. Yet there was that part of her that remained defiant, and she'd found a particular pleasure in her little sins: truffles stashed in the back of the freezer, a cigarette in the bathroom at midnight. She envisioned trips into Fife for groceries, a quick detour to the bar for a margarita—the icy tang, the savory salted rim—and her mouth grew moist.

Thomas made his way to her side, and she let her head loll back so that she could gaze into his gray eyes.

"It feels like the edge of the world," she said. "Like you could step off and disappear."

"It's an omega." Thomas traced the horseshoe shape the river took around the jut of basalt.

She arched her back. "I wish I had a cigarette."

"No you don't."

She smiled. "You're right. I've given that up." She didn't tell him that she'd hidden a pack of Kools in the Limoges cookie jar still stashed in the car's trunk.

Thomas touched her knee with the tips of two fingers. "You'll be okay while I try my luck?"

"Let me come with you." The rough landscape and the unfamiliar balance of her body had made her hesitant to attempt the path down to the river.

Thomas looked from her to the trail and back. "We should drive, then. I don't want you falling."

Even with the windows down, the little car was hotter than

Helen had expected, the morning cool giving way to the canyon heat. She shook her hair from its braid and refastened the large silver barrette—a gift from a former boyfriend. She had fallen in love not with him but with the barrette's engraved sketching of a horse at full gallop, its mane and tail luxurious in the wind. When they reached the beach, Thomas spread the blanket in the shade of a large cottonwood. Across the railroad track was a spring. He filled a canteen with water and set it beside her before stepping into the river.

Helen lay flat against the cool sand, stretched her arms above her head, and tried to take a deeper breath. She could hardly remember that other body that Thomas had first known, light and quick. She'd never been thin but had always loved the strength of her shoulders, the solidness of her legs. Over the last few weeks, she'd felt weighted, anchored in place. Like she was the anchor itself. Her breasts were outrageous, her cleavage the décolletage of some plump Elizabethan paramour.

And still she was hungry. She wondered if there was any food in the car that they might have overlooked. On their trip across the country, Thomas had been strangely protective of the kitchen box nested with jars of pickles, tins of deviled ham, and cans of syrupy plums, as though the trunk of homely staples were a pirate's chest of pilfered dainties. At first it was the sardines she'd craved, and she'd eaten more than her half of the briny fish, feeding him pieces while he drove, licking her fingers, leaning over to run her tongue along the corner of his mouth and down his chin. Maybe he had known what an undertaking it would be to gather groceries: a trip in and out of Fife was a full hour's drive. She thought of the little market a short walk from her parents' home in Southport, its bins full of fresh fruits and vegetables, the butcher case in the back corner with its shelves of cutlets and tenderloins. She loved red meat, as raw and as tender as she could get it. She loved it spiced and cured—salami, pancetta, mortadella. "My beautiful carnivore," Thomas called her, even as he ate bologna with the same relish he did prosciutto.

She wished she could jump in the car and drive into Fife for a hamburger, but she had never gotten her license—the man's role, her mother had said. It was Thomas who had stayed at the wheel as they logged sixteen-hour days on the highways west, even as she protested that she'd once steered her girlfriend's Chevrolet down the country club road without mishap.

Helen ran her fingers through the sand, found a small round stone, placed it on her tongue, and sucked until it moistened and the grit loosened against her teeth. Thomas had moved back into her field of vision and was casting upstream. She envied the ease with which he entered the river. She wished she were there in the water with him. What harm would it do? She saw that he was facing away from her. She rose and walked down the short beach to where a rise of rock caught the water in a deep pool and sheltered her from Thomas's view, then stripped to her panties. Just shedding her clothes allowed her to breathe easier. She stepped in to her waist and let the water buoy her faceup to the sun. Her breasts bobbed at the surface like fishing floats, her belly a white island. She and the baby were both weightless now, the river carrying them on its back, effortless as sleep. Bliss until she heard Thomas call her name, then again, louder.

She swam the few yards back to shore. Thomas stood on the beach, holding a willow branch strung with two trout. He was looking out over the river, fear etching his face.

"Here," she called and waved. For a moment, he seemed not to recognize her, as though she were some naiad come up from the water, but then he walked toward her with such quick urgency that she realized he was angry.

"What are you doing?" he demanded.

"What does it look like I'm doing? I'm swimming."

Thomas glanced toward the road as though he feared someone might see her there, her swollen belly and breasts wet and glistening. "I thought something awful had happened. Where are your clothes?"

Thomas rested the fish in the shallows and began dressing her as though she were a child, tugging her top over her head, brushing the sand from her feet, tying her shoes.

"It's okay, you know. I'm a strong swimmer."

"You should have told me, that's all."

"I didn't mean to frighten you."

He straightened her collar, then stopped, took a deep breath before moving his hands to her face. "I can't lose you. You're all I have."

"You won't lose me. I promise." She kissed him, let him taste the river still wet on her lips. "I'm hungry. Can we eat now?"

Thomas picked up the fish and turned to look out over the stretch of sand. "I think we'll call this Home Beach. That's what it feels like. Part of home." He steadied her as they made their way to the car. "And this place. Omega Bend. The last place we'll ever need to be."

Back at camp, Helen watched him gather the kindling and start a fire the way Stubb had taught him: a tepee of thin sticks around a few twists of paper. The flame caught quickly, and she smiled, remembering their first night in camp when, cold and shivering, they had stood peering at a large chunk of cottonwood.

"Where's the axe?" she'd asked.

"What?" Thomas had looked at her blankly, as though she had asked him to produce a manatee.

"What do we have? A saw?"

Thomas had shrugged. "I thought we'd buy tools as we needed them." Nothing but their hands, then, with which they had gathered enough limbs and dried grass to make a small fire. They were learning.

Helen set the skillet to heat, added oil and the last of their potatoes. They ate sitting on a log, fish skin crackling between their teeth. When the air had cooled enough to make them shiver, they slipped into their tent and warmed together beneath the heavy blankets. Thomas was asleep before Helen could move against him, and she rested her ear on his chest, listening for the steady cadence. She closed her eyes and began planning the spring garden: pole beans and yellow squash, corn and tomatoes, hollyhocks and marigolds bordering the edges. She'd found a book on canning and imagined the lids pinging shut. It was a life no woman in her family would have chosen. Her mother and sisters had warned her that she didn't know what she was getting into, moving to such a desolate place. They expected her to fail. She would send them jars of jam for Christmas, made from blackberries she had picked herself, show them how wrong they were.

She licked her lips and savored the ashy char. Fish from the river was like nothing she had ever tasted before—like sweet water. Maybe Thomas was right: everything that they could ever need was right here. An entire world that money could never buy. A life they could call their own.

Chapter Five

Manny opened the door to the pearly light. Early frost had licked the mullein dead, and his breath wafted out in little puffs. He gathered his hat and jacket, felt under the mattress for his gloves, found one, the wool eaten through. He tucked it back. Better to feed the mice.

When Dog started to follow him out, he pointed her inside. "I'll see what I can fetch you from the Bateman place," he said. "Guess I'm the breadwinner around here now."

He knew it was a lengthy hike along the railroad. He could cross the bridge and hitch on the highway, but he preferred to keep moving and wait for the Monday log train, counting the ties, the cadence taking up room in his head.

Berry canes threaded beneath steel. Patches of poison ivy, bitten with frost, reddened the pockets of browning fern. The building of the rail decades before had necessitated blasting cliffsides to make way, then using the debris as fill where the shoreline dipped and slewed. The disruption of ancient soil had given rise to miles of bull thistle and loosestrife. It seemed to Manny that the railbed was a place unto itself, unlike any other—a fairway along which he stooped to inspect the seed-laden scat of bears. Coyote spore might contain rabbit fur, mouse skulls amazingly whole, or the wing joint of a bird. Beneath the cottonwood branches, he looked for the regurgitated pellets of owls—masticated bits of bone, hair, and feather. Atop the boulders closest to water, he found the crawdad claws left by the great blue herons that kept monastic watch over the shallows. He prized the hollow bones of killdeer and the indigestible incisors of rabbits, gathered them as he did the abandoned wasp hives and the teacup nests of hummingbirds. Once home, he would empty his pockets of treasures, place them along the single windowsill, add them to coffee cans and Mason jars already layered with remains, like the miniaturized strata of fossils.

As he walked, he stayed vigilant not only for the leavings of animals but for the animals themselves. Every living thing came to water. The shade beneath brambles sheltered rubber boas and alligator lizards. Each copse of ocean spray and locust breathed with the respirations of sparrows. Deer held in their lays until he was nearly upon them, and then crashed into the open, some making their way into the nearby draws, others taking to the river, swimming for the far bank. Once, he had come upon a badger, mean-faced and hissing, having backed itself against the hillside, no clear avenue of escape. It had made short charges, as though it might win the day by way of sheer ugliness. Manny kept a safe distance, aware of the thin leather of his boots. He coveted the teeth and imagined how he might first boil the meat from the skull, then leave it in the sun to bleach.

Behind him, he heard the deep whine of a railcar, the driver doing track inspection, surveying for fallen rock, beaver-dragged branches, coyote-killed calves—anything that might jump the train off its tracks.

"Mornin'," the man said as the vehicle's hum slowed. He lifted his hat, wiped his face with his sleeve. "Sure be glad when we get some colder days."

"Won't be long," Manny said. He understood weather talk. Something they could agree on up front.

"*Farmer's Almanac* says early winter. Hard one." The man licked his lower lip and spat. His broad face was ruddy with grit. He'd probably been working hours to clear the rail. Manny thought it seemed like a lot of responsibility for one man.

"Seen lots of woolly worms. Guess they know what's coming."

The man squinted toward the horizon, the sun topping the V of the canyon. "Where you headed?"

Manny tipped his chin downriver. "Got work at the Bateman place."

"Those new folks I saw in town?"

"Yes, sir." Manny knew the locals were already betting on failure. It was the kind of land that needed more than one generation to claim, more years than money to own.

The man waved off a deerfly, settled his hat a little farther down on his head. "Hop in. I'll drop you by."

"I'm thinking I might just stay afoot."

"Suit yourself."

Manny watched the railcar disappear, took a deep breath, and let his shoulders loosen. When, a while later, he heard the rumble of the train approaching, he waited at the curve of a sharp bend where the engine slowed and swung himself aboard.

Deracotte was waiting at the campsite and waved when he spied Manny shortcutting across the field.

"So," Deracotte called. "The rich. Are they different from you and me?"

"I'm sorry?" Manny saw that Deracotte had been working a pile of stones into a neat row. It was an odd way to fence, Manny thought, and wondered why Deracotte chose rock over post and wire.

"The rich. Gatsby. Daisy Buchanan. What do you think of her?"

Manny wanted to say that he had fallen in love with Daisy—her lightness and the tinkling of her voice—from the first, but he sensed that Deracotte would not find the answer satisfactory.

"I guess she had it better than some." Manny stepped to the pile, noting that the tent was pitched in a gully, perfect for a washout in sudden rain. Manny didn't think he'd ever seen anything so orange and wondered where Deracotte had found such a shelter. Nearby were the fire pit, coffeepot, and skillet. He imagined he smelled potatoes and onions fried in bacon grease.

"And Gatsby. Can you think of a vice in which he didn't indulge?" Deracotte placed his hands on his hips, leaned back until his spine popped. "So, tell me. What are *your* vices?"

Manny wasn't sure what kind of job interview he'd expected, but he figured he could prove his ability to carry rocks while he considered Deracotte's question. He thought at first to say he had no vices, and that, perhaps, may have been the most truthful of answers. But then Deracotte might think him dishonest. Forced Sunday school attendance at every church in town (each mother of every domination determined to have him confirmed, saved, baptized, washed clean) had taught him that no human is without flaw, and he figured he was nowhere near pure, but *vice* had a permanent ring to it, as though a man had settled into his sin and intended to stay a while.

"Dr. K says I'm lazy. Guess that's my vice."

"You don't seem lazy to me." Deracotte stripped off his gloves, slapped them atop the stone. The exposed flesh of his wrists was sunburned a raw pink. "Of course, we've only just met. Let's see what coffee we have left."

Deracotte led them to the warmth of the campfire and handed Manny a delicately painted teacup and saucer. Deracotte settled himself on a rotten piece of yellow pine and pointed for Manny to sit on another. Manny balanced the hot coffee on his knee, wary of his seat, which tottered unevenly and threatened to throw him. The firewood had not been split but heaved whole into the pit, giving off more smoke than flame.

The side of the tent rippled, and Manny looked quickly as the woman stepped out barefoot, braid of dark hair over her shoulder, stomach bulging. She was younger than he had imagined, close to his own age, beautiful. He might have looked longer, but his ears began to burn, and he moved his eyes to the ground. He lifted his cup by the dainty handle. The first sip scalded, and he bucked forward to spit, the cup falling from his hands into the hot ash. He made a grab for the handle and held on for a split second before dropping it, the burn helped only a little by his impulsive sucking of both fingers and thumb.

The woman pulled a handkerchief from the pocket of her skirt, folded Manny's hand into her own, and began dabbing.

"I'm sure he's fine," Deracotte said. "Although I fear the same can't be said of your grandmother's china." Deracotte cocked his head over the shards as though he were reading tea leaves.

"I don't care about the cup, Thomas. Here." She knelt and examined Manny's palm, her warm breath on his skin like a second burn.

"He claims he has no vice but laziness, Helen. What do you think of that?"

Helen stood, brushed the dust from her knees. "I think you should leave him alone with your ideas. At least let him settle in first." She winked at Manny. "You'd think he was a philosopher instead of a physician."

Deracotte rose. "Let's leave the rocks for a while, and I'll show you the work we're after."

Manny followed Deracotte along a broken fence line, the pickets and poles derelict in their station, the wires sprung loose, twined with morning glory. The occasional pine or hackberry had been used as a post, the staples festered with sap. In the distance, Manny saw the new barn and the men already working. Dewey and Stubb. He'd known them for years, or at least of them. They lived at the margins of town, each with his family in a trailer house. He sometimes saw them having coffee at the Ox or tilting away from the Jet Club. The batter of their hammers filled him with excitement.

Deracotte stopped at a small outbuilding, its door yawed open and split. "This will need to come down." He picked up a Mason jar full of nails, rattled it lightly, and began to ferret about an old workbench. Manny had hoped he'd be working on the barn with the other men. Instead, he'd been relegated to kids' duty. He felt a sudden longing to be back at his place along the tracks, the coppery air coming in off the river, instead of on the dusty bluff, talking with a stranger who didn't know enough to keep his head down, his eyes open, his fingers out of dark places. It was all Manny could do not to caution Deracotte about black widows, just as he'd wanted to warn him about stepping across the doorjamb without first checking for snakes.

"So," Deracotte said. "What's your opinion? New house here when the time comes?"

Manny figured he could gauge the risk of snakebite or spider nest, and he supposed he might even be a good judge of building sites, but he had never had an elder request his guidance in anything.

He knew this: old man Bateman's clan had been wise as to where to build and why. Manny looked west to what had been the property's sole barn for more than a century. Tucked against the shoulder of a hill, out of the way of spring runoff and rogue winds, facing east for first sun—it and the farmhouse beside it had lasted longer than most. Deracotte's new barn sat at the mouth of a dry run, rich flat ground for crops but a a goner should a cloudburst hit.

"What about over there?" Manny asked. "Where the old house was?"

Deracotte furrowed his brow, pretended to consider something he'd already decided. "It would take more work to clear." He turned back to his small window. "And the view isn't as good."

Manny thought that Deracotte had better be more of a doctor than he was a farmer. The unsplit firewood, the piled wall of rocks—he wondered if Deracotte had arrived with anything other than a suitcase full of vials and bandages. He shivered at the thought of needles. It had taken two men to hold him down while Dr. K stitched his knee, opened to the bone on a shard of basalt. He remembered the boy who had caused his fall: Shirley Renfrow, slick-haired and bulging at the waist. They'd been racing each other back from the river, Manny in the lead until Shirley pushed him off the trail and into the rocks. He still felt rage whenever he thought of it, the unfairness of the shove, the meanness, the trickery. And then the blood, which he knew would draw unwanted attention. What he had not expected was the burn of the needles: the first meant to deaden, and then the curved one that Dr. K hooked through the skin and pulled tight as though whipstitching a hem.

Deracotte returned to the trail and seemed headed for the river. Manny could see Helen moving in and out of the tent, and he knew that he'd take what little cash he had to Duggy's Department Store, where Duggy's wife, Roxie, had filled a corner with candy dishes and tea towels. It wouldn't be exact, but Manny was sure he'd find a teacup that might pair with the one he'd broken.

He stepped into the small building, surveyed the roof, the few shingles still intact. Better to burn it, he thought. But it wasn't his to decide. He began clearing the bench, careful of his blistered fingers and thumb. He separated the jars carefully so that he could see between before reaching for the next. Most held nails and staples; some kept the degenerate dust of rubber washers; one came up heavy, full of ball bearings of varying size that Manny saw right away could be steelies—the marbles he'd most coveted as a child and still did. Deep to the back of the bench was a coffee can of bolts, and when he pulled it away from the wall, he saw the glossy black body of the spider. Egg cases the size of peas clung to the erratic web she'd woven beneath the window. She was one of the largest Manny had ever seen, easily the size of a half-dollar, legs included. He admired the hard glint of her, the stealth. He knew that had Deracotte kept up his fumbling, she'd have made herself known to him.

Manny found a small jar, emptied its tacks into the coffee can, and shook her in before punching the lid with a screwdriver. She seemed unperturbed by the capture, and he set the jar in the lee of a tree so that the warming sun wouldn't scorch her.

When he'd emptied the contents of the shed, he went at the roof with a crowbar he'd discovered leaned into a corner. The blisters on his fingers and thumb burst, and he wiped them against his jeans. The shingles took little time, the walls only a little more. He hammered the larger brads loose, found a cat's paw to pry the smaller ones, dropping each nail into a can so that no animal would come up lame. He organized the rough lumber into uniform stacks, cleared the packed dirt floor of litter, and added it to the burn pile, which he hoped Deracotte knew enough not to light until first snow lest the entire county be set ablaze.

Dewey and Stubb stopped by on their way to the pickup, both grinning and tired. "Would've saved you some lunch if we'd known you was coming," Stubb said, and Manny realized no one had called him to eat. He could see Helen outside the tent, rising every now and again, closing her book to look out over the river. Manny wasn't sure what had become of Deracotte, and he did not feel he should go to the tent while the woman was there alone.

"Not hungry anyway," he said, but he was thinking of the dog and what he would feed her. He waved to the men and felt a wince of longing to be with them, headed home or maybe to the Jet Club for a round before dinner. Even though Dr. K said he was too young to be thinking in such a way, what Manny desired was not a girlfriend but a wife, the same person to come home to night after night, a family to gather and feed and keep warm. "I want a bunch of kids," he'd told Dr. K. "Boys and girls. A bunch of them." The pharmacist had surveyed him with one eyebrow raised, then shook his head. "Might want to join up with the Mormons," he said. "They support that kind of foolishness."

Manny picked up the lidded jar and held the spider to the light. She'd settled to the bottom, and he could look beneath and see the hourglass. He turned to the road that would lead him to the tracks.

He could have grabbed a ride with Dewey and Stubb, but this way he didn't have to talk to anyone but the spider. The jar rode ably in his shirt pocket, like a rocket ship. He remembered the comics he'd read as a boy, Buck Rogers traveling through space.

Buck, Manny thought. Not much of a name for a girl. "Buck," he said, and tapped the jar. "Yea or nay?"

All eight legs held still, each delicately hinging the glass.

"Buck it is, then."

Manny lengthened his stride. The train would be pulling its seven o'clock load. He'd hitch if he could make the bottom of the hill in time.

As he rounded the corner, he could see Deracotte, hip-deep in the river, casting toward where the cottonwoods rimmed the pools. Did he know of the deep holes that cratered the riverbed? How a man could take one step and be in over his head, the current whirling him away?

He heard the train's engine, felt it vibrate up through his shinbones. He began to run, telling himself he'd have to remember the jar in his pocket when he swung himself aboard. He did not want broken glass in his chest, did not want to have any doctor's needles visited upon him. He did not want a black widow loose upon his person.

And even as he ran, he watched the road. The air was cooling, the rocks held heat. Rattlers would lie out on their bellies, blend in with the dusk-darkened gravel. It was a lie that they had to coil before they could strike. Manny had seen one go after a dog, its body arrow-straight, head erect. He'd seen them long as a harvest table, thick as a baby's arm. He'd seen the new hatch like a knot of worms and the hawks carrying them away in their talons. He'd seen them in all seasons, sloughing their skins, smoking out from ditch fires, paralyzed by fall's first frost. And when the railroad had blasted a new bed for the track, he'd seen their ruptured dens rain down, the men screaming, flailing and stomping, snakes dead and alive hanging from them like their own shredded flesh.

He made the track ahead of the train and waved to the engineer, who slowed as best he could. Manny waited for the caboose. He held the jar tight to his chest with one hand, grabbed with the other, and felt himself lifted off his feet, the brakeman's strong arms pulling him aboard.

They stood facing each other for a moment, grinning in recognition, and then the brakeman hollered, *"Tea?"* and motioned to the kettle racketing atop the stove. Manny nodded, checked the glass jar in his pocket, felt the tremor of the train and perhaps the shudder of his own heart.

The tea settled in his empty stomach, and he realized that he was hungrier than he had been in a long time. His hands were raw and prickly with splinters. He felt the tightness in his back and down his legs. When the brakeman offered him half of his olive loaf sandwich, Manny shook his head. He'd keep his hunger and his ache, savor them awhile. Once in town, he'd hit the Ox, order a cheeseburger basket and chocolate malt with the money Dr. K had paid him.

When he jumped off the train at Fife, Manny was hoping to see lights, but the street was closed down, only the bar still lit. It was past dinnertime, and the sidewalks were empty. Manny leaned his forehead against the café's window and peered inside. His stomach clenched and growled. He moved to the drugstore, tapped on the glass, waited, and then walked around to the alley, where a stairway rose sharply to the apartment.

He'd never done this before, come to Dr. K like the orphan he was, looking for some comfort, but the work had loosened something in him. He wanted someone he knew he could talk to, to tell about Deracotte and maybe about Helen. All day, he'd watched her as she lay on a blanket in the sun, reading, every now and then moving to the canyon's lip to look out over the river. When she'd gone into the trees at the edge of the clearing, he'd turned his head to give her privacy; from his elevated point above camp, he might have seen everything.

He set the spider beneath a riser, climbed the stairs, and looked around to see who might be watching, as though he were visiting a bordello under cover of night. The door itself was the bright red of parade flags. People speculated as to what mysteries lay behind it but supposed that there was little any man could do in such a small town that would escape notice of some kind. Whatever it was, if it didn't smoke, scream, or smell, it was probably best left be.

Manny leaned in and listened. The sound of a radio playing opera. He guessed that Dr. K might be readying for bed. He imagined a little room with sink and toilet, a bathtub—luxuries that Manny seldom missed but now did: water hot from the tap, enough to soak in while you listened to the nine o'clock news.

Or maybe the druggist was just sitting at the table, enjoying a cigarette, a sin he claimed he needed; otherwise, he said, he was in danger of becoming smug. "Look at these hands," he'd say to Manny, holding them out for inspection. "Ever seen anything so lily white?"

Manny knocked and heard the radio go silent. When the door opened, he saw the cobwebs lacing the corners, strands silvering between his face and the narrowed eyes of Dr. K.

"What?"

"It's Manny."

"I can see who the hell it is. What?"

"I was wondering if you might have some dinner left over."

The older man snorted, opened the door a bit wider. "Come on, then. You're letting in the flies."

The room smelled of burnt sugar. On the small drop-leaf table a pecan pie cooled in its tin.

"Pie's for tomorrow's auction, but I guess one piece won't cost you."

"What's the cause?" Saliva pooled behind his teeth as Manny watched Dr. K cut a wedge and set it on a blue saucer.

"Richardson girl. One who got burned so bad at church camp."

"She still in the hospital?" Manny remembered her tight blond pigtails, the mole on her neck he always had to look at twice to make sure it wasn't a tick digging in. The fire had taken her hair, her ears, and most of her nose. The skin off both shoulders. The mole.

Dr. K opened the refrigerator, pulled out a jar of heavy cream, poured a little over the pie. "You haven't ever been burned bad, have you?"

Manny sat down in one of the two wooden chairs, folded his hands, and felt the rawness of his fingers and thumb. "Few blisters here and there. Not much more."

"Hurts, though, doesn't it?" Dr. K handed him a spoon. "Eat it while it's warm. Best that way."

The first bite, Manny closed his eyes, the better to concentrate on the buttery sweetness, the toasted nutmeat, the salt lard crust. Oh, Lord, he thought. Aw, Jesus.

"Well, hell," Dr. K said. "Maybe I'll just donate a hot-water bottle." He moved the pie in front of Manny. "Just promise me you'll never throw white gas on a fire. You know better, don't you?"

"Yes, sir." Manny took the cream Dr. K offered, poured a little, then a little more.

"Might as well empty it."

Gratitude was something that Manny knew and understood, but he'd never felt quite as grateful for anything as he did the pie. It fed something in him that was more than appetite, more than an empty stomach. It was the movement of hands over dough, of fingers fluting the edges. It was just the right temperature and length of time in the oven. It was the whole round pie itself, pulled out perfect, set to cool.

"Good enough for the fair?" Dr. K had settled back into his soft chair and rested his feet atop an embroidered hassock, the pink-petaled flowers strange beneath the flagging toes of his wool socks.

"Blue ribbon," Manny said.

In normal times Manny would have been looking forward to late nights beneath the shriek and whirl of the Ferris wheel, or maybe a double trip on the roller coaster. He often worked setup and breakdown, earning enough for a few free rides, cotton candy, caramel apples, taffy pulled and pulled until it glistened. The exhibition barn held a special fascination: platters of fudge, cakes, peanut brittle. Canned pheasant, moose jerky, smoked trout. Pumpkins too large for a wheelbarrow, hauled in with tractors, unloaded and positioned with great tenderness by the men who had raised them from seed. Tomatoes unblemished by too much water or too little sun. Eggs by the gross, white and brown and pale green. Relishes, compotes. Bread-and-butter pickles, sweet, dill. Watermelon rind. He examined each display to see what portion the judges had taken: from the gooseberry pie, a smallish wedge; from the jar of apricot jam, enough to slather ten biscuits; from Mrs. Bledsoe's famous rum cake, an entire half, replaced by an enormous purple ribbon, Best of Show.

Manny rose to take his dish to the sink. Through the window he could look out over the lesser buildings, see the steeple of the Methodist church and what he knew to be the silhouette of Clifford Lott's house with its pigsty built right on back, given over now to the hubcap collection that Clifford hung on the weathered boards and polished to a superior shine. A little farther, Manny could see the dark band of the railroad and the glint off the moon-splashed river. He believed he could make out his shack, a grainy blackness where nothing else was.

"Mrs. Deracotte. She's going to have a baby."

Dr. K considered this for a moment. "Guess she'll go to Folgate."

Manny rinsed his plate. "Sure was good pie."

"Tell Mrs. Deracotte I got anything she needs."

Outside, the good kitchen smells were replaced with the familiar incense of woodsmoke and the smell that was the canyon at night when cold was coming on: compost of syringa, dogwood, ninebark. Duff of larch needles and bear moss. An undercurrent of horse manure. The lesser odor of old man Burgdorf's outhouse, holdout against city plumbing and water fees. Carrying it all along was the river, the scent of it bright and metallic, blended with bitterroot and silt.

Manny breathed in, felt fine with a full belly and the night's promise of sleep. Knowing there was hard work ahead allowed him to feel the pleasure of his meantime leisure. He rolled his shoulders, sore from the biting weight of lumber. His breath hung before his face, then ghosted away. He thought of Helen's bare feet, the thinness of her dress. Maybe he should have stayed longer, split a rick of wood, put a store of kindling by.

He picked up the jar at the bottom of the stairs, held it to the moonlight, and discerned the black orb suspended. He followed the sidewalk, crossed over to the alley behind the Ox, and pulled a gnawed steak bone from the garbage. Back at the shack, Dog was waiting for him. He motioned her outside, waited while she snuffled and squatted. He lit the candles and pulled the bundle from his coat pocket.

"Compliments of the chef," he said. "Aged to perfection." Dog took the bone between her teeth as daintily as she had taken the cracker. By the time Manny had washed his face and undressed, she was cleaning her feet.

"Don't know where you came up with such manners," he said. He crawled in bed and moaned with the goodness of it. He remembered how he had slept in the hut with his mother and father, all of them bundled together on a mattress flat on the floor. It was the same low bed on which his mother had given birth to his sister. Manny recalled little of that time, only that the midwife had arrived and asked him to stay outside until she called him. He had listened through the canvas wall until the sun had set. Then things had grown quiet until that moment when his father threw open the plywood door and ran for the pickup. Not a word to Manny, who stood shivering in the evening dew until the midwife stepped out and told him to follow her to her car, which he did. He never saw his mother or his father or his home again. His father had returned, doused the canvas with kerosene, and burned the hut to the ground. That Christmas, an envelope arrived with a twenty-dollar bill and a handwritten note: "Tell my son I'll see him come summer." But that summer had been years ago.

Manny thought of the Deracottes in their fiery orange tent and hoped that the downriver wind didn't rip it from its moorings. He couldn't imagine why a doctor wouldn't buy a nice house in town, plumbed and wired, windows tight. He thought of Helen and was embarrassed by the quickening of his pulse. He knew that she was beautiful. He knew that any man could see that it was so. He knew that he shouldn't think of her the way he was thinking.

He blew out the last candle and listened to the dog's breathing deepen. She huffed a closemouthed bark, growled low in her chest. Manny reached out, laid a hand on her side, and she lifted her head to lick his sore fingers. He looked to the window and the spider in her jar. She seemed content enough, hung like a black star in her sky of glass. "It's getting downright crowded in here," he said quietly. "Going to have to add on." Maybe a kitchen. A room for nothing but books and bones, with a fat chair in the middle. He'd pad around in his socks, smoke if he wanted. Become a man with some vice to keep himself humble.

The dog resettled her shoulder against the plank floor. He let his fingers trail along her side and thought of his father's horses and the great heat of their bodies. His father had sat behind him in the saddle and taught him how to direct the horses into a walk, trot, canter, gallop. Manny remembered how proud his father was of the geldings, their hair the color of buttercream, how he laughed when people expressed surprise that such large animals could be so graceful. "They don't know how big they are," he'd answered. "It's the bigness of the heart that matters."

To rest the whole of his hand against the dog's chest, feel it rise and fall with each breath, felt like something Manny had lost and finally found. Like the pie, how he recognized with his first mouthful that it was the perfect answer to the question he didn't even know he was asking.

Maybe someday he'd have a wife, he thought. Maybe even a daughter. A bighearted horse that would carry them well. "It's not impossible," he said to the dog, and she sighed beneath his hand.

Chapter Six

The Give-n-Get thrift shop stood next to Freddy's Feed, and the smell of straw permeated the secondhand clothing—one rack of children's, one of men's, another of women's. Musty suit coats, faded flannel nightgowns, pajama tops missing their bottoms. Shelves of mismatched dishes, pot lids, and ashtrays from Las Vegas. A rack of shoes still bearing the shape of their owner's particular stance: heels broken down, toes curled up, soles unevenly worn. A table in back held board games and puzzles marked with the number of pieces missing. Who would log so many hours determining such vacancy?

Deracotte had stopped in to see what bargains he might find. The barn was mostly finished, the house started, yet his toolbox was still empty. Hammers, screwdrivers, saws, shovels—the list that Stubb had given him seemed endless. But he didn't want to borrow each time a chore arose, which was nothing like self-sufficiency.

The clerk, an elderly volunteer with thinning white hair and an enormous brooch pinning her bosom, watched him closely as he dug through the bins.

"Can I help you?" The woman walked toward him on sore feet, wincing with the effort.

"I'm just looking for tools, thank you." The bin held little of any worth: a level with two bubbles broken and a ball-peen hammer with a cracked handle.

"All proceeds go to the animal shelter. Feeds the dogs. Spays the cats. People have too many, you know."

She was studying him, and he tried not to stare back. Her eyebrows, long lost, had been replaced with two exaggerated black lines that reached from her nose to her temples, like the wings of an albatross.

"That Dr. K. I love cats, I tell him, but I don't like what they do in my flower beds."

The woman had taken on the smell of the shop—damp straw, singed wool, an undercurrent of rose water. She followed him as he made his way around the room. He kept his head down so as not to invite further conversation, to no avail.

"We got a call that there's a bunk bed coming in. You got kids? Kids love bunk beds. Always a fight who gets top. Someone gets his head cracked."

He wondered if he would ever get used to the quick conversations that the people of Fife seemed likely to spring upon him without benefit of acquaintance or reason. Deracotte wished that Helen were there with him. She welcomed such chitchat and had an easy way with strangers. He knew that he should talk to the woman and ask if she knew of any vacant office space that might serve as a place to see patients. Yet he hesitated, and why? It was something about the way the people looked at him with sudden expectation when they discovered he was a doctor. The way they eyed him with something between respect and suspicion.

"Think we're headed for a weather change." The woman rubbed her shoulder with a hand twisted by arthritis. "Alice . . . you know Alice? Alice and Gwen, they've taken to stinging each other with bees. Says it helps the inflammation. I never heard the like."

Deracotte discovered a hoe, leaned into the corner by the books, its handle rough with splinters. "How much?" he asked.

"One dollar," the woman said. "Most things like that are one dollar."

He followed her back to the counter, the hoe large and awkward in his hand. He'd have to keep a window down in the VW to accommodate its length. He gave her a five and waited for his change.

"You could donate. Tax deductible."

"I'll keep that in mind," he said, and folded the ones into his pocket. "I'm looking for an office to rent. Do you know where I might inquire?"

The woman folded her eyebrows into a single wing. "What kind of office?"

"I'm a physician."

"Is that right?" Her eyebrows flew up.

"My wife and I moved here to take over the Bateman place."

"Ah," the woman said, and nodded. "I heard about you."

He waited but she offered no other information. "Is there a Realtor in town? Someone who might know about rentals?"

"Closest real estate is . . . well, I don't know. Folgate, I'd guess. Not here. Know that for sure. Most folks do their own business or have Jasper Jones do it. He's the lawyer. Guess you could ask him."

"Thank you. I will." Deracotte had seen the office next to the Blue Ox Café.

"You get settled, maybe you could help with the castrations." She looked out the window as though she might lay her eyes on a wayward tom. "You could ask at the drugstore. Dr. K. He's the one I go to. Helped me with my rheumatoid. He's got a special salve that really works. Burns like fire when you first put it on, but then it's good. Anyone knows anything, it'll be him."

"Maybe I'll stop by," Deracotte said, though he had no intention of doing so. The druggist's role in the town wasn't something he had anticipated, and he wasn't yet sure how to respond when the townspeople referred to the man as "Doctor," which he wasn't. He found their smug faith in him irritating, although he sometimes wondered if he himself might not have made a better pharmacist than physician.

He directed the hoe handle through the Volkswagen's window, then realized that someone could easily reach in and unlock the doors. Helen teased him about his insistence that something might be stolen. "What?" she'd ask. "What do we have that anyone could ever want? Besides, Thomas, we're in Fife. People don't lock their doors here. It's like you're saying you don't trust them."

Rolled tight, the window left only a two-inch gap. Deracotte hesitated before checking the lock. The thrift-shop woman had followed him outside and was watching from the doorway. She pointed down the street. "Dr. K's *that* way," she hollered. He waved in response and turned quickly, aware that the few people on the sidewalks were now looking at him. He walked to the attorney's office. The door was unlocked, but there was a note taped to the window: "Ox for coffee. Back in 30." Deracotte peered into the café for only a moment before realizing everyone inside was peering back.

How was it, he wondered as he walked to the car, that such a place could seem both friendly and hostile? The people were quick to smile, say hello, strike up a conversation about something as unlikely as feline castration, yet they watched him as though they believed *he* might be the one come to mark the corners of their property.

"This is a small town," Helen had chided him. "We're newcomers. Some of these families have been here for generations. Give them time."

Maybe Helen would come back with him the next day, help him talk to these people in a way that wouldn't seem foolish. He thought of her inside the tent, bundled in blankets. It would be a week before they had the walls of the house finished. It wouldn't matter if those walls were raw and the floor nothing but plywood: it would be warm and dry, and that would be enough for a while. They had what was left of the gift money from their wedding. He could wait a bit longer before opening an office.

It was always a relief to leave Fife and drive alongside the river. *A Field Guide to Western Birds* indicated that, by first snow, the osprey would have left their nests and fishing grounds, making way for the bald eagles, a brilliant balance of supply and demand. He was nearly to the bridge when he realized he had forgotten the groceries. If he turned around, it would be another hour before he reached home. Better to use that hour catching the fish that would feed them just as well.

He took his time up the hill, slowing for a run of quail, stopping long enough to watch a rabbit ricochet from ditch to burrow. He wished he had this day and all the days to come to do nothing but watch the sky and fields. It wasn't that he needed the barn, or even the house, he thought. Just a place to stay warm, fish from the river, and Helen. He knew that the baby would change things, and he felt a twinge of regret. They should have been more careful, taken precautions, but Helen seldom gave him time to think about such things.

Manny waved as Deracotte drove by the house, beams rising at four corners. Dewey and Stubb had left for the day, but, as was often the case, Manny had stayed on. No smoke wafted from the fire ring. Deracotte would have to split more kindling, something he was no good at. No matter how many times Stubb had showed him how to feather the wood into tinder, he couldn't do it. He feared the proximity of the sharp bit to his fingers and let go too soon, missing his mark. His kindling fell into thick chunks that spat and smoldered. Maybe Manny would take that task.

He parked the Volkswagen at the barn and pulled the hoe from the car. He'd stow it along with the odd assortment of other tools he'd bought and scavenged: a keyhole saw, slightly bent, and a posthole digger that Stubb said would be the most important tool he ever owned, next to his axe. The axe itself was a double-bit that terrified him: he dared not swing too far back for fear of embedding it in his spine.

Inside, he breathed in the smell of fresh-cut lumber. A riser would soon hold steps leading up to an apartment for the hired hand. He liked the idea of someone to caretake the land while he was working in town, someone to keep an eye on Helen and the baby. He rested the hoe against the wall, pleased with his growing hoard of implements, then stopped, cocked his head, and listened. A raven, or maybe a magpie, mimicking sound. But then he heard it again. The tent was over two hundred yards away. Could Helen's voice have reached him?

He stepped outside, began walking and then running, tripping over roots, cursing his slick shoes. He stumbled into camp and tore open the tent flap. Helen lay propped on her elbows, face flushed, breathing hard.

Deracotte stripped off his jacket, rolled his sleeves, even as he calculated the numbers he had been so sure of, the days until delivery. This was too early, premature by how many weeks? He fought the impulse to count on his fingers.

He hadn't attended a birth since his days as an intern, and then only one, when he'd been shuffled aside by a large nurse who cooed over the panting mother, scolded her, finally ordered her to push, then stepped aside at the last minute so that he could guide the already emerging head and shoulders. "Nice catch," the nurse had said, then moved her attention back to the mother and child.

"I'm afraid, Thomas. I want to go to the hospital." Helen's dark eyes grew large, and she began to moan, low and ascending, a sound so animal that it made the hair on Deracotte's neck rise.

He knew that he must check cervical dilation, the baby's position. "I've got to scrub," he said, but Helen grabbed his arm and shook her head. She was naked, and he attempted to cover her with the blankets she had kicked to the corners. "No!" she ordered. "I'm burning up." But then she was shivering, her skin cool, sheened with sweat.

He remembered the nurse, her mix of encouragement and

command. "You're doing fine, Helen. You just do what I tell you, and we'll be fine." He stepped out just long enough to run a few yards back and call for Manny to build a fire, bring water. By the time he returned, the moan had started again, deep in her chest. She did not blink but kept her eyes on his, and he could not look away. Her fingers wrapped his wrist, and he was surprised by the strength of her grip.

He heard kindling being split, the striking of a match. Helen's groan became a growl, loud and building to a pitch that was alarmingly similar to the sounds that accompanied their lovemaking. Deracotte leaned over her, as though he might buffer the noise with his chest.

"Hush," he said. "Manny will hear you."

The bite came so unexpectedly and sank so deep that he yelped. She had taken him by the flesh of his forearm.

"For God's sakes, Helen!" He pulled away and saw the crescents pool with blood.

Helen fell back, eyes closed, breathing fast and shallow. Deracotte stepped out to see Manny filling the few pots, balancing them atop the rocks. Deracotte stripped to his waist and began scrubbing his arms, including the bite Helen had given him, which would need to be watched for infection. He backed his way into the tent, hands held high and dripping, never saying a word to Manny, whose eyes seemed filled with a kind of sad fear that reflected Deracotte's own growing distress.

"Thomas, Thomas, Thomas." Helen wasn't looking at him but at a corner where the tent poles came together. "Thomas, Thomas, Thomas." She brought her head forward, chin to chest, and raised her knees. The sound was no longer a wail but a resonant drone in the back of her throat.

"Are you pushing? Helen? Wait." He worked his way between her legs, wary, now, of the proximity of her teeth. He saw that the bag of waters had broken, and, to his astonishment, that the baby was crowning, the dark whorl of hair showing itself. It was happening too fast.

"Wait," he ordered. *"Not yet."*

Helen unfolded, fell back to her pillow. The baby's head disappeared.

Deracotte remained kneeling, hands outstretched, eyes fixed on the sex of his wife, now altogether unfamiliar to him.

And then she was tensing again, as though her body were strung to a bow, as though it were the bow itself. She curved upward and braced herself on her elbows. Lips drawn back, teeth bared, she bore down, every muscle and tendon in her body straining with and against itself. Again the head appeared, slick with mucus and blood, and this time Deracotte reached his hand to touch it. There was the groan, the growl, the roar of the animal Helen had become, and then the head was turning beneath his fingers, the rotation he knew would happen because the books had told him it would, but nothing had prepared him for that moment when the child, half-birthed, opened its eyes and rested those eyes upon him.

He felt his heart grip like a fist, a sudden, gulping sob escape his throat. Then one shoulder, and the other, and the baby came into his hands.

Deracotte cradled the small body. Beneath the waxy vernix, the skin was a healthy pink. The face became a tight pucker that erupted into a howl.

"A girl," he said. "Helen, it's a girl." But Helen wasn't listening. She was panting with new pain. The afterbirth, Deracotte thought. The final contractions to expel the placenta. He'd almost forgotten.

He laid the baby girl at Helen's breast and tugged gently on the umbilical cord. He expected depletion, release, but what he felt instead was solid and firm. He wished for more light, the intensity of his headlamp. He prodded with his fingers, and then sat back, confounded. Another head had begun to emerge.

"Not possible," he said under his breath. Helen pushed once, and the twin slipped into the space between Deracotte's knees.

Two. One hidden behind the other. The heaviness. The early labor. He should have known.

"Thomas." Helen was holding the firstborn, who rooted vigorously for the nipple just out of reach. "Show me."

Deracotte slid his hands beneath the child, a boy, much smaller than his sister. The infant opened its mouth as though to cry, and Deracotte realized that there was no sound. He tilted the head, jiggled gently.

"What's wrong?" Helen demanded, on her face a look of wild intensity.

He turned the baby's chest onto his palm, slapped gently between the shoulder blades, then turned the small face upward, ran his fingers between the gums. The baby's head fell back, its lips blue.

Deracotte knew how to pound a man's chest with his fist, hard enough to break ribs, hard enough to get the stilled heart beating. But the bones of this being felt hollow, like the bones of a bird. He tested two fingers against the sternum, pressed once, twice.

Then Helen was laying the girl aside, leaning forward, pulling the baby boy into her lap, covering the tiny mouth with her own, sucking, spitting, sucking, clearing the airway. She placed her fingers atop the infant's rib cage and rubbed as though calling forth fire. The infant's head lolled, the skin fading from blue to milky gray. Even as Helen pulled the child to one breast and held the girl to the other, Deracotte could see there was no use.

"I need to examine the boy," he said quietly and reached out his hands.

She raised one shoulder against him. "No."

Deracotte sat back on his heels, momentarily unsure what to do, but then he remembered from his books that Helen still needed his care. He moved to her soft stomach and began the aggressive massage that would tighten the womb. She closed her eyes against the ebbing contractions, the echoing pain.

"What about names, Thomas?" Helen turned her gaze back to

the babies and lifted them toward her lips. "What shall we name you?" she whispered.

"Elise," Deracotte said. "Elise Rochelle Deracotte." He'd planned that it would be Elise—the name of no one he knew—but the second was his mother's name. Until that moment, he'd believed he'd forgotten.

"Elise Rochelle," Helen said. Her eyes shone with weariness.

Deracotte lowered his head. He found his bag, clamped and cut the umbilical cords. Helen watched silently as he gathered a thin blanket and wrapped it around the depleted placentas. When he stepped outside, he saw Manny standing stricken, dead still. Deracotte realized that he didn't know of the second birth. It would be easier to leave it be.

"The baby and Helen are both fine. It's a girl."

Manny's shoulders dropped with relief. "Good," he said. "That's *good*."

"Tomorrow doesn't have to be early."

"No, sir."

Deracotte watched Manny and the dog until they reached the embankment that dropped to gravel. He found the spade, walked to the three-trunked hawthorn, set the bundle on the ground, and began digging. The earth rang as though he were striking steel. The soil fractured as it gave, more rock than dirt. Deeper, it became less friable, turned to a kind of clay. He went deeper until the dirt moistened, until the bit sank into the ground soft and silent. He wrapped the blanket tighter and laid the afterbirth in the depression. Still, there was enough room for his son.

Deracotte studied his hands, caked with soil and blood. He could feel the tiny body gone limp, the pulse fading beneath his fingers. It was what he had known all along, something he had whispered to himself in the dark while still in Connecticut, hours after Helen had fallen asleep, the textbooks and practice exams scattering the floor around them: *This is not who I am.*

He wiped his face free of sweat and looked to where the new barn rose from the ground like a landlocked ark. He looked to the river. There were larger stones there, rounded and lovely, some shot through with color. They would hold down the grave.

The ribbon of water reflected the day's last light, and he walked quickly, skirting the brambles. The prints of animals marked the beach—deer, raccoon, the tri-toed trek of a heron. At the river shallows, Deracotte undressed, tucked his socks into his shoes, folded his pants. His skin tightened against the cool air as he squatted. An umber lather grubbed his wrists, the crease of his elbows, the beds of his nails. He cupped his hands full of water, worked it along his arms, the back of his neck. He rubbed himself with sand, let the mica and schist scour the blood and carry it away. He was a boy again, elbow-deep in the muck of the small pond behind his grandmother's house. The fishy redolence of shallow water, and in his hands, the pebbles and small bones of dead things, which he turned and petted beneath the sucking mud. Those days, he would return home begrimed and tell his grandmother what he had learned of the underworld, and she would nod solemnly as she kneaded the dough for bread.

Deracotte waded out into the current, then stopped. The water no longer held the sun's warmth, and he shivered before turning back for shore. Helen would be waiting. And Elise.

Elise. He said the name as a whisper at first, and then louder, giving it to the river and the wind, until his voice echoed against the canyon walls, and he believed that every living thing must hear.

Chapter Seven

Helen tucked Elise a little closer and lay in the near-light, listening. October, and the robins were gone. The birds that would stay through the winter were large and hardy: raptors, ravens, and owls. Only the mourning doves remained to soften the dawn and soon they, too, would migrate.

A little over a month since the birth, and already the memories seemed more like dreams. When Helen tried to recall the sharp pain she thought would split her in half, she remembered only moments of awareness between stretches of foggy exhaustion. "You forget," her mother had told her when she'd called from the pay phone at Fife with the news. "Otherwise, no woman would have more than one."

She hadn't told her mother about the dead baby boy. Maybe it was her punishment, the fulfillment of her mother's predictions—all that willful desire. Only she and Thomas knew—a truth they never spoke. She sometimes dreamed that she was moving the stones, digging to find the bones, looking to convince herself that there really had been another child.

The sound of Stubb's pickup, the coughs and low laughter of the men as they moved to the barn. Thomas had been gone for hours, up before the light hit their bedroom window, bare of curtains and trim. No water, no bath—nothing but a swaybacked bed, a table and two chairs, a potbellied stove with rusty hinges.

She needed a refrigerator, an oven. She'd tried cooking corn bread in the frying pan and ended up with a mess of batter that was scorched on the bottom and raw on top. Even coffee gave her fits: boiled too hard, it flooded itself with grounds; not long enough, and it tasted like ditch water. Nothing was as she had imagined it might be.

You've got no one to blame but yourself—her mother's words, and maybe true. She could hardly recall the logic that had led them to Fife. "What do we have to lose?" she'd asked Thomas. Out of some sort of misplaced pride, they had rejected every offer of help her family had extended, and even if Thomas were to approve of her request for more money, there was no guarantee her parents would give it. She thought of her mother's stiff admonishment: "You made your bed, now lie in it."

More and more, it seemed she slept in that bed alone. Thomas stayed up late to read, rose early to check on the men's progress, to walk the ridge, to fish—to do anything, it seemed, except spend time with her and Elise. The night before, he had lain cool and distant beside her. When she moved her hand to his chest, he'd sighed, as though her touch were not an erotic invitation but a summons to duty. She'd rolled away and peered into the dark, tears wetting her pillow, until Thomas's steady breathing filled the silence. And then who was there to cry for? No one but herself.

What made it worse, and what she could not tell her parents, was that Thomas still hadn't opened his medical practice in Fife. They had all the food they needed, he argued. Fish, berries, and wild plums. Stubb brought them a dozen eggs each Friday, free because he couldn't keep up with his hens. "Just a few more weeks," Thomas said, "and we'll have our own chickens, a cow for milk. How does that sound?"

Awful, Helen thought. After weeks of little more than trout and beans, she craved chateaubriand with bordelaise sauce, fresh asparagus with béarnaise, new red potatoes with rosemary. Those meals at her family's table, ridiculously lavish, came to her in dreams: the gravy hot and savory, the fresh peaches and scones with clotted cream. She often woke with the memory of cinnamon in her mouth.

Elise whimpered and kicked. Helen snugged her closer to nurse, felt the sharp tug. Her mother had championed formula and warned of sore nipples and sagging breasts. "You're not a primitive," her mother had said. "You don't want to look like those women in *National Geographic.*" Maybe her mother was right: maybe she wasn't cut out for this kind of life. Her heels were cracked, her hair a constant tangle. The blackberry jam she envisioned had gone the way of other dreams. Who could pick berries with a baby in her arms?

She imagined her parents on their sunporch, sitting down to plates of poached salmon, bowls of cucumber soup. She was surprised by how much she missed her father: the times he knocked on her bedroom door when he heard her crying over some boy and entered with a quart of maple nut ice cream, which he fed her in alternating bites—one for me, one for you—until they both were happier. He would return from his travels bearing Nougat Gerbe d'Or, Porcelana, tough stalks of Brazilian sugarcane that she shredded between her teeth. His homecomings were as sweet as his leavings were bitter, when Helen's mother would lock herself in her bedroom, Sinatra's voice crooning softly through the house, carrying with it the scent of cigarettes and Chartreuse. Helen wished she missed her mother more.

She missed her friends more than she thought she would, although she had always been outside the most intimate circle of girls, less comfortable with makeup and shopping than with a game of flag football. She hadn't had a best friend since grade school. She missed her piano—a Steinway of ribbon mahogany so dark it looked like blood swirled in black oil. It had belonged to her grandmother, a steely woman of great patrician airs. Helen missed the melody rising from the strings that contained more than she herself could ever give, as though hammer and felt had been possessed of the notes all along: *sereno, legatissimo, staccatissimo.*

She rolled the blankets on either side of Elise, then rose and stepped through the door, shivering in the frosty air, fighting the need to pee. The outhouse that Stubb had built was colder than the air outside, and she hated its rank odor. She didn't care that they were feeding the earth what the earth had fed them. She wanted a simple lever to push, enough water to flush it all away. Instead of a bucket full of soaking diapers, she wanted a washing machine, a dryer to replace the rope lines that flapped with a dozen white flags.

Breakfast, but what? The fire was dead, and there was no kindling. She rattled the oatmeal box, pulled out a fistful, and ate it dry. She peered out the window, and when Manny appeared on the trail, she smiled, always glad for his company. He stepped in, tawny with sun, his arms and shoulders muscled from work. He doted on the baby, toting her about with the ease of a doula. Helen sometimes believed that he might be the better father, and the thought filled her with guilt.

"I was wondering," Helen said. "Could you stay with Elise for an hour or two? I need to run some errands in town. We're out of groceries."

Manny looked toward the car.

"I can drive," Helen said. She wasn't sure it was true, but she remembered how her girlfriend had taught her to work the clutch and shift from first gear to second.

"Mr. Deracotte . . ." And here Manny trailed off. "Well, maybe he'd need to say it was okay."

"Where is he?" Helen was sure that Manny didn't know. Who did? And who would be willing to traipse the canyon to find him?

Manny looked out over the river, shrugged. "Guess I could use a break."

Getting ready to go to town was both simple and complicated:

a quick sponge bath, a search for a change of clothing that was neither too stained nor too wrinkled. She chose a cotton skirt and a simple olive-colored sweater, pulled her hair back and clipped it with the silver barrette, feeling the minutes of her freedom ticking away. Soon, Elise would awake and need to be fed. And again. And then again. Helen sometimes felt shackled, any desire she might have to read, explore, even look out over the river stymied by the weight of her breasts emptied but already swelling with new milk, Elise's cries for more.

Helen waved to Manny, who stood in the doorway a little unsure. She toed the accelerator and turned the key, then revved the Volkswagen to a high-pitched rattle. When she released the clutch, the car bucked and died. She tried again, working slower this time, and eased onto the dirt road before shifting into second, then third. Even at twenty-five miles an hour, the narrow highway was terrifying at first, river on one side, rock wall on the other. She pushed the accelerator up to thirty, then forty, rolled down the window, and let the cold wind catch her hair and pull it from its braid. When she saw her face in the rearview, she realized that she was smiling.

She'd been in Fife only a few times since their arrival, and it all seemed new again: the gas station, the library, the café where they had stopped for brambleberry pie. The grocery store, where the checkers called everyone by name and where you could put your bill on credit—an oily ledger with names and numbers dating back several decades. She parked on Main Street, opened her purse. She hadn't carried money since leaving Connecticut. She rummaged and counted the change: $2.36. Enough for a hamburger, fries, and a milk shake.

Enough for a margarita and a pack of cigarettes.

She walked to the Jet Club, its high, dark windows illuminated with neon beer signs, its front door open to the morning air. She was relieved that it was the kind of place that understood the need for a drink before noon. The dark bar smelled of damp ashtrays and beer-soured rags. She made her way to a table in the corner, glad that only one other customer shared the room with her: an older woman, her hair pinned into a reddish mass, who never looked Helen's way. The bartender reminded her of her father's barber: ruddy cheeks, plump fingers. He greeted her as though he'd expected her all along. "Yes, ma'am. What can I get for you?"

"A margarita, please. And a pack of Kools?"

"You got it."

Helen moved the ashtray a little closer, tried to keep from counting the seconds used up by the blender's whir. When the bartender set the salted glass and cigarettes in front of her, she pulled out her wallet.

"I'll go ahead and pay now, if that's okay."

"Sure. Let's see. With the smokes, that'll be seventy-five cents."

"For *all* of it?"

"That's it."

"I wish I'd known," Helen said, only half joking. "I'd have ordered another margarita."

"You got it." He was gone before she could protest.

Helen lit a cigarette, inhaled deeply, welcoming the sudden dizziness. She drank the first margarita before the second one came. When, at one point, the woman at the bar turned to look, Helen waved pleasantly, the glass at her mouth.

When the second margarita was gone, she stowed the cigarettes, stood, and looked for a bathroom. The bartender lifted his chin toward a hall behind the pool table. "Ladies' that way," he said.

Helen was glad for the narrowness of the corridor that kept her corralled and moving forward. The thin door clapped shut before she could find the light switch, and for a moment she was lost in the darkness. She felt for the toilet and sat with her face in her hands, her breasts throbbing, heard the muted wail of the jukebox, and then a woman's voice, drawing closer, singing "You are my sunshine, my only sunshine" in a true soprano. Helen realized too late that she had forgotten to lock the door. The wedge of dusky light caught her just rising, a twist of toilet paper in her hand.

"Sorry, hon." It was the red-haired woman. She squinted through the smoke of her cigarette. "There's a light. You want it?" She stepped inside before Helen could answer, flipped the switch. Helen saw that there wasn't one but two toilets, separated by a plywood partition. The woman yanked down her jeans and squatted, the cigarette pinched tight in the corner of her mouth.

Helen washed her hands quickly. The powdered soap left grit that stung the raw skin around her nails. She heard the toilet paper unwind, the clatter of the woman's belt as she stood and zipped. She shuffled back to make room at the sink.

"You're new here." The woman's hair was held by a thicket of bobby pins, lacquered with spray. Her skin looked cured.

"Almost two months."

The woman snapped the towel loop, dried her hands.

"My name's Esther. Friends call me Eppy."

"I'm Helen."

"You want another drink, Helen? I'm running a tab."

"Thank you, but I've got to get home. I have a hungry baby to feed."

"Ah." Eppy nodded, inhaled deeply. Her eyes were the same faded blue as her jeans. "I remember those days. Hard to get away and nothing you need worse."

"Well, maybe just one more," Helen said, but Eppy was already leading them back down the hall as though she'd known the answer all along. She had the lean legs of a cowgirl, the hips of a boy. Helen noted the way she straddled her stool with ease. When Eppy lit a cigarette, Helen pulled the pack of Kools from her purse and laid it on the bar like a ticket.

"So," Eppy exhaled in a long syllable. "You must be the doctor's wife. Where you from?"

"Connecticut." Helen licked the salt from the corners of her mouth.

Eppy shook her head. "I've never been farther than Denver. Went with my dad once to a rodeo. Three days' drive there, three days back. We ate peanut butter and jelly sandwiches for a week. Haven't eaten one since."

Helen laughed and felt some of the stiffness leave her shoulders.

"You ever work in a sweet shop?" Eppy continued. "Same thing. That sugar smell gets in your nose and never comes out. It'll break you of any cravings, I'll tell you that. A month behind the counter at the old soda fountain down the street, and all my hankerings turned to salt." Eppy hiked one boot to rest on her knee. "Got me my first husband there, though. Came in for a cherry phosphate." She held the smoke so long that Helen felt her own lungs ache. "He was the best one. Maybe I didn't want him bad enough. Too good at keeping my own company." Eppy snuffed one cigarette and lit another. "How's that Bateman place treating you?"

"It's fine," Helen said and knew that Eppy saw the lie for what it was. Niceties seemed some kind of sin in this place, and Helen should have been relieved: she had never been one to engage in chitchat. "It's beautiful. The river."

"River's pretty," Eppy agreed.

Helen took a swallow of her drink and then another. The bartender had gone to the back room, and she heard the rip of cardboard. She lit a second cigarette and settled herself more squarely on the stool. When she looked up, she saw that Eppy was watching her in the mirror.

"The canyon, it's so big," Helen said. "I feel lost in it sometimes."

"Some like it for just that reason. It's all I've ever known."

Helen tried to imagine what it was like to have lived your whole life in a town so small.

"Do you ever have any desire to leave? Go someplace else?"

"Never found anywhere else I'd rather be. Kids grew up and

got out so fast it'd make your head spin. Both living in California now. First husband followed the kids. I've got grandkids, and I'd like to be with them, but not there."

"I miss my family more than I thought I would." Helen closed her eyes. "I guess I didn't really know what I was getting into."

"Who does?" Eppy leaned her head back and blew a stream of smoke toward the ceiling. Helen saw some hint of the beauty she had once been. "Doesn't really matter how old you are or how many times, every decision is a new one. You just got to go with it sometimes, right or wrong. Find a way."

"I don't know if there is a way."

"There's a million ways." Eppy tipped her face toward Helen and her eyes took on a new seriousness. "You sure you're all right out there?"

How to answer? Helen knew better than to complain about the outhouse, the bare floors—the only kind of life that many of the people in Fife had ever known. Loneliness seemed a part of the landscape. If you bartered for one, you got the other. And what could she say about Thomas? He was to be the doctor, she the doctor's wife. She felt a sudden fear that she was making a terrible mistake being at the bar. What would the people think? She lifted her glass and realized it was already empty.

"I'm sorry," she said. "I have to go."

Eppy watched her gather her cigarettes, her purse. "Listen," she said. "I'm here this time most days. If you need someone to talk to."

Helen wished she could stay all afternoon. Already, she'd been gone too long. She stepped out, grateful for the gray sky that threatened rain. It calmed her, slowed the racing of her heart. She climbed into the Volkswagen, straightened the rearview, checked for traffic before slipping the clutch. She needed to go slow, stay focused, but Main Street wavered and dipped. Her stomach clenched—other than the handful of oatmeal, she hadn't eaten anything since dinner the night before.

She wasn't sure what made her think that Main was one-way. It was Fife, after all, the street as wide and open as a parade route. And there she was, *taking her half right down the middle,* her father would have said, and the pickup truck coming straight at her.

The impact was slight—*only a fender bender,* she repeated over and over as she opened her door and tried to stand. But a man wearing a white shirt was pushing her back to the seat. He smelled familiar, like hard soap and just-waxed floors.

"She was just there, Doc. Comin' right at me."

Helen looked up to see the driver of the pickup, his arms held high as though in surrender.

"It's okay, Dag. I saw it. Wasn't your fault."

"Mine," Helen said, nodding her head. "My fault," and then she felt the wave of nausea. She leaned forward and heaved.

The other driver seemed unfazed as he surveyed his pickup. "Don't think I got anything but a ding. I can pop that out. She all right?"

"She's just shook up."

Helen leaned her head back against the seat, wiped her mouth with the sleeve of her sweater. "Is he okay?"

"Who? Dag? Hell, he hasn't been okay since the day he was born."

Helen watched the green pickup back away. She lifted one hand as Dag passed by. "Sorry," she called, and felt the nausea building again.

"Go ahead," the man said. "Best get it all out."

Helen leaned forward, but there was little left for her stomach to bring up. She took the handkerchief he offered and saw that people had gathered at the sidewalk.

"It's just a fender bender," she said too loudly. "Not much to see."

"In this town, it doesn't take much," he said. "Why don't you let me get this buggy parked, and we'll get you some coffee."

She waited on the sidewalk, then let him cup her elbow as they stepped across the street to the Blue Ox. "I should clean up that mess," she said. "It's awful."

"It'll be gone in no time," he said. "Dogs will think it's Christmas. I'm Dr. K, by the way. Burt Kalinosky. I run the drugstore."

"Helen Deracotte." She slid into the booth and leaned her head into her hands.

He motioned the waitress over, a woman with twisted blond hair who smelled like drugstore perfume. "How you doing, Julie?"

"Can't complain. Got Bobby home."

"How's his leg healing?"

"Still got the cast on. Another month."

"Why don't you bring us two cheeseburger baskets. Cokes." He leaned forward as the waitress took their order to the kitchen. "Nice girl. Husband left her after the boy busted his leg falling off the monkey bars. She's better off anyway."

Helen pulled out her cigarettes. "Do you mind . . . ?"

"I'll join you." He moved the ashtray between them. "Hard habit to break. Got me at fourteen."

"I should have known better," Helen said. She rested her head back against the booth and closed her eyes.

"Life's oldest story. It's done now. No harm."

No harm. But she could have ruined everything. She sucked on the ice from her water as Dr. K asked how the building was going, what classes she'd taken in college, who her favorite composers were. It was an easy conversation, just like with Eppy. She liked these people, their straight questions and honest concern. When the burgers arrived, she stubbed her cigarette and breathed in the hot-grease smell.

"God, I'm hungry."

"Sounds like a good enough blessing to me." Dr. K salted his fries and thumped out a puddle of ketchup.

Helen knew she should hurry, but she wanted to savor every bite.

"Good?" Dr. K was smiling, his broad face lifted into a pleasant pattern of wrinkles.

"*Very* good." Helen wiped her mouth, took a long sip of

Coke. "Sometimes living off the land isn't all that it's cracked up to be."

Dr. K laughed. "Hard to grow a good cheeseburger." He waved to the waitress. "Just put this on my tab, Julie." He stood, brushed off the front of his shirt. "I've got to get back to the store. Probably already missed the Merck rep."

"Thank you." Helen held out her hand, and he took it shyly, pressing it between his large fingers.

"You might have that doctor of yours take a look. A little neck strain, maybe. You didn't bump anything?"

"The food helped."

"Always does." He hesitated, looked across the street, then back at Helen. "I've got a room in back. Not big, but he could see patients there. Might be a good setup for both of us."

"Thank you. I'll tell him." She lowered her eyes. "I guess I'm not very good at being alone."

Dr. K leaned forward. "No reason you should be. You come on in to town anytime. I'm always good for a cup of coffee."

He helped her inspect the Volkswagen's fender: a sharp crease, scraped with green paint. Maybe Thomas wouldn't notice. She pulled onto the highway, the clutch more familiar now, and held the speedometer to forty. She moved her neck to the right and left and felt the stiffness settling in. The closer she got to the bridge, the more sorrowful she felt. Since Elise's birth, what had once felt like solitude now felt like isolation. If she were back home in Connecticut, she'd have help with the constant diapering, bathing, feeding. Elise would have aunties and cousins galore. A closetful of Irish linens and satin gowns. A nanny. She'd have Helen's life all over again. And was it so bad, that life? Which was worse, Helen wondered: the sadness of staying in the mess she had made for herself, or the shame of returning home having failed, just as everyone had predicted she would?

She dug around in her purse for a stick of gum, found an antacid and hoped its chalky mint would mask the smell of tequila.

When she reached the house, she puttered into the driveway. The house was empty, and she made her way to the barn. She took the stairs leading to Manny's apartment, which was just big enough for a bed and dresser, a corner kitchen, a couch. The windows were in, and the room held the afternoon's warmth. Manny sat on the raw floor, Elise in his lap. He looked calm, content.

"Hey," he said.

"Hey." Helen squatted down beside them. Elise was sucking a damp cloth. "Sorry I was gone so long. Did she cry much?"

"Only when she woke up. I made her a sugar tit." Manny blushed with the word. "Hope that's okay."

"It's okay." Helen touched her daughter's soft hair. "Are you ready for Mama?"

Manny shifted the baby into Helen's lap and averted his eyes as Helen lifted her sweater.

"Guess I'd better get back to work."

Helen surveyed the walls, the rectangle of light. The river seemed a mile wide, the whole of the canyon's horseshoe opening below. An omega, just like Thomas had said.

"Do you think you'll like it up here?"

"Sure." Manny rose and brushed the seat of his jeans free of sawdust. "Best view around."

"You'll have to have some furniture. A table."

"Dr. K says he's got extra."

Helen smiled. "I had coffee with him today. He seems like a nice man."

"Always been good to me." Manny hesitated at the stairs. "Well, let me know next time you need a babysitter."

"I will. And Manny?"

"Yeah?"

"Don't say anything to Thomas. He'd worry, I think."

Manny considered a moment, then nodded before disappearing.

Helen moved Elise to her other breast, so swollen that it was difficult for the baby to latch on. Elise whimpered, her small fists fighting the air, her mouth opening and closing like the fish Thomas pulled from the river. Helen rocked to the rhythmic suckling. She wished that Manny had stayed a little while longer.

The tears came so unexpectedly that the sob broke from her throat before she could stop it. She rocked faster. How could she have foreseen this kind of loneliness? Those months with Thomas before the move, she'd felt satisfied, just the two of them with time enough to talk, laugh, question. He'd broken the back of her boredom, thrilled her with his odd intelligence. There had been something feral about him, exotic, as though he had come to her from some faraway country. "Not our kind of people," her mother had said, and that had made it even better.

Helen looked down to see Elise gone still, her gray eyes focused, as though aware and knowing, a look of such intensity that it startled Helen. What was going on in that small brain? She kissed the tiny fist that gripped her sweater. "Go ahead, baby. Eat. It's okay." The rosebud mouth resumed its pull and then slowed as the baby drifted into sleep. Helen wondered if her daughter had any memory of her twin. What was it like to have never been alone?

When Helen heard Thomas calling from the bottom of the stairs, she tried to answer in a whisper, "Up here." But he called again, and the spell was broken.

"Here!" she hollered, and Elise jumped, her arms and legs jerking out, her face twisting into a grimace before the wailing began.

Thomas's socks were burred, his shaggy hair matted with tree moss. His shirt hung loose across his shoulders, as though he'd been on some wilderness pilgrimage. He looked like a character from a fable, Rumpelstiltskin or Rip Van Winkle. She groaned at the thought of trying to work the pitch out of the knees of his jeans.

"Where have you been?" she asked before stopping to consider that she already knew.

"I found a place where the sand is full of arrowheads. Look." He leaned forward and held out his hand to show her the three broken points of obsidian.

Helen rocked to calm Elise, to calm herself. He'd been playing at the river like a child. She hung her head over the baby, whose cries had grown louder, as though the tension in the air were feeding her own anger. "I drove into town today."

Thomas looked out the window at the car. "Not with Elise."

"I asked Manny to watch her."

Was it concern or confusion that crossed Thomas's face? He stood with the arrowheads in his hand.

"I talked to Dr. K. He says he has a room in back of the store that he'd let you use to see patients."

"Dr. K?"

"He's a good man. He's willing to help us."

"We don't need charity, Helen. We don't want to be in anyone's debt. We need to make our own way."

"You mean *you* need to make your own way. Your way is the river, fishing, doing *nothing,* Thomas. That's not making a living. This isn't a vacation. And it's not your money that's keeping us from starving."

Helen saw his jaw tense, his lids drop low over the grayness of his eyes.

"This is crazy, Thomas. What are we doing? I can't stand it. Something has got to change. Maybe we can find a house in Fife. I can't live here like this."

Thomas laid the arrowheads on the windowsill and looked out over the river. "Maybe you're right, Helen. Maybe you don't belong here. Maybe you need to go home."

"And you'd prefer that? You'd rather lose your wife and daughter?"

"Elise is not going back."

"You're insane." Helen held Elise closer, struggled to her feet. "I'd never leave my baby with you."

His head jerked up, and she backed to the wall, fearing he might lunge at her, tear Elise from her arms. But then his face screwed up, his mouth pulled down, and he began to make little panting noises, grunts of pain. The sudden transformation was as alarming as the overt anger. She covered Elise's head with the palm of her hand, as though protecting her from a driving rain.

"Don't do this, Helen. Please." He held out his arms. "I'll do whatever you want. Just don't leave me."

"Thomas." Helen shifted Elise to fit against her hip. "We just have to talk to each other, that's all. I feel so alone here. I don't even know where you are most of the time."

"I'm here. With you and Elise. That's where I am."

"No. You're fishing. Or in the canyon. I don't have anyone else to talk to, to be with. I'm so lonely, Thomas."

"I'm sorry. I didn't know." He dropped his face into his hands, then lifted his eyes to meet hers. "I love this place. I don't ever want to leave it. But I couldn't survive without you."

Helen leaned into his shoulder and let him pull her close. "Wait," she said and nestled Elise on the floor, tucking the blanket tight. She touched his chest, his arms. There was less of him now, less softness. His bones felt solid beneath her hands, knowable. She felt his breath in her hair, his fingers at the back of her neck, a gentle cupping.

"I miss you," she whispered into his mouth. "I miss you."

"I'm here," he said. He laid his hand against the swale of her back and took her gently down to the hard floor. She wondered if he smelled the smoke on her, if he tasted the sharp bite of tequila. She could still feel the tingle in her toes, the warmth in her lungs. He moved one hand beneath her sweater, touched each breast lightly with his fingertips, moved over her, in her, and she breathed the smell of just-broken pine, of rainwater come down off the fields.

Chapter Eight

Manny rotated his wrist, and the spider swayed inside the jar. Everything else was packed: some clothes, a few novels. What he left behind would be little more than what he'd found in the shack to begin with. He didn't have room for all the books. Maybe the next squatter would find them and be glad.

"Wonder if we should take Buck along or let her go?"

Dog raised her ears, studying him as he studied the spider.

Manny slid the jar back to the window, tapped lightly on the glass. "Maybe we'll leave her here. Gives us reason to come back for a visit."

He carried the boxes one on top of the other, kicked the door shut behind him. He made his way through the grass, broken with first November snow, to where Deracotte waited in the Volkswagen.

"Is that it?" Deracotte opened the trunk, and Manny positioned the boxes, pointed Dog into the backseat.

"Yes, sir. But I'd like to stop by Dr. K's."

When they pulled in front of the drugstore, Deracotte kept the car idling at the curb.

Sunday, and Manny figured he'd find Dr. K in his apartment, but the pharmacist was filling a bottle from a long tube that ran from a jug of water set high on a shelf.

"Moving day, huh?"

Manny nodded. "Thought I'd see if I could get some cough drops before I go."

"You got a cold?" Dr. K pinched the tubing and peered at Manny.

"Not yet."

Dr. K laughed. "Might as well stock up on Ex-Lax, then. Maybe some Pepto and sinus tablets. If you're really planning ahead, how about a box of Trojans? And maybe some Preparation H and PoliGrip."

"How about a magazine?" Manny perused the rack, though he'd already read every issue of *Sports Illustrated* and *Field and Stream* it held.

"Take what you want. Going-away present."

"I'm not going far."

"Sure seems like it." Dr. K moved from behind the counter, pulled a thick sheaf of magazines from the stand. "Besides, I missed your birthday. Can't believe you're eighteen." He piled the magazines against Manny's chest and moved back to the counter.

"Mrs. Deracotte made me fried apples. Pretty good, too."

"That doctor of yours making business yet?"

"Haven't heard."

"Cal Lytle's got another ear infection." Dr. K tipped the bottle and shook it.

Manny rolled the magazines. "Well, I'm going."

Dr. K wrapped his arm around Manny's shoulders and gave a rough squeeze. "You know where to find me if things don't work the way you want them to."

Deracotte pulled onto the highway, and Manny watched the buildings of Fife disappear into the distance. He thought about his new home. It had taken most of the fall to finish the barn and dry-in the little two-bedroom house. The house was blocky and plain, but the barn was beautiful, high-beamed and tight. Still, Manny wasn't sure he wanted to be leaving his shack along the river, moving into the room above the barn. But it was a good trade. Dr. K had told him so. "You're a grown man," Dr. K had said. "Better start acting like one."

Hills the rusty color of rufous hummingbirds. Manny cracked the window, just enough to let in a thin slip of air. Deracotte began to whistle some low tune, a waltz maybe. Manny had come to believe that Deracotte was a good man but lax when it came to his duties. And Manny understood, as well, that he was not the only one who observed this. The townspeople knew without having to be told. They could see the fields lying fallow, the ditches choked with weeds that needed to be burned.

They turned right onto the bridge at Omega and started up the grade. Deracotte slowed the car, and Manny saw the covey of quail run for the cover of bramble, their topknots bobbing.

"I wish I had a gun," Deracotte said. "We'd have partridge for dinner."

Manny envisioned Deracotte in a tweed jacket, a leather patch at the shoulder, a funny cap.

Deracotte pointed to a larger bird, standing alone even as the others disappeared into the hedge. "What's that?"

"Fool hen," Manny said. "Dumb as a shovel. You could probably kill it with a rock."

Deracotte looked at Manny, then back at the grouse. He pulled off the road, eased his door open, and stepped out.

Manny had killed enough grouse in his time, but there was something peculiar about watching Deracotte in his low shoes sneaking toward the bird, a special kind of fascination in watching him bend slowly to choose a rock. The stone hit the grouse just at the wing.

"Got him!" Deracotte bellowed, then slipped and stumbled the few steps to where the bird twirled in the dust. Just as he reached the hen, it rallied and took off at a dead run for the brush.

Manny laughed, delighted by the grouse's unexpected recovery and Deracotte's struggle to climb the barbed wire fence, his slapstick scramble to keep his footing as he followed the bird down the steep and rocky hillside. Deracotte stooped once to grab a handful of rocks and pitched hard as he ran, missing each time. Manny whooped directions through the open window when the bird dodged, cheering Deracotte on.

But then Deracotte stopped, arms outstretched as though he himself were about to take flight.

Had he lost a shoe? Manny wondered. Had the grouse died at his feet?

Deracotte slowly lowered his arms and lifted his shocked face toward the car. Manny saw the look of confusion in his eyes, a kind of sad pain.

Manny threw open his door, cleared the fence, and reached Deracotte in a few long bounds. The rattlesnake remained coiled, its tail trembling. It extended and hissed as Manny lifted a large stone and crushed the snake's head. Even in its death throes, it rattled and rattled, the blood curdling from beneath the rock thick as syrup.

Deracotte was breathing hard, his eyes fixed on the river, as though he were on fire and might bolt for water. Manny knelt to examine the two punctures that oozed watery red.

"We better get you to town."

Deracotte didn't respond. The muscles of his jaws clenched. He turned and began walking toward the car.

Manny helped him with the fence, holding the wires high and low so that Deracotte could crawl through, guided him into the passenger seat. Deracotte kept his gaze fixed on the road as Manny worked the unfamiliar clutch.

"We'd best get you to Dr. K. You need that medicine."

Deracotte shook his head. Manny didn't know what to do.

Deracotte was his boss, his elder, a doctor. How could he overrule such authority? He turned left at the junction, eased the car into the driveway, hit the horn. Deracotte was pale, his breathing quick and shallow. He struggled out of the car and leaned against the fender as Helen appeared outside the door. She moved slowly toward them, then began running, the baby clutched against her shoulder.

"What happened? What is it?"

"Rattlesnake," Manny said. "He needs to get to town. I told him. He won't go." Deracotte's ankle had begun to swell, the wound bluing around the edges.

"Thomas," Helen said, "let Dr. K help."

"No," he said. *No.* The only word he would utter, even as he fell into bed, buried himself beneath the covers, and began shaking so violently that the bed frame rattled against the wall.

"What do we do?" Helen whispered. Elise had begun to cry, her wails growing louder the longer they stood in their indecision. Manny wanted to drag Deracotte into Fife, tie him if they had to, but Deracotte was the doctor, not him. And maybe it would be all right. He'd heard of a ridge runner who had gotten through more than one snakebite with little other than turpentine and whiskey.

Manny waited as Helen stood with the wailing baby in her arms, her eyes fixed on the window that looked out over the river, listening as Deracotte called her name from the bedroom. She lifted her sweater as though in slow motion, moved Elise to her breast, and Manny saw the fear and helplessness in her face. He wanted to kill Deracotte himself for not paying more attention, for causing her such pain, but maybe he was as much to blame as anybody. How many times had he started to warn Deracotte, but didn't?

"Let me take Elise," he said and held out his arms. Helen looked at him and began to cry. "Here, now," he said, and pulled them both toward him. "It's going to be okay. We'll make it okay." He held them against his chest, wishing he could keep them there, keep them safe. But Deracotte was calling louder, "Helen! Helen!"

Manny eased Elise from Helen's breast and began a gentle sideways swaying. "Go on," he whispered. "We're okay."

Helen touched the baby's head, then raised her palm to Manny's face. It happened so easy that in the days to come Manny would believe he had dreamed it: Helen's mouth pressing against his. He closed his eyes, the breath gone from his lungs, but still he could taste the sweetness as he listened to her step out of the room.

Over the next twenty-four hours, Manny kept watch over Deracotte as the skin of his swollen leg split and seeped like a tree blazed for pitch. It was too late for antivenin, but Dr. K sent medicine for the pain, and Deracotte's moans became weak whimpers and, finally, nothing more than the guttural breathing of deep sleep. As the days passed, the snakebite festered and crusted, then dried. The leg shrank back to its normal size, sloughed its skin as though it were the snake itself, and took on the color of sunburn. Deracotte seemed caught in a dim twilight of awareness and recognition. Often, his only words were to ask which direction he was facing, as though he were on a raft set adrift, at the mercy of wind and current to carry him toward landfall. Finally, he requested his compass, which he kept in his palm, his fingers opening, closing over the glass face as he checked the needle's hold, like some captain whose ship had been blown off course.

The day after Thanksgiving, winter set in with dead seriousness, sealing the seams of autumn with an icy meld. Manny closed his book and stepped to the window of Deracotte's room. A thin slurry of snow pasted the sill. Even in the dark he could make out the solid body of the barn, and he longed to be there in his apartment, reading beneath the small lamp Helen had found at the Give-n-Get—a base made of antlers, the shade of parchment stitched with rawhide and printed with a hunting scene: men dressed in red jackets astride fine horses, following the hounds who trailed the fox. It was the look on the riders' faces that entranced

Manny. Their lips were prim beneath their manicured moustaches, their eyes calm and kind. They looked as though nothing more than afternoon tea was unfurling before them, while the horses and the hounds and the fox itself leapt and scrabbled, necks and legs wrenched into impossible positions, tongues panting out, eyes wildly rolling. Manny had studied the shade, the small bulb illuminating the hedgerows and thickets, the copper fox and chestnut horses. He'd tried to imagine the sounds of the hunt—the dogs baying, the hooves clattering the ground, the call of the trumpet held high—but the placid look in the men's eyes belied it all.

Manny looked at the clock on the nightstand, its face luminously leering. He'd wait for Helen to wake, then sleep for an hour, maybe two, before beginning the chores. He settled himself against the hard back of the chair, planning what came next: the wood he'd need to find, buck, and split; the tending of the few hens and the cow that Stubb had given them. He'd already asked a nearby rancher for the loan of his bull in return for graze. Together, he and Helen had formulated a list of what they would need, how they would get it, who would provide. It was a plan that Manny trusted, one that demanded work and attention but guaranteed return.

Manny closed his eyes, startled awake to the sound of Deracotte coughing, asking for water. Manny refilled the glass and held it as Deracotte drank. Afterward, they listened to the radio—songs skipping in from El Paso, Johnny Cash and Merle Haggard, Patsy Cline crooning her sorrow as the snow ticked against the window and the land turned itself toward sleep.

Elise's cries, Helen's soothing words. In the silence, Manny knew she had drawn the baby to nurse. Even with Deracotte snoring lightly beside him, he felt suddenly alone, more alone than he had felt all the years since his parents had died.

He turned off the radio and went into the kitchen. He chose a chunk of larch, densely grained and well seasoned, fed it to the woodstove, and tamped the draft, then stood at the window looking out over the river. He imagined his shack, the spider bundled in her web, witness to moonlight and the meandering of animals through willow. When he heard Helen behind him, he felt the loneliness fade.

"Will you take her while I wash up?" Helen's face was soft with sleep, a single strand of hair come undone from its braid.

He held Elise close and breathed in her scent of sweet milk and talcum. He heard the makeshift curtain drawn closed around the corner by the stove where he had set the china washbowl and a jug of river water to warm. Manny imagined Helen for only a moment before turning his attention back to Elise. The slight weight of her steadied him, and he hummed a low tune, "The Tennessee Waltz," stepping, sliding. He remembered being balanced atop his father's feet, their graceful dip and swirl around the kitchen. He lifted on his toes, floated forward, and turned to see Helen, her hair damp and undone. She smiled and joined him, her hands on his shoulders, and they continued their dance through the tawny dark, gliding along to the silent music, the child held between them, dreaming on.

Chapter Nine

Two boys kicked a red ball along the sidewalk, oblivious to the last skids of early-spring snow. Five years old, maybe six, each intent upon the target, ignoring Deracotte, who had stopped to watch. They hollered in high-pitched voices, scrabbling, feinting, trying out the curses they had heard between men. He tried to remember if he had ever played with such abandon, if that was the reason for the knot in his chest.

It sometimes seemed that the snake had poisoned his memory both forward and back. The Dilaudid injections he'd self-administered had eased him into sleep and kept him there, but those first weeks of winter had evaporated into hazy recollections: the thin turkey soup at Thanksgiving; the Christmas tree decorated with paper snowflakes and popcorn. He sometimes felt he'd watched from behind a partition, as though he really wasn't there at all, as Helen and Manny went on about their lives—the life he had imagined for himself. From his bed, he could see into the kitchen, see how they moved in easy proximity, how Manny took Elise into his arms with the familiarity of a father. His appreciation for Manny's presence was tinged by a jealousy he couldn't bring himself to acknowledge: the boy had nursed him back to health, taken on the chores he himself couldn't perform, stayed after Dewey and Stubb had taken the last of their meager wages and gone home. How could he feel anything but gratitude?

Deracotte keyed open the door to his office. The mail that had dropped through the slot was for Mrs. DeLong, the dead mayor's widow. Nearing eighty but still a beauty—a head full of silver hair pinned into languid ringlets. After his recovery from the bite, he'd been stalling, trying to find a way around the pharmacist's offer of a room, when he'd seen the FOR RENT sign in the upstairs window, where the widow had sequestered herself to "live out her remaining days, and may they be few," she'd told him. He could lease the downstairs if he gathered her mail, but he wasn't to try to save her. She locked the stairwell door from the inside, opening it only to receive the brown paper bags stocked with praline ice cream, cigarettes, and gin that the grocery boy brought in through Deracotte's office. The bags and cartons she burned in the upstairs fireplace; smoke rose from the chimney at such a predictable time that people set their watches by its plume. She dropped the empty bottles out the window into a perfectly positioned trash can that a neighbor dumped and carefully repositioned each week. Patients often startled at the sound of shattering glass.

Deracotte was glad for the telephone's silence. He still had no home phone, the cost of stringing the line for miles more than he could afford, and he wasn't sure he wanted the intrusion. Though there was little money for luxuries, he liked the balance he had struck. What other doctors could claim that their fishing time exceeded their office hours? When Clearwater Mental Hospital had contacted him, saying that, although they weren't required by law to have a medical doctor on staff, they could certainly use one, Deracotte had flatly declined. Attending to the body was trial enough. He had no desire to muck with already muddled minds.

Only two morning appointments: Mrs. Malcom, balancing her heft atop impossibly small feet, had twisted her ankle and needed to hear once again that, even though the pain was severe, the ankle wasn't broken; Mr. Telecky, an old Czech lumberjack with a finger gone from each hand, said his arrhythmia wasn't responding to digitalis. The one o'clock was Dewey, who'd been complaining of his bunion. After that, the appointment book was blank. The people of Fife seemed loath to give up their time and money for preventive treatment, and when they did present themselves to him, it was often too late, their last stop before intensive care in Folgate. Until then, they consulted the pharmacist for free advice or doctored themselves: horse boluses of sulfa swallowed three at a time; livestock caustics swabbed on a patch of ringworm that burned a hole bigger than the fungus. They lanced their own boils and drilled through smashed thumbnails to release the aching buildup of blood. Deracotte found himself admiring their self-reliance and sometimes wondered if they wouldn't all be better off tending their own wounds.

Lunch was an apple and cheese. Deracotte ate standing, checking his watch. Five minutes for a cigarette on the back porch, sheltered from the alley by a high cedar fence. He had taken up the habit while he was convalescing because it kept his hands busy and filled the time. The first one Stubb had offered in a gesture of comfort, and he had inhaled tentatively, familiarizing himself with the initial bite, the rush of dizziness, which he patiently endured and then came to love, just as he loved the ritual of it: the tamping of the tobacco, the striking of the match. Each inhalation, each brightening of the ember. The stop-beat moment before the next breath. He had marked the calendars with dates he planned to quit, but each target had passed.

He stubbed out the ember and stepped inside to wash his hands, rinse his mouth with Listerine. The slamming of the door announced Dewey's arrival.

"Hey, Doc." Dewey appeared bloated and pale. When they shook hands, Deracotte felt the fingers plump with edema. Instead of his usual work boots, Dewey wore house slippers, broken at the heels and stained with mud. He held out a grocery sack. "Picked some brains for you. The wife says they ain't woody."

"How is Gladys?" Deracotte took the bag of forest mushrooms and waited for Dewey to position himself on the examination table. In the months since they'd first met, Deracotte had watched Dewey's face collapse in on itself, the toothless gums recede, his hair thin and wisp, his eyebrows disappear. An odor of overripe fruit filled the room.

"Have you been checking your blood sugar?"

Dewey shrugged. "Mostly."

"Insulin?"

"Sometimes."

"Let's see that bunion."

Dewey grunted, reached to pull the slipper from his right heel, and winced. The sock was damp with sweat and pungent, the bandage stained with blood. Deracotte peeled the tape carefully. The skin was broken, ulcerous. He resisted the urge to scold. How many times had he told Dewey to come in if a simple scratch became inflamed? He could attempt to clean and trim the wound, but it would not be enough. Surgery, perhaps even amputation. He considered Dewey's toenails, yellowed and thick, the heel fissured and grimed. He wished for another cigarette.

"You need to check yourself into the hospital." Deracotte moved to the sink and ran his hands beneath water so hot it scalded. "You may need surgery."

Dewey shook his head. "You just go ahead and fix me up, Doc."

"I wish I could, Dewey. I'll call Folgate and tell them you're on your way."

Dewey lowered his head, rubbed his knees. "Thing is, I don't have no way to pay."

Deracotte turned with the paper towel in his hand. It had never dawned on him that the reason Dewey failed to keep his injection schedule was because he couldn't afford the insulin.

"What about assistance?"

Dewey shrugged. "Can't say I'm disabled, Doc. Worked hard enough for you, didn't I?"

The foot dangled, sore and pulsing. Deracotte could imagine the infection spreading, traveling the length of the leg. He wished he'd been able to keep Dewey working a little longer, pay him more. Even now, he didn't have the money to help Dewey with what the hospital would charge him, and even if he did, he wasn't sure that Dewey's pride would allow him to accept such charity.

"I can clean the wound, give you penicillin. I've got enough insulin here to last you a month, but you've got to promise me you'll take it."

"Gladys and I will find some way to pay you back, Doc. We're not scroungers."

Deracotte nodded. He understood how pity caused its own festering ache.

"I'll deaden it first, but you'll feel some discomfort." Deracotte inserted the needle into the Novocain, dreading the procedure nearly as much as Dewey.

"Got any whiskey, Doc? Whiskey always helps."

"I wish I did," Deracotte said, and it was the most honest thing he had felt all day. By the time he had finished, they were both sweating. Deracotte dressed and bandaged the foot, filled a paper bag with insulin and syringes. He helped Dewey limp to his pickup, then watched him drive away. Friday, the end of another week, and he was glad. He'd have the weekend to fish. It would take his mind off of Dewey. He knew he should call Folgate, see what arrangements could be made. He tried to imagine such a blow to the little man's pride. There was no doubt in Deracotte's mind that Dewey would find death preferable to such betrayal.

He was filling the autoclave when he heard the front door open, the murmur of voices. When he stepped into the waiting area, he saw a woman with graying hair and a little boy he guessed to be seven. Both had the wind-chapped look of farm people. The boy's left arm was nested in a dish-towel sling.

"I wonder if you could take a look at my son. He was jumping on the bed. I told him not to, but you know kids . . ." The woman attempted a smile.

Deracotte started to say that his office was closed, but he knew what options remained: the pharmacist, or a trip into Folgate. He motioned the woman and child to follow him into the examination room. Beneath the brighter light, the woman seemed even older. Children caused him the greatest unease, their fear and frightful tantrums often more than he believed he could bear.

Deracotte patted the examination table. "Can you sit here so I can take a look?"

The boy didn't fuss or hesitate but pulled himself up with his one good arm, then sat waiting with an air of great patience. He smelled crisp and peppery, like spring radishes.

"Can you show me how high you can raise your arm?" Deracotte raised his own to show the boy how it might be done. The boy looked at him with eyes the color of agates—a swirl of green and brown and blue.

"I can't lift it at all," the boys said. "It's dislocated." His words were clear and even, as though he were being asked to recite a science report.

"Any pain here?" Deracotte started to palpate the radius, but the boy pulled back.

"It's not broken. It's dislocated. Complete subluxation."

Deracotte looked at the woman, who stood with her own arms crossed in front of her, her simple housedress bunched beneath a once-white sweater.

"He's had it before," she said.

The shoulder felt swollen beneath Deracotte's fingers, the humeral head separated from the clavicle.

"I'll need to get your arm back in its socket. It will hurt for a minute, but then it will feel better." He touched his own shoulder as though to comfort the pain he was feeling there.

"I know," the boy said.

"What's your name?"

"Lucas. Lucas Jainchill."

"Lucas, I'm going to pull on your wrist and push on your chest, pretty hard. Okay?"

"Yes." The child tilted his head to the side and closed his eyes. Deracotte took the small hand between his fingers and rotated the arm until he heard the unmistakable *clunk* of the joint reconnecting, as though a cog had fallen into place.

"There. All done." Deracotte realized the muscles in his own arms were trembling with the exertion. "Is that better?"

Lucas didn't open his eyes but nodded.

"It's going to be sore for a while." Deracotte looked at the woman. "You say it's a chronic condition?"

"I don't know about chronic. It's happened before, that's all."

Deracotte turned his attention back to the boy, who had opened his eyes and was staring out the window.

"Why don't you lie down here and let me see how that socket feels."

Lucas lay back, and Deracotte worked his hands over both shoulders. The boy kept his eyes turned toward the square of light. Deracotte directed his voice toward the woman.

"You say he fell from the bed?"

"He was jumping. He likes to jump."

Deracotte felt his way down both arms. At least two hard knots in the left humerus indicating previous fractures. He palpated the chest, felt the mend of broken ribs. The spleen and liver felt normal, but when he raised the boy's shirt, he saw the scars, some elongated, others like polka dots cratering the skin. He lifted his eyes to the woman's face.

"It wasn't me," she said.

He should have the child disrobe, check his back, genitalia, and buttocks, but he couldn't bring himself to discover more. He sensed that the boy was glad for this. It felt like an act of mercy.

Deracotte fitted Lucas with a sling and helped him off the table. "I need to talk with your mother for a minute. There are some comic books out front." He waited until the boy had closed the door with his good hand, then looked to the woman, who raised her chin.

"I know what you're going to say. But you don't understand."

"I understand that this child is being abused." It was all he could do to keep from raising his voice. He felt the rage in his chest. To have such a son. To do *this* to your son.

"It's not me," she said again. "He's safe when he's with me." The woman looked less frightened than simply drained, as though it were a story she had told before, devoid of any emotion. "He's not really my son. He's my grandson. If his father finds out we've been here, Lucas will be in worse trouble yet."

"I have no choice but to turn this in," Deracotte said. He wanted to do more. He wanted to find who had done this and kill him.

The woman's mouth hardened, and she lowered her gaze to his. "Now you listen. They take him away, put him in them homes, then his father gets sober for a while. Then it's worse than before. They keep taking him away like that and putting him back, they're going to be what kills him. At least now, when it gets too bad, he's got me."

"What about the pharmacist? Does he know about this?"

The woman straightened. "This isn't some city where a do-gooder can come in and make it all right. This is Fife. Things go deeper here."

"He's failed in his duty to protect this child."

"You turn us in, you'll be the one who's failed. That boy's blood will be on your hands."

"I don't even know that what you're saying is true. Not any of it."

The woman rested heavily against the table. "Lucas is my only grandchild. Lord knows where his mother is. But his dad . . ." She swallowed hard, fighting back the tears that had finally come. "It's not just the alcohol. My husband had that demon. There's something else that's got my son. He's a good worker, knows construction. He can mechanic. He'll sober up for a while, start coming to church, but then it comes back on him. When money's gone, that's when he gets crazy. He brings the boy to me, and I give him all the cash I got. I can buy Lucas that little bit of time." She leaned toward Deracotte. "The state takes Lucas away, I can live with that. It's when they give him back that I pray." She wiped her eyes, then ran her hands down the front of her dress. "I came here because you know things Dr. K don't. You can fix him up when it gets real bad. The Lord's promised me. I have faith that Lucas will survive until he's old enough to run or fight back."

Deracotte wanted to tell her how little had come of his own mother's faith, how he despised such ignorant rationalizing, but he turned instead to his notes. "He can take aspirin for the pain. An ice pack will help the swelling."

Lucas sat in the waiting area, back straight, feet dangling above the floor as he read an old issue of the *British Medical Journal.* The comic books were untouched, the few toys still in their wicker basket.

"Come on, Lucas. We'll stop by the café for ice cream," the woman said, but the boy didn't answer. He simply closed the magazine, opened the door, and held it for her, as though such times called for nothing more than chivalry.

"Lucas," Deracotte called, and the boy turned. Deracotte hesitated, his hands empty, then scanned the room for something he might offer. He reached to a high shelf and brought down a medical encyclopedia.

"Here," he said. Lucas looked to his grandmother before cradling the heavy book in his good arm.

"Thank you," the boy said and moved out into the light of the afternoon.

Deracotte stood for a long time after the mud-streaked pickup had driven away. He wanted to keep the boy with him, keep him safe from harm. He locked the front door, closed the blinds, and made detailed notes in the boy's chart. When he was finished, he moved to the back porch, where he sat in an old kitchen chair and smoked until the widow's empty bottle shattered into the garbage can only feet away.

As he walked to his car, he heard the distant throttle of the train and imagined it pulling its heavy load through the outskirts of town. Sometimes he wished he could ride the rails like the hoboes he'd found when he was a boy wandering the hours alone. They'd offer him the last cup of stew, made from the wilted leaves of cabbages and sprouted potatoes. Sometimes it was a T-bone that the bums charred over their cans of Sterno, the greening meat thrown to the restaurant's trash. And once it was fish-head soup, ladled into a tin bowl and handed to Deracotte with great ceremony, the gelatinous eyes rolling up and over to peer at him from the milky froth. He'd been surprised at the taste of salt and earth, the clean mineral broth sweetened with a rare can of cream. He ate it all, even the eyes themselves, which the tramps insisted would bring him a clear vision of his future.

Deracotte waited for the Volkswagen's engine to smooth out before pulling away from Fife. He reminded himself that nothing had changed, but the sadness that had settled into his chest was familiar and haunting. It reminded him of all his other hesitancies, his failures. He had no idea what was the right thing to do. To act might prove fatal. To not act might prove the cure.

He crossed the bridge at Omega, turned left, and found the faint ruts leading to Home Beach. Just downriver, a basalt flow thumbed out into the current. The osprey would return soon, replacing the bald eagles that he often saw topping the trees. Manny told him that he'd once seen a full-grown eagle towed under, its talons locked around the backbone of a salmon. Deracotte loved the detail of the bird reemerging, land-bound until its feathers dried, preening on the beach as though unaware of how close it had come to death.

Deracotte pulled on his waders and stepped into the current. Even after all the hours spent with a rod in his hands, each strike seemed a surprise rather than the end result of his studied experiment: the fly carefully selected to match hatch and season; the cast so nearly perfect that the feathered hook whispered down like a caddis dipping its wings; the placement at the lip of current just shy of stone; the rise and roll and set. He would bring the fish in, cradle it just below the surface, and rock it softly until it spasmed free.

He watched for the flit of insects, something he might imitate, but the still-cold nights had frosted the first hatches. Color, then. An enticement to strike rather than feed. Orange or red or yellow. The sun wouldn't give him long. He stripped and loaded the line, his arm clocking the familiar rhythm. The most perfect thing he had ever done was to land the fly and see the fish rise up to meet it. It was something he could teach Elise, when it was time. He thought of the two young boys kicking the ball down the sidewalk. He thought of Lucas Jainchill. He thought of his own son buried beneath the hawthorn, and the tears came as the line furled out behind him and the sun settled against the western sky.

On the ridge above, smoke rose from their evening fire. It was late, and he should be home. Manny would have the animals fed, the chicken yard locked against foxes. Helen would have Elise bathed, his dinner kept warm in the oven. He imagined them sitting together in the living room, reading, listening to Bach. What place was there for him? Sometimes Deracotte wondered if they missed him at all.

Chapter Ten

A Mozart concerto. Allegro, andante . . . Helen closed her eyes to feel the melody's rise and fall. How long since she'd touched the keys? Like so many other things since they'd left Connecticut, her ability to play the piano seemed a lost memory, a useless remnant of her former life. Even if she had an instrument to play, who would listen?

The first Sunday of April, and, instead of fly-fishing the river swollen with snowmelt, Thomas had taken Elise in the backpack for a hike up Bedrock Creek. Helen had needed some time alone, she'd told him, but the truth was she needed time to do anything other than nurse, diaper, and rock the baby. She wished she had the courage to drive back into Fife, have another drink with Eppy. Instead, she sat at the kitchen table and opened *Ladies' Home Journal* to the page she'd dog-eared to read again. "Are you in need of change?" the article queried. "Improve your life by improving yourself!"

First, the article said, she was to talk to three different people who knew her well. Ask them to list what they admired about her. Then ask them to list any negative characteristics they saw in her personality. "What do you feel good about?" the article asked. "Bad? What do you wish to change?"

Three people who knew her well. Helen wrote down Thomas's name, hesitated. All the friends she'd had back home seemed as distant as shirttail cousins. There's my mother, she thought, but she wasn't sure her mother knew her at all. Maybe her grandmother. Who could guess what bare truths might arise from the old woman's senile brain? The last time Helen had called, the grandmother had shrieked, *"You toad-spotted strumpet! You Tin Lizzy!"* The epithets had held in Helen's mind. She couldn't help but believe that the name-calling contained a riddle. She could write, "My grandmother claims I have certain mechanical characteristics that are potentially admirable, but she finds my complexion to be the outward manifestation of moral vacuity."

Instead, she wrote: "THINGS COULD STAY THE WAY THEY ARE OR THINGS COULD CHANGE."

She looked at the choices and thought she might cry. She longed for friends, for companionship, for a phone to call someone. But all Thomas needed to be happy, he said, was the love of his wife and daughter. Why couldn't she be so easily satisfied?

"He's not like us," her mother had warned. Helen thought that he wasn't like anybody—not like her, not like the people of Fife. So what if he only had two or three patients a day? So what if those patients could only pay five dollars a month? What did it matter if she wanted linoleum for the kitchen, a trip home to visit her family? So what if no one came to their door at Christmas, bearing champagne or even fruitcake? He was content to fish for hours, to walk the ridges for no other reason than to see what birds rose at his feet.

What did she need to be happy? She didn't envy her sisters their manicured nails and hours at the club. She didn't envy them their grand homes along the golf course, their sons and daughters bound for Yale. She could not say she would trade her life for theirs. Even the former boyfriends whose names she had listed and considered didn't move her to wish to be their wife. What, then?

She sighed, gathered her hair at the nape of her neck, and clipped it back with the silver barrette. She licked one finger, ran it across the top of the saltshaker, and sucked. Between the jam jar and sugar bowl lay Thomas's compass, so long unmoved that it had stuck to the table as though tacked there with glue. She remembered how, after the snakebite, he had grasped it in his palm as though the world were swinging wildly away. When she pried at it with her spoon, the needle spun, and, for a moment, she felt dizzy.

There was a quick shuffle on the porch, a knock before Manny stepped in. His hair was thick and clean, cut tight. Each time she saw him, he seemed new to her, his eyebrows darker, the line of his jaw more distinctly drawn, as though he were coming into sharper focus.

"Anything you need?" he asked. "I'm headed to town for oil."

Anything. What would he give if she asked? Ever since their first and only kiss, Manny had remained chaste, like a priest in his cell. Not unkind but simply unavailable. Helen admired his instincts even as she wanted to test his resolve. What harm was a kiss?

"Maybe I'll ride in with you," she said. "I need to get out." She'd leave Thomas a note, tell him she wouldn't be long.

"I could have had the rig warmed up." He brushed at his sleeves. "Can't decide if it wants to rain or snow. See your breath out there."

She straightened her skirt, pulled on her shoes, grabbed her jacket. "I don't mind," she said. "It will wake me up."

Manny whistled Dog into the bed of the old pickup—a retired rig that a rancher had bartered Manny for breaking his colt. They drove the river road in silence, only the heater huffing. Helen took in Manny's smells—the faint spice of shaving cream and clean scent of cotton. He was a man that any woman might pine for, yet she seldom heard him speak of anyone in Fife other than Dr. K. It was as though his world, like hers, was made up of nothing but this place.

"Manny, can I ask you something?"

"Sure."

"Why do you stay with us?"

He glanced at her quickly, and she thought that she had astounded him.

"I work for you and Mr. Deracotte," he said.

"I know that. Of course, I know that. But you could probably make a better life for yourself some other way."

"I don't know that I could. Maybe."

"Why, then?"

He licked his lips, looked out his window, then back at the road. "It's just the decision I've made," he said.

"Can I ask you another question?"

"Is it okay if we get some lunch first? I could use a cup of coffee."

He parked in front of the Ox and ordered Dog to stay. They found a booth toward the back as the customers watched, leaned over their tuna melts and pickle spears. Helen realized she hadn't eaten breakfast.

"I'm starved," she said, and ordered a cheeseburger basket and a large chocolate malt.

"Make it two," Manny said. "Thanks, Julie." The waitress smiled at him as she took their menus.

Helen envied the ease of the locals who had settled in for refills, waving at others who happened to pass by on the sidewalk. Even if she were in the hometown she'd known all her life, she'd not encounter such camaraderie. Who are *my* people? she wondered. She was no longer sure where she belonged.

Manny looked across the street to the pharmacy. "Maybe we should visit Dr. K's. Won't hurt to let the oil go a day or two."

Helen understood for the first time that the errand might have been a ruse. She wondered if he looked for excuses: a broken chain, a run for feed, a haircut. What desires did he have? What longings did he keep hidden? She realized how little she knew about him. Nothing, really, at all.

The drugstore was closed, but Manny led her to the alley and up a narrow stairway to a red door. There was the strong smell of urine. Helen had a sudden memory of her grandmother, pants bunched at her ankles, squatted incredibly and peeing on the pristine white sofa she had guarded for years.

"He can't turn away a cat," Manny noted. "Must be twenty of them hanging around." He knocked lightly and turned the knob.

"You in here?" he called.

"Where the hell else am I going to be?" The druggist was in his recliner. In his black-and-red-checked shirt, he looked more like a logger than the pharmacist who had helped her with her car.

"Thought maybe you'd upped and moved to Florida," Manny said.

"Sure you did. Sure."

"I got a visitor with me. Mrs. Deracotte. You remember?"

"It's been a while," Helen said.

"Not that long." He motioned them toward the sofa. "Go ahead. Sit down. Make some coffee, if you want."

Manny shuffled magazines and offered the seat to Helen, then leaned against the refrigerator. "Just had lunch at the café. You hungry?"

"No, hell. I'm not hungry." Dr. K settled back into his chair.

Manny crossed one boot over the other, and Helen thought he looked like a cowboy. She felt a quick lick of lust between her legs. It wasn't just that he was handsome. It was the ease with which he moved, the way he took in other people, really *saw* them. It was what she had loved about Thomas in the beginning, but now, even when they made love, he seemed distant, pulled away by the sound of the river.

Dr. K shifted his weight in the chair. "Bring my smokes?"

Manny pulled a pack from his pocket, then pointed to a bottle of whiskey on the counter. "Want me to pour?"

"Why not? Give yourself some, too. Both of you."

Manny poured shots into three coffee cups and handed them around. Helen took a small sip and felt the pleasant burn down her throat. She wanted a cigarette but reminded herself that one indulgence was enough.

The druggist took a long drag. "Julie still working over there?"

"Yep."

"How's that going?" Dr. K held the cup to his chest like a warm stone.

Manny cleared his throat, took a drink. "Guess it's going okay." He turned his cup in the palm of his hand.

So that's the reason the waitress smiled at Manny but wouldn't meet my eyes, Helen thought. How could she have missed that he had a lover? She'd let herself become so shut off, shut in, shut down. They *all* could have lovers, Thomas, Dr. K, Manny. How would she ever know?

She listened to the affectionate banter between the two men. She envied the ease of the friendship. They had known each other for years, were bound by something other than blood. Something other than money. They loved each other, Helen realized. It was that simple.

Manny drank the last of his whiskey. "Got a few other stops to make. Better get going."

The druggist lifted one hand toward Helen. "Take care of him. He only thinks he knows what he's doing."

She smiled and left her empty glass near the sink. The chill wind was a respite from the close odor of the apartment. The dog heard them coming, yapped once, then set up a high-pitched howl when two cats darted from beneath a car and charged around the corner. Helen climbed into the pickup and waited while Manny cleared the slush from the windshield. The neon rocket ship of the Jet Club glowed, and she wondered if Eppy was sitting at the bar. She could tell Manny she needed another hour. She could ask that he wait for her. Or join her.

"How long has it been?" she asked.

"Since?"

"Since we left. How many hours?"

"Closing in on three, I'd guess. Maybe four by the time we get back."

Helen thought about Thomas and Elise, hiking the draw. The wet snow would have hurried them home. She remembered the magazine she'd left open on the table, her scribbled note.

"Sometimes I wish I could just stay here in Fife a little while longer."

"Why don't you?"

"Maybe I just need to go home. Back to Connecticut. Back to my family."

Manny looked at her quickly. She closed her eyes and swallowed hard to keep the tears from coming.

"Can we stop by the phone booth? I haven't talked to my parents for a while."

Manny waited in the pickup while Helen closed herself into the booth and dialed collect. It was her mother who answered, her voice woozy with Chartreuse.

"Your father's in Greece," she said. "Don't ask me why."

Helen wanted to say that, of course, he was there on business, but now she wondered if he had a mistress as well. Maybe he had always had one. And who would blame him?

"Elise is sitting up now," Helen said. "She'll be crawling soon."

There was silence and then the sound of her mother exhaling smoke into the receiver. "It's really too bad," she said, "that we can't watch our granddaughter grow."

"You could visit," Helen said, but they'd had this conversation before. The closest airport was hours away. And where would they sleep? Helen tried to imagine her mother's matched set of luggage in the little bedroom. Maybe the barn.

"Helen, you could come home, you know. There is nothing there for you."

"Mother, that's not true. This is where I live now. Thomas has his office open. It's doing very well." A lie, one her mother might have already guessed.

"It's neglectful to raise a child in such a place. You'll regret it someday."

One word, Helen thought. Just one word of encouragement.

"Thomas loves it here, and so do I. The river is beautiful. Dad could come and fish." What would she give to have her father close again, comforting her with ice cream?

"Maybe he should just move out there with you. Maybe you'd both be happier without me."

Helen leaned her forehead against the glass, felt the cold, something true. "I just wanted to call and say hello. I should go now."

"Nobody has time for me anymore. You don't care." There was the rattle of ice cubes, glass clicking against the receiver.

Helen looked toward the pickup where Manny waited. She raised her hand, and he waved back. Even through the streaked windshield, she could see his smile.

"I've got to go. I need to get dinner ready for Thomas."

"He's ruined you, you know. I'm sure your figure is gone."

Helen stood silent, the rain softening to snow.

"It's his fault, Helen. Not yours. He's a con man, a charmer. He knew how to turn your head. As soon as he realizes we won't give you more money, he'll be gone. You should bring the baby and come home now, before it's too late."

The phone was heavy in her hand as Helen set it carefully into its cradle and walked to the pickup. Why had she thought anything had changed? There was a reason why her father was never home, and it was the same reason she herself had felt a need to escape. This was her life now. What choice did she have?

Manny let her keep her silence until she shook her head. "Sometimes I wonder if no family at all would be better than this."

"I wouldn't say that," Manny said.

"I'm sorry." It was selfish of her to complain when Manny had lost everyone once dear to him. "Do you have any more of those cigarettes?"

Manny smiled, pulled another pack from his jacket. They smoked together, waving at the fishermen who stood at the river's edge, bundled in wool. The April snow was beginning to stick.

"Dr. K doesn't have anyone but you, does he?"

"I try and stop by every week or so. Just to make sure he's still alive."

"He's not that old."

"Seems like he's always been old." Manny lifted two fingers to an approaching truck, and the driver waved back.

"Don't you think that's sad?"

"Doesn't really matter what I think." Manny switched the heater to defrost. "Not my sadness."

Helen gathered her coat tighter across her chest. Elise nursed less often now, but her breasts still ached. Manny turned the fan up a notch.

"What about Julie?" she asked.

Manny lifted one shoulder, let it drop. "What do you want to know?"

"Do you love her?"

"Julie?" Manny's face showed surprise, or puzzlement, Helen wasn't sure which. Maybe even alarm.

"I think she loves *you*."

"Well, that's a different thing."

"Tell me about her."

"I don't know what to tell you that you don't already know."

It was the details that she wanted—the very thing she realized he wouldn't give. He was a gentleman, after all. She knew that about him. Helen looked at Manny's hands on the wheel, the strong fingers she remembered holding hers as they waltzed. She allowed herself to imagine his lean hips, the tightness of his stomach, and felt her pulse quicken.

As they crossed the bridge at Omega, Helen pointed downriver. "Let's stop at Home Beach."

"It's snowing."

"I can stand it if you can."

Manny swung the pickup left and followed the shallow ruts to the point where grass gave way to sand. Their tracks were already disappearing, their path erased. She opened the pickup's door, stepped out, wrapped her jacket tighter. Her shoes would get soaked, but she didn't care.

"Come," Manny said, and Dog ran between them, prancing and nosing. Helen led them down the familiar path, sliding a little. She wanted to witness that split second when the snow touched the water and disappeared. She crossed the narrow beach and stopped at the river's edge. Manny stood beside her, his hands buried in his pockets.

"Used to know an Indian," he said. "Lived in a shack, just about here. He'd sweat in this hut he'd built, then run buck naked into the river, sometimes right through the ice."

"Purification," Helen said. She'd learned about it in her history class. "They believe that it's good for the soul." She thought of her own sins. She thought she might confess, tell Manny about the dead baby boy, how well she remembered the small crease between his eyebrows, the bow of his lips. The shame that came of his short life had never been spoken, his death never acknowledged.

She couldn't stop shaking, the air around them colder. Manny was shaking now too, his jaw clenched against the chill.

"I guess we'd better get home," he said.

She looked into his face. Would he despise her if she kissed him like she'd done before? But longer this time. More. It would ruin everything, but maybe everything was already ruined. Or maybe he was what she had wanted all along.

"We could take off our clothes and dive in." She unclipped the barrette, laid it on a nearby rock, shook her hair free. "Come on. I'll make us a hot toddy when we get back." She watched his face for some sign, some hint of desire. When had she become such a romantic? Maybe she should just grab him, rub him hard. What man would say no?

She leaned a little toward him, and he looked down into her face.

"I'm not sure this is where we should be."

"Where, then?"

"Not here." He wrapped his hands around hers.

"Is there anything that you would say yes to?" She pressed herself against him.

He looked toward the ridge, to the house he'd help build, the fire he'd kindled, its smoke lacing the trees.

She cupped his face, drew his mouth to hers, tasted the snowmelt, the warmth of his breath. All familiar, as though they had been lovers from the beginning. He lifted her, laid her down. The wet sand, so unlike the loose till of summer beaches, was dense and solid beneath them. Helen felt it molding the small of her back, bracing her shoulders, as Manny moved into her, careful at first, as though he wasn't sure, and then she felt every muscle in his body take hold. She wanted to cry out, or to cry, or to whisper something that would keep them in this moment just a little while longer, no fears, no regret. She welcomed his weight, wanted it to press her down harder, to make her believe that her presence in this place was real. She turned her face to the sky, closed her eyes against the snow.

The catch of his breath, his body's release. She held him until he braced himself on his elbows, brushed her hair free of snow. He was going to say something, something she didn't want to hear. If he was sorry, she didn't want to know. She set her lips against his, not a kiss, but something else, something closed and sheltered, then stood, smoothed her skirt. She looked to the ridge. Thomas might be there even now, watching her in the dusky light. She turned toward the river, stepped into the shallows, felt the lap of water little different than the chill air. She took another step, felt the current at her shins.

Behind her, Manny said, "Hey."

She felt in her pocket, found the compass, and threw it as hard as she could across the river.

"That's probably far enough," Manny said.

Her feet wedged between rocks, and she fell forward, wet to the shoulders. She laughed because she felt some part of her old self coming back—that girl she'd once been, who wasn't afraid to climb the hotel fence and skinny-dip in a pool of moon-glazed water. She lowered her face. There was cold like a quick burn, then an aching numbness. Good for her circulation. Her soul.

She stood and kept walking. When the water reached her thighs, she bounced once, twice, then kicked out. All the lessons of her girlhood summers came back: the scissors kick, the breaststroke, the crawl. The current made it easy, pulling her along.

She laid her head sideways to match the reach of her arms. She saw the dog racing back and forth along the sand, but Helen couldn't hear her, only the resonant churn, like a giant turbine pulsing. And then she saw Manny dropping his coat, shedding his boots. She yelled at him to go back, but he couldn't hear. When she raised her hand to wave that she was okay, she was surprised by the weight of her arm swathed in wet cotton. She should have stripped before plunging in. She brought her feet forward and began treading water, felt one shoe let go, then the other. The river's current, so unlike the lakes of her youth, had carried her farther than she had intended. She would need to let the eddy catch her, swing her closer to shore, but she was no longer sure of her direction.

Hair tangled at her neck. She pushed it from her eyes, but she couldn't feel her fingers, her hands like blunt clubs. Even the skin of her face had lost sensation—was she smiling or frowning? She willed her legs to move, her feet to kick. Left side, right side, left side, breathe. She rolled to her back, let the water carry her, fill her ears. She remembered her parents' pool at midnight, a boy but not his name, the silken glide of his skin against hers, the way her head rested in water so that she seemed to be of two worlds, her body anchored by the boy's strong legs, his hands holding to the rigging of her hips, her gaze cast upward to the black bowl of sky. How long since she and Thomas had taken their blanket, spread it on the ground, eaten cheese, drunk wine, and lay on their backs to watch the meteors careen across the horizon?

Had they ever?

The current tugged. When she closed her eyes, she saw striations of black and gray, pockets of illumination and shadow. She thought she could see the touch of snow like stars. She thought she could hear Manny churning toward her, drawing closer, long, strong strokes that made her feel something like love.

There was still time—she wanted to tell him this. Tell him that she was going to rest, just for a while, and then give it another try. She was a strong swimmer, after all. She knew what to do. But the water was sucking at her legs, pulling her under.

She thought of Thomas, making his way back from the canyon, the baby on his back. Elise would be hungry. She would need to be fed. Someone would need to find her clean pajamas. She would need to be danced in a slow circle, to be rocked, to be nursed one last time. A lullaby. A nursery rhyme. A *toad-spotted strumpet Tin Lizzy.* Whatever meaning the words might have had was gone, swirled away in a wash of sound that rose and fell, grew soft, then loud. Like music, she thought. A symphony. Now a single violin playing. Which, would she argue, was more beautiful?

How could she ever choose?

A warmth took hold of her toes and filled her lungs and rushed into her ears, such sweet relief that she forgot about everything else and had only to let go. There was a last breath she might have taken, a last kiss in the dark. A memory of a boy, now gone.

Part Two

"It all evens out," Nick said.

—ERNEST HEMINGWAY

Chapter Eleven

1976

Elise waited for the first morning light to lift her from hearing into listening—that moment when the noise became something outside of her body, rose from her chest and blossomed into air, like the impatiens Manny had planted around the steps, folding into themselves each evening, opening each day. She often thought of them as little mouths, closed but humming, then unfolding into color—something that she could almost hear, each waking a melody of purple, a lullaby of blue.

A wan September sun caught the edges of her dresser, the chenille spread tatted with the sweeping plumage of a life-size peacock—an early birthday gift from her grandmother, who had sent it wrapped in tissue paper that smelled faintly of White Shoulders. It wasn't rock bands or movie stars that decorated her room but the salvage of found things: an iridescent brush made of magpie feathers; sprigs of dried lupine; wreaths of vine maple. It was because she'd been tutored at home, her father said, that she had never been tainted by high fashion or low ideas. No boys had ever pitched pebbles at her window. No kissing beneath the bleachers during football games or band trips fueled by lemonade spiked with rum. No television or radio or phone to allow the world in. Until she'd turned sixteen, one or the other of two aging twin sisters—Elise was never sure if it was Effie or Edith—had visited once a week with a sheaf of Chopin. She'd composed her own melodies to make sense of it all—a protégée, her father said, as he sat facing the river to listen, his eyes closed.

Although her father preferred jazz, or maybe because of it, he had given her a stack of her mother's classical recordings, which she listened to with the lights off and curtains drawn, the color flowing, cartwheeling, fading against the ceiling's darkened theater. She thought she might hear in the music something of the woman she believed her mother had been—moody, excitable, daring. In the absence of friends her own age, she often imagined bedtime talks that lasted late into the night, during which she shared with her mother her secret concerns about boys, the shape of her breasts, her dreams of becoming a veterinarian. Her father only nodded when she talked about her plans for college. Even Manny seemed unsure about how such a transition might take place.

She'd never questioned her homeschooling until the fall she'd turned twelve. When she'd complained of having no friends, her father had agreed to the "experiment" of seventh grade at the Fife middle school. Finally, it was the very children she thought herself lonely for who had driven her away. She was fat, they said; she walked like a chicken. The knitted caps she loved to wear were stupid. She didn't know how to whisper about boys, didn't know how to make them like her. When Manny picked her up after school, she burst into tears, and he took her to the café for banana splits. Finally, it had been her father who had decided. "You were happy enough before," he said. "Why make things worse?"

The floor was cold beneath her feet as she pulled on her jeans, stiff with horse sweat. They were tighter than they had been. Over the last two years, her body had become something strange to her.

She welcomed the new weight of her breasts but wished her hips had stayed thin, her legs lean. She grabbed her jacket and pushed into her boots, scuffed and soft in the soles. Outside, the air smelled of sour grass and chicory. The old mare grazed at the far corner of the pasture, cowbirds cresting her neck. Dew had licked her flaxen forelock into a spit curl. Elise would need to wash and brush her, braid her mane and tail, before she herself could get ready for the Fife County Fair. She would compete in Western Pleasure and enter Costume dressed like a gypsy, trailing scarves, her horse a-jangle with coins and little brass bells.

"Come on, horse." Elise rattled the coffee can with its cup of oats. "Allegro, come on, girl."

The halter, the bit and reins, the dusty blanket, the denim-shined saddle, all came into her hands with a familiar weight. She led the mare into a few tight circles before toeing into the stirrup, but there was really no need: they'd shared this routine for a long time, and the mare had come to accept the fingers latching her throat, the knees directing her shoulders.

They practiced their paces, walking the pasture's perimeter, reversing, backing, kicking into a canter. Elise sang Allegro the songs she believed might match the horse's markings: sorrel body a deep and coppery bass D; the white blaze down her face a siren at high G; three white socks sopranic accompaniment as they traced figure eights in three-quarter time—a four-legged waltz, a fluid movement that would stay in Elise's hips for hours after, a rhythm that rocked her dreams.

As she worked the horse, Elise wondered if anyone else could sense it—that part of herself she felt forming, approaching like a strange figure in the distance. Not yet comfort, not yet threat. It came as desire, as something held open and empty, waiting to be filled. And it was this that she believed she must cloister, this curiosity, this *wanting.* Her father would define for her once again that delineation between *want* and *need,* between indulgence and necessity. But what name could she give the itch at the base of her spine, as though a cheatgrass awn had made its way there, or the quickening of her heart for no reason, as though she had come from the pasture to find the church people with their pamphlets, the boy with his slick hair and white shirt, who met her eyes just for a moment before his elders turned him away?

She slowed to a walk, let the reins loosen in her hands, felt the easy sun on her face. She closed her eyes and imagined that she was circling the arena, that the other girls were watching, a little jealous. That the boys were watching. That she was beautiful in her silk and satin, her silver and gold. Who is she? they would whisper, having already forgotten.

When the horse raised her head, Elise listened, too, and heard the whine of a distant machine. The caw of a raven. More. She opened her eyes and was blind with sun. Someone was walking toward the pasture, his heels striking the dirt in precise and steady rhythm—Manny, coming to help with the grooming.

They led Allegro to the barn, where Manny soaped the saddle while Elise lathered the horse's hide. They did not speak but worked together, each knowing the other's place without looking. She accepted this help just as she accepted his morning offerings of oatmeal. The way he accepted her presence on his stairs some evenings, in the barn where she came to escape her father's immutable sadness that descended with the sun.

"She's not the spring chicken she used to be," Manny said as he shined the horse's hooves.

"Not so old," Elise said. "Maybe twenty."

"She's twenty-five, at least. Horse years, she's an old lady." Manny busted his cap against the leg of his jeans, shrugged out of his canvas jacket. "Mornings cold, afternoons hot. Can't keep up with the weather."

They powdered and wrapped the mare's white legs, left the barn, and walked together across the grass to the house, the old dog beside them. The kitchen smelled like damp dirt, the last carrots pulled from the garden. She hung her jacket next to Manny's, heeled out of her boots, and sat down to her oatmeal, toast with blackberry jam.

"I'm making soup for supper," Manny said. "Those carrots you planted. Nice and even. You did a good job. Hard to seed straight rows."

"Straight doesn't matter," Elise said. "Space apart, that's what counts."

Manny filled their glasses with milk. "Never trust a man whose rows aren't straight."

"I'm not a man." Elise smiled around her spoon.

"That's nothing I need to hear." Manny folded and pinched his toast, sopped it in the oatmeal.

Elise had recently discovered that Manny could be teased into blushing, a power she hadn't realized she possessed. She tore the crust from her toast and laid it aside.

"Best part," he said.

"I'm tithing. That's my ten percent for Dog."

It was a running joke between them: May Dog bless, they said. May Dog be with you. Praise Dog. The dog would raise her head, prick her ears. "Dog can hear *everything*," Elise would whisper, and they'd laugh.

She watched Manny tip his bowl, the concentration on his face as he spooned the last of the cream. She studied his hands, the scar where a shoeing nail had caught. She'd been holding Allegro when the mare had twitched a deerfly and jerked her hoof from his grip. He'd cursed softly beneath his breath, but not at Elise and not at the horse, just at the pain. When he pulled off his glove, the tear ran the length of his palm. He wrapped his bandanna around the wound and finished the shoe before heading into the house for peroxide and bandages. She'd known better than to say her father could tend the injury. It was as though he was a doctor only in some other life, a story she had heard told about him but never quite believed. She'd visited his office as a young girl but seldom went there anymore. The smell of Betadine made her head ache. The way people waited so quietly for their names to be called and entered the secret rooms behind the dividing door made her queasy with dread. She was glad she'd always been healthy, that Manny had doctored her with chicken soup and calamine. She preferred knowing her father as she did: as someone who left in the dark of morning and returned in the dark of night, ate the dinner Manny had prepared for him, smoked his cigarettes, read his books. A few words of inquiry about the next day's chores, a question or two about how many hours she'd practiced her piano, what period in history she was working through in her studies. All three of them, she believed, were relieved when he finally made his way to bed. Sometimes, swinging in the rope hammock Manny had strung between two pines, she'd watch the last light flick off and wonder if he'd forgotten about her. Still, she missed him in a way she couldn't quite say. Maybe, more than anything, she missed him missing her.

Manny moved their bowls to the sink, ran water. "Let's leave these to soak. I'll hitch the trailer while you get ready."

The gypsy costume she'd put together from the bins at the Give-n-Get was already on hangers and wrapped in a plastic bag. Elise had polished her good boots the night before and zipped them into a duffel so that she could take extra time in the shower, washing her long hair with the same shampoo she'd used on the horse, then combing it into a tight knot while it was still wet. Her father wouldn't have to know about the mascara and lipstick she'd bought at the grocery store. As in years past, he wouldn't attend the fair, wouldn't see her in her low-cut blouse with the flowing sleeves, the skirt and scarves.

It was Manny who was always there. He'd taught her how to milk the cow, how to take eggs from beneath the docile White Leghorns and the peckish Rhode Island Reds. They made pancakes together Sunday mornings, fried chicken Sunday afternoons. When she'd turned ten, he'd helped her steer the tractor across the flats; at fourteen, he'd let her take the wheel of the pickup because her father refused to let her drive the old Volkswagen that was still his only car. It was Manny who had taken her to Duggy's Department Store for her first bra, shrugging when the lady asked what size, what color. When she started her period, it was Manny who told her that they should stock up, and they'd filled a grocery cart with tampons and pads, neither caring that the other customers smiled indulgently or that the box boy had blushed with embarrassment as he bagged their goods.

Elise pulled on her new jeans and red snap-button shirt. She wrapped her good hat in a pillowcase and folded a denim jacket into her duffel. Manny had promised that after the horse show, he would take her on the Ferris wheel and maybe the Octopus. He'd buy her a snow cone. He'd win her a bear if he could.

By the time they reached the fairgrounds, the sun was hot, and Elise could feel the sweat between her shoulder blades. Manny helped her back Allegro out of the trailer and spread fresh straw in the stall she'd been assigned. On either side of her, other young riders were clipping tails, knotting manes. They watched her out of the corners of their eyes, but she kept focused on her work. Allegro dropped her nose, dozing, but Elise knew she'd freshen once she was saddled, that she'd arch her neck and step out like the good horse she was.

Manny stayed close by, chatting with the other men who took turns leaning at the door of the big barn, spitting and kicking manure from their boots. Like him, they were dressed in jeans, T-shirts, and caps. When the announcer called Western Pleasure, Manny helped Elise toe into the stirrup.

"Remember to keep her attention," he said. "She's a wise old gal, but some of those other horses are knuckleheads. Watch for trouble coming from the sides."

Elise smiled. "I know. You've told me a hundred times."

"Hundred and one," Manny said.

Elsie looked out at the arena, at the crowd in the bleachers, at the pennants and flags waving from the tops of the stands. The air was thick with dust and chaff, alive with the sounds of the carnival barkers and music blaring from the loudspeakers. The noise and its attendant flurry of color excited her, and she felt a moment of panic, of being overwhelmed by the screams coming from the rides, the calliope's strange cadence. She felt her heart pound as the announcer called her name, and she clucked Allegro into place with the other horses circling the arena.

As Allegro stepped out, Elise felt the mare's shoulders swell with purpose, the head come up, the ears flick forward and back, listening for Elise's quiet commands. The horse's sure posture steadied her, and she felt the calm that always came when the two of them were working together, the signals between them so subtle that they seemed transmitted through thought rather than the nudge of a knee, the turn of a wrist. She kept her toes pointed, her thighs tight, her back straight, her chin up. Cool as a cucumber, Manny would say. What a team. When the judges announced that they had won third place, Elise wished she had pushed the mare a little harder. Maybe they made it look too easy.

And then they were back in the barn, Manny rubbing Allegro with a rough rag, Elise in the trailer where Manny had covered the floor with an old sheet, stripping her jeans, pulling on the skirt and the belt with its strange coins. She took off her cowboy hat, shook out her hair, and applied her makeup in the little mirror Manny had hung from a hook. She pulled a gossamer scarf over her head and let it fall around her shoulders. Her veiled face reflected back in the glass, her eyes lined in black pencil, her lips newly red. By the time she stepped out of the trailer, Manny had draped Allegro's saddle with a bright green blanket.

"I don't know which of you is prettier," he said, considering Elise's costume. "But I'm sure glad I'm not riding in that getup."

Elise hiked into the saddle, adjusted the layers of material, and looked around her. There was a medieval lady, a scarecrow, a magician, an angel-winged fairy riding a Shetland pony with a paperboard horn sprouting from its forehead. Like Halloween, she thought, a holiday she had always loved but that made her lonely, the Fife children running from house to house, screaming out boasts about their take, while she held tight to Manny's hand, mute with wonder as the candy dropped into her plastic pumpkin. She'd hide the sweet stash in her sock drawer and nibble at it for weeks, even as she swore to her father she had thrown it away. Sometimes, she'd sneak Manny a Milky Way or Butterfinger, and they'd eat together while sitting in the barn, wiping their mouths carefully before venturing back into the house.

"The scarecrow is good," Manny said. "Could use him in our garden."

Elise patted Allegro's neck and adjusted the reins. "After this, the Ferris wheel, right?"

"And cotton candy. Maybe a hot dog, if they don't look too bad."

Elise nudged Allegro into the arena, less nervous this time and glad for the veil. The scarves and makeup made her feel pretty and daring. She pushed back her shoulders and let her hips rock in the saddle as she fell in behind a girl wearing a beige dress and moccasins, a turkey feather in her beaded headband. There was nothing to do but circle the arena, pull to a stop while the judges conferred, then circle again. First place went to the Shetland and his tight-lipped fairy, even though the pony's skittish trotting had loosened the horn, which hung beneath its throat like a malevolent goatee.

"Second place to the gypsy!" the announcer crowed, and Elise urged Allegro forward to receive the ribbon. The mare was tired, Elise could tell, slow to respond and dropping her nose. "Come on, girl," she said. "It's almost quitting time."

Back in the barn, Manny hung the ribbons from the rail and offered Allegro a wedge of apple, but the horse only lipped the fruit and let it fall to the ground.

"She worked hard," Elise said. "She's ready for a nap."

Manny nodded but kept his eyes on the mare. "Let's get her some fresh water before we hit the carnival," he said. "Might should blanket her." He stroked the horse's white poll. "You go ahead and change. I'll rub her down."

As Elise hung her skirt and scarves, the mirror caught the surprise of color on her face. She tilted her head, pursed her lips. She brushed her hair smooth and decided against the cowboy hat. Outside, the air was dusky and cool.

"What first?" Manny asked. In years past, they'd come to the fair together, but this was their first nighttime trip to the carnival. The lights of the Tilt-A-Whirl buzzed above their heads.

"Octopus," Elise said.

"Can't start there. I'll puke."

"House of Horrors."

"You up for that right off the bat?"

"It never scares me." Elise wanted to skip ahead as she had as a child, but she kept her pace slow to match Manny's as they walked down the gauntlet of barkers shouting their promises of stuffed pandas and extra chances. At the ticket booth, they bought two wristbands, good for a night of unlimited rides.

"Okay," Manny said. "I'm ready."

They found the House of Horrors and waited in line with a group of teenagers, loud and jostling. Elise remembered some of them from her short stint at the middle school, but the boys were taller, the girls thin and prettier than she recalled. She was almost seventeen, but in her barn boots and jeans, she felt like a kid. She kept her eyes down and hoped that they didn't recognize her, suddenly aware that they'd think that Manny was her father. She looked at him quickly and saw that he was watching her.

"You know," he said, "I'm hungry right now. Maybe I'll get me one of those hot dogs. I'll meet you at the Octopus in twenty."

"The Octopus," she said. She watched him walk away before turning back to the line, which had started to move. She didn't want to be glad that Manny was gone, but she was.

She was almost to the ticket taker when she felt a tap on her shoulder.

"Hey."

It was the Bible boy, the one who came to the house in his stiff white shirt, carrying a fistful of pamphlets like some insurance salesman. Elise had never seen him this close. He'd let his hair grow a little.

"Hi," she said. They stood for a moment, grinning at each other, then jumped in unison when the barker called them forward.

"I'm Todd," he whispered. "You're Elise, right?"

Elise nodded but kept her hands in front of her, feeling through the dark for what she knew would come: the jigging skeleton, the green-faced witch.

"Wait," Todd said. He pulled her to the wall. They let another group pass—a howl of grade-schoolers pushing and pulling their way down the corridor. One girl was crying, being dragged along by her friends. "It's all fake," a boy yelled, and then gave a shrill scream when the skeleton's bony hand touched his shoulder. When Todd and Elise laughed, the children shrieked away. Elise hadn't realized that they were invisible.

"I'm not supposed to be in here," Todd whispered. His breath smelled like strawberries.

"Why not?"

"It's against my religion."

Elise snorted, and Todd took her arm. "If my dad finds out, I'm in trouble."

Another group was stumbling through, and Elise pressed herself against the wall. Two men and a woman, laughing loudly, sloshing cups of beer. One of the men kept goosing the woman from behind, hollering "Boo!" each time he poked her. When the dangling spider dropped down, the woman pitched her beer straight up.

"Goddamn it, Marlis!" the other man said. "Goddamn it to hell."

"I can't help it," the woman said. "Tell Larry to quit jabbing me."

"I'm not jabbing nobody," Larry said. Elise wanted to reach out and touch his ear just to give him a taste of his own medicine, but she stayed still. Todd grabbed her hand and squeezed. They waited until the bickering fell off into the distance.

"Come on," Elise said. "I've been through here a hundred times." She pulled Todd after her, dodging the rubber snakes and cobwebs. The closer they got to the exit, the louder the racket became. Music rasping, the whoosh of hydraulics, the screams of riders rising and dropping through the night sky—she wanted to cover her ears to stop the noise, the colors, but Todd still held her hand in his, and she didn't want that to stop at all.

She led him away from the din, through the livestock barn to Allegro's stall. The mare nickered. Most of the other horses were already gone, only a few held over for the next day's stone boat pull. Elise loved to watch the Belgians throw themselves into the traces as the weight was added to the sleds, the big horses leaning so hard into the collars that they fell to their knees and still kept digging.

Elise showed Todd how to extend his palm as he fed Allegro a sugar cube. Their shoulders rubbed, and Elise wished he'd put his arm around her, pull her close.

"I've got to get home," he said, "or I'm in big trouble." He wiped his hand down the leg of his jeans. "My dad's the minister at Gospel Lighthouse. I'm not even supposed to be here, but he's leading revival in Folgate." Todd looked across the fairgrounds toward town as though he feared he was being watched. "Sometimes I just want to do what the other kids do."

"Yeah," Elise said. "Me too."

He shuffled the straw beneath his feet. "Maybe you can come to church with me sometime."

"Sure," Elise said.

"What about tomorrow? Service starts at eleven. I could meet you out front."

Sunday. The horse pull. She'd watched it with Manny every year of her memory. "Do I have to wear a dress?"

"Should, but they won't kick you out."

Elise imagined showing up in her gypsy skirt, the jingling belt, the scarves and veil. "Okay," she said. "Eleven."

Manny was waiting at the Octopus. He had two hot dogs wrapped in napkins. "I'd about given up on you," he said.

"I met a friend who wanted to see Allegro." She bit into the cold hot dog, sweet with relish and ketchup. She liked the sound of the word *friend.*

"What's next? Ferris wheel?"

"Maybe some cotton candy," she said. They walked to the

trailer. Manny got a caramel apple, which he ate in a few bites before wrapping the core in a napkin and sticking it in his pocket for the mare. The line for the Ferris wheel wrapped around the enclosure, so they walked to the Tilt-A-Whirl, but it was swarmed by teenagers giddy for a third or fourth time on the ride.

"Maybe we should just go home," Elise said. The desire she had felt for the rides was gone, replaced by a yearning to spend more time with Todd.

"We can always catch the Ferris wheel tomorrow," Manny said. "Prettier during the day, anyway. You can see all the way to Montana."

They trailered Allegro, mucked the stall, and hosed it down before climbing into the pickup. Elise held her ribbons in her lap. She might have forgotten them if Manny hadn't reminded her.

They didn't talk as they followed the highway back to Omega, comfortable in the familiar silence. The Volkswagen was in the driveway, the house already dark by the time Manny had backed the trailer and unloaded Allegro. Elise took Dog and locked the chicken coop against raccoons and foxes. She came around the barn to see Manny sneaking a cigarette. She liked knowing this secret about him. There were times that Elise forgot that her mother and Manny had been only a few years older than she was when the drowning happened. She tried to imagine them young and together, easier than imagining her father. She knew that Manny was the last one to see her mother alive, that they had been alone at the river. Watching him in the soft light of the moon as he struck the match and cupped the flame, she saw him as her mother must have, young and handsome. He stood looking out over the canyon until she scuffed a few rocks, then snuffed the cigarette and buried the butt in his pocket. He motioned toward the house.

"Let's heat that soup."

"Too much cotton candy," Elise said. "I think I'll just go to bed."

Manny considered a moment, then nodded. "You should have gotten first in Western Pleasure."

"I didn't back right."

"Better than most." Somewhere over Angel Ridge, a coyote took up its song, and a chorus joined in. "That must be some kind of party," Manny said.

Elise lifted her shoulders. "My friend wants me to come to church with him tomorrow. Will you take me into Fife? I'll have to miss the pull."

He looked at her, then at the moon. "I guess a little religion won't hurt you."

As Elise walked to the house, she wondered what she would wear. Maybe she'd see what was in the boxes that kept her mother's old clothes. Other than a few photographs, it was all she had. She sometimes wondered how her life might be different if her mother hadn't drowned. It wasn't that she missed her but that she missed the idea of her. Someone like Manny, but different. Someone she could talk to about Todd.

Elise stepped into the kitchen and buttered a piece of bread, sprinkled it with sugar. It tasted good, and she buttered and sugared another slice and took it to her bedroom. The boxes were in the back of her closet, and when she opened them, she smelled nothing but the dust that had settled in the seams. She pulled out a few blouses, a sweater that fit just right, a skirt that bunched at her hips. She stood in front of the mirror and tugged the zipper, but it was no use. Ten pounds, at least. She turned to the side, narrowed her eyes. No more butter and sugar, she thought. She'd had more than enough cotton candy.

She hung the clothes and pulled on her nightgown. She wasn't sure why, after so many years, she'd begun to wonder about her mother. She thought about her father alone in his own room, already asleep, and felt an unexpected loneliness, maybe his, maybe her own. She lay on her back, then her stomach, then one side, and then the other. It's no use, she thought. She craved another slice of bread spread with sweet butter, folded and pinched soft. Maybe a drink of water. She rose, walked to the bathroom, saw herself reflected, and was taken with the tangle of her hair, the welt of her lips. She leaned toward the mirror, pressed once, twice. I *want,* she whispered. A wing of breath feathered the glass, then evaporated, leaving only the print of her kiss. In the morning, her father might find it. Remember that she was there.

Chapter Twelve

The mare stood straddle-legged in the evening dusk, trembling, her breathing gone from quick and shallow to a deep, prolonged moan. Manny leaned against the tractor's bucket, shouldering deeper into his jacket. He'd risen at dawn and found Allegro down. She'd been showing signs for the last two days, ever since the fair. He should have been paying more attention, but Sunday had been filled with dropping Elise at church, and then the stone boat pull, and then the carnival. He'd encouraged the mare up and walked her out into the pasture, whetted her with sweet-feed, but she'd stepped away, pulling her legs forward as though they were mired in mud, and made her way to the hawthorn, where she leaned into its thick trunk. He'd called the only vet for miles, who injected her with penicillin, but both understood what came next. Manny had started the tractor, dug the grave only a few feet from where she swayed and shuddered like a thin-ribbed ship, each hoof a weak and tremulous anchor.

He lit a cigarette and cupped it for warmth. The horse stumbled but did not lift her head. Dog rose to a sit, then curled back down, tucking her old bones tight against the chill air. This mare had been with them a long time, ever since Elise had read the ad in the paper for the Tennessee walker. Allegro had been delivered to them with her head poked through the canvas roof of the trailer like a circus giraffe. "Damned stubborn," her owner had groused. It had taken him an hour to shag her into the trailer, and she had kicked and reared, denting the side panels, tearing the roof.

"She doesn't like trailers," Elise had countered, reaching her hand to stroke the mare's withers. "She's afraid of what's inside."

"She needs to be more afraid of *me.*" The man slapped the greasy thighs of his jeans, shook his head over the ripped roof. "How in the hell am I going to fix that?" Manny could have told him—a patch, a heavy curved needle and industrial thread—but he didn't like the man's temperament or the smell of his clothes and wished him gone.

The first year with the mare had been a test of patience, more time spent recovering the animal's good instincts than was spent riding her. She'd been hit in the face and shied every time a hand was raised, had been spurred and whipped until her hide began its tender rippling before she was ever mounted. Finally, the horse was intelligent and kind by nature, and Manny had taught Elise how to start her over, just as his father had taught him, working the mare in the round pen with gentle ropes and gunnysacks slipped across her back, a plastic bag at the end of a stick to get her used to noise and movement. "*Here,*" Elise would say. "This isn't going to hurt you. No one here is going to hurt you." Manny had felt pride in the truth of her statement.

The mare coughed, a strangled sound. He checked his watch, then wished he hadn't. He knew that Elise stood vigil at the kitchen window. He looked toward the barn, its cedar weathered to gray, and remembered the autumn it was built. Maybe it would have been better for Dewey to have died there, the Lemonhead wedged in his throat, rather than the way he did, carved away a joint at a time, until, both legs gone, he had drowned in the fluid of his own lungs. It was Stubb's death that Manny thought he would choose over all others. The big man had stepped back into the house after having gone out to admire the sunset and collapsed into his wife's arms, taking her to the floor with him, and they'd lain that way, like lovers, until the wife found the strength to free herself from her husband's cooling embrace.

Manny's memories of that first season at Omega seemed a lifetime ago. Sometimes it seemed little more than habit that had kept him on the place all these years: the land must be tended, Elise fed, Deracotte maintained. Sometimes he understood that it was the grief he and Deracotte shared that bound them fast as blood ties.

There was silence, and Manny thought the mare was done with it now, but she lifted her nostrils free of the dirt and wheezed. He glanced toward the window and saw Elise's shadow. When he turned his gaze back to the mare, she was sinking, going down one knee at a time. She rolled to her side, stretched her lovely neck toward him, and he understood that she *saw* him, and that he was the last thing that would ever be in her vision.

"It's okay, girl," he said. "It's okay now. You've done good." She heaved violently, and then she was quiet. He felt some wonder, as he always did in the presence of an animal's death, at how quickly the sheen was gone from her eyes, as if the soul resided in that thin reflective membrane.

In the window, Elise's shadow shifted, then disappeared. He waited to see if the door would open, if she would join him, but, instead, he heard Helen's music drifting out across the pasture. The melody came to him like those spring mornings he woke to the first new trill of the meadowlark. He remained still until the melody faded, until the silence was full of sound again: the rhythmic call of chickadees; a truck along the highway gearing down for the curve; the river. He gave the mare a final caress and climbed onto the tractor.

As he pushed the mare into the hole and the dirt fell in, Manny could see some interest in the way the dog followed the tractor's movement, her head held high for scent. She nosed forward, too close. "Dog! Out!" he ordered, but she kept her stance, deafened by age and the rumble of the tractor. He was nearing the last bucketful when he saw the white glint against the dark earth.

Manny climbed down to examine what he'd uncovered, and in the near-dark he saw the small bones of an animal. He knelt at the edge of the berm, raked the cold dirt, and pulled free the skull pieces, which fit the bowl of his hand as though molded there. The shoulder blades, the dainty finger bones, which he sifted like nubbish gems. An Indian baby, he thought. Some kind of sacred grave.

He took off his jacket, gathered the bones inside, and wrapped the sleeves into a knot. He restarted the tractor and lowered the bucket onto the mounded earth, killed the engine. It would be enough to keep the scavengers away until he could do more.

"Come on, Dog." He carried the bundle up to his apartment and set it on the table. He wanted to show Elise, but not tonight, when things were already so gloomy. He wondered if Elise had cooked something, or if she had warmed up leftovers, or if she'd eaten at all. He still remembered the meals that Helen had fed him, simply prepared but laced with surprise: the chicken and noodles sparked by a red dash of paprika, a generous pinch of cayenne in the stew that set his mouth aflame. The first few weeks after Helen's death, he and Thomas had eaten nothing but the casseroles brought by distant neighbors who had never seen Helen's face—tuna-and-potato-chip casserole, chicken-and-rice casserole, spaghetti-and-hot-dog-casserole—even as Elise screamed with hunger. It had taken most of two days for Manny to urge the bottle's nipple between her lips, and he remembered how he had wanted to cry with her, his own stomach knotted with loss and regret.

"Let's go see what's in the cupboard," he said, and Dog raced ahead toward the light of the kitchen. It wasn't that he was uncomfortable around Elise but that she recently had become strange to him. Maybe, with the horse in the ground, she'd be willing to talk about the next one—maybe a filly, young enough to last her a while.

The dog nosed in and the door swung open. Elise sat at her place at the table, wrapped in what Manny at first thought were blankets but came to see were scarves, covering her hair, her shoulders, belted at her waist, some with fringed bells and punched coins—her costume for the fair. She had let the fire die, and her feet were bare. He wanted to scold her but knelt instead and crumpled newspaper, found a few sticks of kindling. The woodstove did not draw well and it took a moment for the flames to catch, and then for the fire to take hold. Dog settled in close and sighed

Manny went to the refrigerator, found butter and eggs. He'd kept the place as well as he could: dishes cleaned and put away; floors swept; bathrooms scrubbed when dirty enough to notice. Only the laundry had been his bane: his own soiled clothing the majority of the load, along with Thomas's underwear and socks, an occasional T-shirt. But it was Elise's things that he shied from. The panties thrown to the floor. The sometimes stain of blood that he folded to the center before adding the small bit of cloth to the stew of hot water and detergent. Her sheets that he pulled from her bed each Sunday, gathering into his arms the woman smell of her, which was lemon and powder and licorice.

He lit the oven's broiler for quick warmth and to brown the toast. When he set the plate in front of Elise, she shook her head.

"Maybe we should have some whiskey instead." She smiled in a way that indicated her pain.

He wasn't sure about the whiskey, but he knew better than to say that she was too young, and he didn't believe it anyway.

"A drink to Allegro," she said, and got up to find the bottle. She poured them each a shot, then moved to the window, the scarves shifting and shimmering. "Here's to you, girl," she said, and lifted her glass. Instead of knocking back the shot as Manny feared, she sipped and grimaced.

"It's not the best whiskey," he said.

She made her way back to the table, scarves dragging the floor, slid down onto her chair, and took another drink, lipstick smudging the glass. Manny thought about how few people her life was made of, how she'd created her world alone. Since the age of twelve, she'd studied only what interested her: third-world religions, the iconography of martyrs, novels written by women from colonized India, Picasso's Blue Period. She was drawn to the exotic, the spiritual, the magical. Astrology, voodoo, faith healing. It was in a book on superstitions that she'd discovered a cure for Dr. K's gout: a paste of salted and baked owl combined with boar's grease. Manny had dutifully carried the recipe to the pharmacist, who said he thought he'd stick with Ben-Gay.

"Winter is coming. It's like death, isn't it?" She settled a scarf into the crooks of her elbows. "Cold and still."

"It's not like death at all. There's a lot of life out there." He gestured toward the dark window as though she might see for herself.

She tilted her head. "Do you have a lover?"

"What?"

She leaned forward, acting more drunk than was possible. "I have a lover."

"No, you don't." It was out of his mouth before he could stop it.

"Don't you think I'm pretty enough?"

"You're more than pretty enough." He took a deep breath. "Listen. There's something I want to give you." He reached in his pocket for the silver barrette. He'd kept it for himself, bringing it out only when the whiskey wasn't enough, or when it was too much.

"Your mother's," he said. "Yours, if you want."

Elise took the barrette, traced the silver mane. "Where did you find this?"

"I've had it for a long time."

She looked at him longer than was comfortable, then pulled back her hair and clipped it tight before gathering her skirts and moving to the door.

The moon was nearly full, shadowing the fields, but he pillaged a flashlight from the drawer anyway. Dog stayed at his heels, a little afraid of the dark, as she had always been. He'd often teased that it was the coyotes' amorous intentions that she feared, although some part of him had halfway hoped that such a mating might occur, provide him with a litter of big-eared pups, rangy and feral, that would run the fields and come back to him smelling of wild fennel, the rabbity warrens they'd plundered. The old dog was beyond that now, her seasons no longer fretted with heat. He knew he would dig her grave next.

Elise stopped at the two largest trees, the rope hammock hung between. She balanced herself, lay back. The length of baling twine was still there, tied to a near sapling, and she tugged herself until the hammock rocked.

"You're not going to tell me I have to go in, are you?"

"Why not?"

"Nothing's there." She looked straight up at the moon, the hollow of her throat like a pearly shell. "Everybody is gone."

He felt that he should argue, but he understood that her words came from some province other than reason.

"Let's go in by the fire. I'll tell you some stories."

She sat up in the hammock, let her bare toes skim the frosted grass. "What stories?"

"We can talk about Allegro."

She turned her eyes away as though she hadn't heard him. Manny felt himself losing ground and pulled out a cigarette to buy time, cupping his cold hands around the flame before realizing he'd given up his secret.

"Can I have one?"

He started to say no, but what did it matter? She was old enough for more things than he cared to think about. He saw by the ease of her inhalation that she'd done this before, which surprised him. Surely he would have noticed her, behind the barn or even here, in the copse of alder. And then he remembered the butts he routinely pinched out and laid on the step to be finished later, how they sometimes disappeared. He'd assumed the wind or even the deer, which were rummy for tobacco. He never suspected Elise.

She let out a breath ragged with chill and tucked her arms. The dirty scarves, her hair knotted with breeze-floated leaves and twigs from the hammock's netting, eyes smudged: she looked like a feral whelp herself, smelling of pine duff and spring-dampened stone, as though she had crawled from the mouth of a cave and brought the webbing of her world with her.

"Tell me a story about my mother. Was she pretty?"

"You know she was."

"Did you love her?"

"We all loved her."

"But did *you. Love* her."

Manny looked at Elise through the moon-dapple.

She leaned back, closed her eyes. "I'll tell a story, then," she said. "One you've never heard before. It's about church yesterday."

Manny let his shoulders settle, his back relax from its stiff posture. The Holy Rollers. That's what they called them. Speaking in tongues and casting out demons. The Lang woman who had taken him in belonged to that church. Manny remembered sitting beside her on the hard polished pew, sliding down, then scooting back up, sliding down, while all around him people stood with their hands raised to Heaven. He'd been momentarily stilled by the sight of Mrs. Durkee dancing down the aisle, large breasts bouncing, high heels kicked off, face flushed and gleaming. And when she'd sung out *hallelujah!* a dozen times, she collapsed like a poleaxed steer. Manny had straddled the pew to get a better look, but all he saw, before Mrs. Lang pinched his leg, was other worshippers gathered around the fallen woman, praising God. She'd been *slain,* Mrs. Lang explained to him later. *Slain by the Spirit, hallelujah, amen!* The next Sunday, he'd asked to stay home with Mr. Lang, whose morose reading of the newspaper and endless cups of coffee seemed less exciting but safer somehow.

"They call me Sister Elise. I kind of like that." The tip of her cigarette glowed briefly, then faded.

"That's good."

"Will you take me again this Sunday?"

"Don't see why not."

"I like Todd. But he's not my lover."

"That's good," Manny said. He pictured the boy who had met Elise at the church door, his hair slicked tight, stiff shirt and tie, like he was the preacher himself. Not the kind he'd imagined Elise would take up with, but better than some yahoo with a letter jacket and car.

They rolled the embers loose, and Manny snuffed them beneath his boot. When they reached the house, Elise walked down the hallway toward her room, shedding scarves as she went, and Manny turned his gaze toward the sink of dishes. He wondered when Deracotte would get home. The night before, he had stumbled in late, then refused the warmed-over dinner that Manny set before him.

"Okay, Dog," Manny said. "We've had our work, our whiskey, and a cigarette. I think the day is done."

Outside, the air was sharp with woodsmoke. He thought he might haul on into Fife for a real drink, some less-demanding conversation. Maybe to visit Dr. K. Or he could take his good book and his good dog and tuck himself into bed.

Dog took the lead, and they made their way through the dark to the barn, where Manny paused to look out over the pasture and see the umber silhouette of the horse. Only she wasn't there, and, for a moment, he couldn't remember why.

A wet snow had begun to fall, covering the newly turned earth, the mare's fresh grave. A great horned owl lifted from the near field, something alive in its talons. Maybe that's the way to go, Manny thought. Your body snatched up and spirited away. Your last memory a dream of flight.

He watched the luminescent wings of the owl disappear, then stepped into the darkness of his room. He thought of the story he might yet tell Elise, how he had dived down in the water again and again, how he believed that what he grasped was not a mossy branch but Helen's wrist, that he would pull her to his chest and swim them back to shore. He remembered the awful deadness of that piece of wood, how he clutched it and could not let go, even as he waved down a passing car whose driver went for the sheriff. It was the sheriff who had finally taken the stick from him. Gently, each finger pried loose, leaving the viscous scum, the larvae that had crawled into the cuffs of his shirt, nested in the hairs of his arms. Back at his apartment he had stood in the shower, felt the worms still alive, the sting of his blood coming back, the questions echoing in his head. All he could answer was that he had tried to save her. That he had failed.

In the weeks after, he felt their eyes on him—at the hardware store, the café. People had seen them come into town together, had seen them alone. Where was Deracotte? Where was the husband? Who was surprised that they had pulled off the road into the cover of trees? Was it loneliness that had sent Helen into the water? Despair? Or was it a lovers' quarrel? Manny sometimes thought that if he knew why she had walked away from him and into the river, he would tell them, but he would never betray Helen's intimacy. He had told Deracotte exactly what he had told the sheriff: that Helen had walked into the river, been sucked under. Deracotte had never asked for details, as though he were afraid what he might hear—his silence its own kind of accusation. There were times when Manny longed to tell it all: not just the truth of their lovemaking, but the pleasure of her as they danced through the kitchen, Elise held between them. How he feared the forgetting as much as he did the remembering. Only Dr. K had accepted Manny's silence, smoking with him in the dark apartment above the store, pouring him another whiskey.

The lights of Deracotte's car skidded across the driveway, and Manny realized he'd been standing in the dark. He switched on the lamp, and in the glow, he saw the bones, still on the table. Tomorrow he would see if he could make sense of them. He could take them to the sheriff, or maybe send them to the museum in Folgate. Maybe he'd dig another grave somewhere in the canyon, mark it with a stone. Maybe he would just keep them for a while, let them rest. He carried the bundle to the closet shelf. When he stepped back to the window, he saw that the snow was settling in, the dark river cutting the white.

Dog moved stiffly toward the bedroom, ready for sleep. "Hey, Dog," he said, and lifted her to the mattress. He stripped to his shorts and crawled beneath the covers, shivering. He moved one foot just close enough to feel the dog's warmth, closed his eyes, and thought he heard the owl, low-throated and calling, the snowy earth a sudden, fertile ground, even as the rabbits began their sympathetic turning, summer brown to winter white, nature's way of allowing them half a chance, a moment's almost, before the flick of an ear, the twitch of a tail, gave them away, and the owl began its precise descent, the shush of wings coming down.

Chapter Thirteen

Deracotte had been watching the ravens for hours, ever since coming upon their black rise off the dead fawn. A warm breeze came up the canyon. The end of January but strangely warm, and he'd shed his jacket. After two months of record snow, the sky, frozen gray since Thanksgiving, had broken to blue. The ravens turned their backs to the wind, and their feathers ruffled and frayed. To the west, a cloud bank was building. Small whitecaps tipped the river's flow.

There had been a time when he would not have been so alone on such a Sunday, only scavengers for company. Once, he and Helen had come to make love while Manny tended Elise, saying they were going for a picnic, trying not to smile. Once? He wished that it had been more. So many things that he wished.

After Helen's death, he'd thought he might lose his mind and wished it so. He'd wished that he might die. He'd taken his father's razor to the river, fully intent upon ending it there. Only the image of Elise when he'd left her, cradled in Manny's arms, had brought him back. He understood the stages of grief, knew that time was what it took. Why, then, had his despair continued to grow rather than dissipate? His memories of Helen became more indelible with each passing year, like a brand burning deeper. Sometimes he wished for no memory at all.

He knew that what everyone said was true: he needed to somehow mend his life, start over again. But none of the women he met in Fife had moved him toward seduction. Each time he looked at them with an eye toward courtship, all he could see was Helen's hair beneath that streetlamp, the way she tilted her face toward him in the light. He might never have known he wanted a woman at all if it hadn't been for her. Maybe he'd have been better off a monk, celibate and sacred in his passion. At least it would have saved him this hell.

But then there was Elise. As a child, she had sometimes followed him down the trail to this place, curious what he was looking for. He'd take her in his lap and stroke her hair, the same auburn color as Helen's, the same warm weight. She knew her mother had drowned, but he didn't know how to tell her that the search for Helen's body had stopped but never ended. That they would never find what remained.

Deracotte tried to remember the last time he had held Elise. He could hardly bear to look at the few photos that Manny had taken and hung on the wall: Elise as a baby in Deracotte's arms, a little girl in his lap, a young woman on her horse, her face tipped down to check the gait, her hair alive in the breeze. Like the pages of a flipbook, those photographs. If bound together and thumbed quickly, the movement might meld: the infant set loose, toddling to the next room, walking to the field, mounting the horse. Deracotte sometimes felt as though his arms were still held in that open position of letting go. Their emptiness struck him as pathetic. No longer a gesture of liberation but of beseechment. *Come back.*

Deracotte knew, too, that even if Elise were to settle into his arms, neither of them would find comfort. How could he tell Elise that as she had grown, become more and more like her mother, what he felt whenever she was close was not consolation but a return of the panic that had come with Helen's death? To touch Elise's hair, even the smell of her, made the loss as fresh and cruel as the moment he'd been felled by the news.

And there was this: what need did Elise have of him? Manny had taught her everything Deracotte could not: how to raise the chickens, how to build a fire, how to plant a garden, how to break and ride a horse. As had always been the case with Manny, Deracotte understood that what he should feel toward him was gratitude. What place was there for the resentment that brewed in his gut, the jealousy that sparked in his chest whenever he watched Manny lift Elise to the saddle, whenever she threw her arms around Manny's neck with such affection? Better to let them lead their lives together. Better that he keep his agony to himself.

The birds watched intently as he rolled his left sleeve, tied the ligature, and inserted the needle, before dropping back to the deer carcass as though understanding what peace descended. Their heads disappeared into the cavern of the belly, already hollowed to spine. They mustered and quarreled over the meatiest parts, the delicacies—eyes, cheeks, tongue—already gone. Deracotte felt the drug begin its work, the calm come into his stomach like warm milk.

When did this ending begin? With the twin birth, his son dying in his hands? The snakebite? Helen's drowning? And then the call from Folgate, the news of Dewey's death, the questions from the resident surgeon: why hadn't Deracotte ordered the man hospitalized? Such neglect courted malfeasance. There was talk of a hearing before the board. Deracotte had stood in his office, the receiver in his hand, unable to defend his decision. Of course, the surgeon was right: he'd ensured Dewey's death. And then he'd gone fishing.

Nights without sleep. Even washed down with whiskey, the sedatives were no match for the rage of self-loathing. The first time he allowed himself to steal an ampoule of Dilaudid home, he'd waited until the sounds of the house had gone quiet. The bright light of the bathroom had steadied him into clinical attention: the vein visible and pulsing, the alcohol swab to prevent infection. He'd stowed everything carefully before making his way back to bed, the drug loosening his muscles, unknotting his heart. He hadn't realized until that moment how long he'd been laboring to breathe, as though the water that killed Helen had filled his own lungs as well. Every few months, then every few weeks. Now, only on weekends, hours carefully timed, evenly spaced. With each terminal patient, he ordered a little more, enough to help their suffering, and his.

Deracotte rolled the vial, syringe, and strap into a red handkerchief, a tight bundle that fit inside his pocket. When he stood, the ravens rose with him, then settled in a nearby elderberry, cranky and garrulous. Deracotte listened to their derelict conversation—short clacks, drawn-out *reeps*—an avian Morse code.

He matched his footsteps to the prints of his coming and saw how the snowmelt had seeped into the indentations left by his boots. Behind him, the ravens took up their meal, glad for his desertion. By the time he arrived at the house, the clouds had pushed east, taking the sky above him, and he felt the sudden rain, strange for the middle of winter. He saw Manny on the tractor, tires chained, plowing an erratic pattern from barn to road, road to house, up and down the ditch. He shucked his coat higher on his shoulders, looked out over the canyon, and began to understand: drifts of snow, solid only hours before, were already eroding in the warm downpour. Deracotte could almost believe that buds and blossoms would follow within minutes, that if he turned his gaze away for too long, he would miss an entire season. The river, gone from the color of smoked glass to milty brown, had begun to heave like the back of some humped animal.

Manny idled the tractor's engine, jumped down, and slogged through the snow to Deracotte. His cap was sodden, his hair slapped against his forehead.

"We've got trouble. Ground's already saturated. Creeks will wash out and take the roads." He wiped a gloved hand down his face, leaving a streak of rust-colored mud.

Deracotte tried hard to think of what might come next, what he should say. "What can I do?" he asked.

Manny shook his head. "I'm doing it."

Deracotte trudged toward the house, the snow settling beneath his feet like wet cotton. He dropped his boots near the fire, hung his jacket to dry, and scooted his chair closer to the window. Uneasiness still held at the edge of his comfort. It wasn't only the rain coming down and the water rising; it was his helplessness in the face of it.

I'm doing it. Always, it was Manny.

In the days after the snakebite, it was Manny who had changed the bandages, fed him broth, stayed with him through the night. Manny who had taken care of his wife, his child, his land. Manny who was the last one to see Helen alive: it was a phrase that haunted Deracotte, yet he couldn't help but repeat it to himself. The torment of wondering why, of wanting every detail, of not wanting to hear any of it. Of blaming himself. Of having others blame him. Deracotte remembered how he'd taken Elise and driven down the hill to find the crowd still gathered on the riverbank, watching as though Helen might step from the water. He saw the way they looked at him, the way they always had: suspicious, distrusting, as though this was what he had planned all along. He'd left them, left Manny shivering and silent, and driven back home, Elise asleep on the seat beside him, only to find himself stopped, halfway between the river and his house, idling in the middle of the road as though he had simply coasted to a halt. He felt like a traveler on a train, the pitch of his body leaned forward in preparation for the lurch, the locomotive picking up speed. How long had he stared out the window, hands limp in his lap, as though he wasn't the engineer of his own machine? Finally, he'd wrapped his fingers around the steering wheel, held on as though the car's acceleration might kick him from his seat and out into the field. But his speed was no speed at all, only a lugubrious creep toward home.

There had been only one call to make, to Helen's parents, and, that night, he'd driven into town and parked at the gas station, left the Volkswagen idling as he dropped coins into the pay phone. He'd hoped for Helen's father to pick up the line, as though the news might be somehow less difficult to deliver to the man who loved Helen nearly as much as he did, but it was Helen's mother who answered. Instead of the cries of anguish he had expected, his words were met with a long silence, then, "You killed her," in a voice so steady and clear she might have been reading a road sign. "I knew you would."

Deracotte closed his eyes and listened to the rain treadling the roof. He heard the *grun, grun, grun* of the tractor and drifted with the rhythmic noise. It felt as though he were sliding into water, up to his ears in nothing but sound. He felt a stark expansion, the room enlarging, taking in more air. He felt as though he were rising, as though gravity might let loose its hold. Is this what it had felt like for her, that letting go?

Maybe he slept, because when he looked again, the roiling water had crept higher up its banks, churning with root-wads, mill planks, chunks of Styrofoam. An entire civilization was floating by: a shed roof; wooden gates and feed buckets; a dead Hereford, udder bulbous and red as a fish float; draperies hung on a wall papered with bright roses; lawn chairs and ornamental flamingos; a child's galloping Wonder Horse; and now the whole of a faded pink trailer, TV antennae still attached. He watched as the trailer was swept into the bridge abutment, where it bent before breaking in half. He felt the impact before he heard the screech of twisting metal. The trailer's contents spilled out like the ruptured guts of a gigantic beetle. Colorful bedding flagged the rapids. An orange sofa bobbed like a cork before sinking, its cushions popping up and rafting away. If they found Helen now, churned to the surface by the rising river, there would be nothing but bones.

He lit a cigarette and leaned back from the window, heard the run of water change its pitch: Elise taking her shower. He'd forgotten she was in the house with him. Although he'd fended off the efforts of Helen's family to gain custody of Elise, he hadn't been able to imagine how he might raise a child without Helen. Manny's offer to care for Elise while Deracotte worked was both a blessing and a curse. He thought about how much of Elise's life he had missed and Manny had witnessed. He remembered how, only days ago, while checking a young woman for hypothyroidism, he'd been startled not only by her question but by his unspoken answer: "What is Elise up to these days?" she'd asked. He didn't know. For so long, it had been enough to be near her, to have her in the next room. He knew it needed to be different, that he should propose some things they could do together—a walk up Bedrock Canyon, or, once the water receded, an evening fishing the close current—but like so many of his good intentions, such plans had fallen by the wayside. How long since he'd taken his rod to the river, cast his line across the current?

He rose, found himself steady enough to walk. He stepped to the small desk where Helen had kept receipts and letters, pulled out the stained page he had torn away from the magazine's folds years before. He read her writing for the thousandth time: "THINGS COULD STAY THE WAY THEY ARE OR THINGS COULD CHANGE." Stay. Change. Again, he tried to make sense of what it might have meant to Helen. What it might mean to him.

The churning of the tractor staggered and ceased. He heard Elise humming in the bathroom. He pushed aside Telemann and Schubert, found Coltrane, and waited for the first harlequin note to color the silence. Out the window, the river had blended with the rain, and he could hardly make out where land ended and water began. A gust of wind busted through the opened door, bringing a waft of woodsmoke.

"Can't keep up with it," Manny said. "It's the barn I'm worried about. Right at the mouth of that draw." His face shone with sweat. Dog slumped to the floor, her fur matted with mud. "It's probably too late to stop it."

Deracotte was no good at running the tractor. He didn't know how to channel a ditch.

"I can fix an omelet," he said.

Manny nodded as he heeled off his boots. "I could use some food."

Deracotte slipped a pat of butter into the skillet, broke six eggs into a bowl, added a splash of cream as Manny shed his coat and hooked it behind the door. Deracotte heard the muffled *click* as something fell to the floor. He turned to see Manny holding the bundled handkerchief, the wrap loosened to reveal the needle, the strap, the vial—all that Deracotte had needed to get him through the weekend, if he was careful.

He turned back to his skillet, the butter browning. "It's for my allergies," he said. "To heighten my resistance." The eggs spat. He turned down the heat, began grating the cheese.

Manny took a step closer. "This is Dilaudid. Says right here. I delivered it for Dr. K. Woman was dying with cancer."

Deracotte topped the eggs with the cheese, added salt and pepper, and reached for the bread. Manny moved closer, his hand tight around the vial. He'd break it if he weren't careful. Shatter it in his fist.

"Listen," Manny said. "What is this?"

"It's what I used for the snakebite." Deracotte divided the omelet onto three plates, added toast.

Manny dropped the packet to the table. "That snake was years ago."

"I've had problems with joint pain."

"I take aspirin for that."

"I don't."

Deracotte pulled out a chair and sat down. The fork felt loose in his fingers, and he buried it in the omelet to stop its trembling. "Your eggs are getting cold."

"You eat them." Manny grabbed his coat, slapped his cap onto his head. "I'm going back out."

"I thought it was too late."

"Maybe it is." Manny motioned Dog outside and slammed the door so hard that the rattle came up through the table.

Deracotte waited until he heard the tractor start. When the engine cut away into the distance, he folded the handkerchief and slipped it back into his pocket. He gathered the three plates and emptied them into the garbage. He was surprised when Elise stepped into the kitchen. He looked at the plate he held in his hands: empty.

Elise went to the window. "What's Manny doing on the tractor?"

"Too much rain. The roads are flooded."

She turned and looked at Deracotte. "But he's supposed to take me to town."

He wanted a cigarette, to settle back into his chair by the window. He wanted another dose, but tomorrow was Monday. He'd need time to let his head clear.

He moved the dishes to the sink, turned and saw that Elise was dressed in a skirt, her hair held back with a silver barrette. Helen's.

"I'm going to church." She reached for her coat. "If Manny won't do it, I'll drive myself."

Deracotte felt the buzz at the back of his skull. What was she doing in Helen's clothes?

"No one is going anywhere. It's too dangerous," he said.

"What does it matter to you?" Her jaw was set, just like Helen's. "We could *all* be dead for all you care."

He was across the kitchen and had hold of her arm before he knew what he was doing. She jerked away and backed to the wall, on her face a look of fear that fanned the terror he himself was feeling. He clenched his fists against the rage, the panic burning through his chest.

When the lights flickered and died, his hands dropped, and they stood wordless in the sudden dark. He heard Elise run to her room, the door slam.

He waited for his eyes to adjust, peering into the dusk as though he might make sense of what had happened.

The tractor churned around the barn. Deracotte felt for his boots and jacket, stepped out into the rain. He started the Volkswagen and found the road, ditched with deep rivulets of mud and gravel. He steered to the highest side, felt the tires gutter and grab as he drove toward the river. It was the direction everything was going, a race of water downhill. Boulders bumped against the side panels. He felt as though he were being carried along, as though the world were joining in his escape. The shaking of his hands was nothing he couldn't ignore, the small weight in his pocket a tease of lips, a fingertip tracing his hip.

He crossed the bridge and pulled the car into the locust grove, felt the tires muck in. The banks were submerged, Home Beach gone. He turned off the engine and heard the river beside him, carrying along the sound of itself, swallowing the racket of stone against stone, of limbs colliding, of sand and silt boiling along the bottom. It was right that no one knew he was there. This was his place, his time. He deserved this fragment of paradise.

Already, he could feel the warmth coming back into his chest, his breath quickening. This was the moment he cherished the most, those few minutes after he had allowed himself to understand that it had been long enough, that the decision had been made. He turned on the overhead and rolled his sleeve, the rain all around him like a veil. He was humming now, a torch song, smooth and easy.

The vein popped smartly beneath the skin, the previous puncture nearly invisible in the forgiving glow. He felt the blood hardening his penis as the needle penetrated the rubber gasket. When he tapped the barrel with his fingernail to release the air, the bubble separated, rose to the top, and he resisted the urge to put his tongue to the drop that quivered at the tip. He pressed the needle lightly against the vein, not yet hard enough to break the skin, and then waited, breathing deeply, faster and faster, until his vision was nothing but stars and the needle going in was a kiss. He closed his eyes, opened them again, and smiled at himself in the rearview, his face touched by light, and in love.

Chapter Fourteen

In the little church by the river, the singing had grown louder than anything the sky might produce. Hands raised, heads thrown back, the brothers and sisters were yodeling their prayers, clapping, stomping up and down. No electricity, the lights lost, candles everywhere, flickering in the windows, stubbed through paper cups, held by the people who moaned and swayed, their faces illuminated and glowing.

In the half-dozen times she had attended the church, Elise had come to love her place in the pew, shoulder to shoulder with Todd on one side, the solid body of his mother, Mrs. Maggy, on the other. It was almost like being held, something she had not realized she was missing until that moment when she felt the warm press of them against her. Mrs. Maggy introduced Elise to the other women as Todd's girlfriend. "Like the daughter I never had," she said, and squeezed her with such affection that Elise blushed with pleasure.

Even in the muted light, the loud singing, banging piano, and tambourines excited a flourish of colors. She'd tried to explain to Todd how the oranges and reds filled her vision whenever she heard music, but he'd shaken his head, a serious look on his face. "I don't know," he said. "Sounds like some kind of vision. Hope it's the right kind."

Elise closed her eyes and let the hallelujah chorus wash over her, grateful that Manny had risked the highway to get her there, saying he'd be back in two hours—long enough for him to fill the gas cans, refuel the tractor, and dig the ditches a little deeper.

The congregation quieted as Reverend Maggy took the podium. He was a man her father's age but seemed much younger, his hair oiled dark and combed back. When he tilted his head and looked to heaven, his face disappeared into shadow.

"Oh, Jesus," he said.

"Lord, Lord," the congregation answered.

"Give me the wisdom to speak your truth. Show me the way."

"Help him, Jesus."

He closed his eyes, took up his Bible, dropped it open, and touched one finger to the page.

"Today," he said, "God has directed me to Deuteronomy, chapter 18, verses 10 through 13: 'There shall not be found among you *any one* that maketh his son or his daughter to pass through the fire, *or* that useth divination, *or* an observer of times or an enchanter, or a witch, Or a charmer, or a consulter with familiar spirits, or a wizard, or a necromancer. For all that do these things *are* an abomination unto the Lord: and because of these abominations the Lord thy God doth drive them out from before thee. Thou shalt be perfect with the Lord thy God.' "

"Amen," Todd's mother said, and flagged one hand toward heaven, waving a white handkerchief embroidered with forget-me-nots. Her faded brown hair hung lank down the center of her back.

"Perfection," the minister continued, "*only* through God. To be perfect is to be like Him. To be like Him, we must be saved. We must repent!"

The clamor of agreement grew louder. Elise looked to Mrs.

Maggy, now holding her handkerchief to her flushed face as though she could smell the brimstone. Elise had grown used to the shouting, but there was something different about revival, Todd had told her. Special things happened.

"Jesus said it. John the Baptist said it. God's apostles said it. What did they say?"

"Repent!" They were shouting now, and the pianist, whose gray hair hung all the way to the bench, hit a chord on the old upright, a player piano with music rolls unfurling from the cabinet.

"And how do we repent? *How* do we repent?" The minister grabbed the sides of the dais as though he were riding out a hurricane. The candles fanned and wavered. "The Lord tells us how. The Lord tells everything. There is nothing that God does not tell us." He licked two fingers, slid them down the pages of his Bible. "In Revelation, God says we must repent of *anything* associated with demons. Necromancers and witches. Unholy prophecies, Ouija boards, horoscopes—all are the work of Satan!"

"Help us, Jesus!" Mrs. Maggy rose from the pew and began waving her handkerchief like a token of surrender.

"*Now* is the day of salvation. *Now* is the day!"

Elise watched as others jumped from their seats. Some skipped into the aisle. Some whirled until they fell backward to the floor, still calling out the name of God.

"They've got the gift of the Spirit," Todd whispered. "They're speaking in the tongues of angels." His breath smelled like peppermint, and Elise sucked in to taste it.

"And *who* among us has not repented?" The preacher had worked his way to the front of the podium. "*Now* is the day to come forward. *Now* is the day to lay your sins at the feet of Jesus. You *must* be born again to enter the Kingdom of Heaven! Brothers and sisters, join me at the altar. Lay your burdens down. Jesus is calling. Jesus is calling all sinners, come home."

He nodded to the pianist, and the congregation stood. Mrs. Maggy swayed as she sang, "Shadows are gathering, deathbeds are coming." When Todd looked at Elise out of the corner of his eye and nodded toward the altar, she felt a moment of panic. She wanted to protest, to say she wasn't ready, but when she shook her head, Todd bent his face close to hers. "God wants you, Elise."

The prayers had hushed, as though they were all waiting for her decision. Mrs. Maggy stepped into the aisle, giving her room to pass. Elise slowly walked to the front and stood looking up into Mr. Maggy's face. He laid one hand on her shoulder.

"Sister Elise, do you want to take Christ as your personal savior?"

The voices rose like the murmur of bees. Elise closed her eyes against the stir of color. The minister rested his hand on top of her head.

"A crown of gold. All the loved ones who have gone on before waiting to greet you." He squinted as though to see into her memory. "Your mother is smiling down from Heaven right now, Elise. She wants you to be saved."

Elise opened her eyes. She had never thought to wonder where her mother's spirit might be.

"She can hear you, Elise. Listen. She's calling your name." The preacher moved his hands to the sides of her head, pressed his palms against her ears.

The piano was picking up tempo. The people had left their pews and gathered behind her. She felt their hands on her arms, her shoulders, her back. Soft and comforting. Holding her up. "Yes, Jesus," they murmured. "She loves you, Lord."

The pastor brushed his thumbs across her forehead. "Dear God, we ask that you accept Sister Elise. She needs you, Lord. She wants to be born again. Take her in your arms, Jesus. Let her feel your love."

Elise closed her eyes as the fingers pressed harder and the voices rose. The color was everywhere, scarlet and smoking, like embered lava. She felt the tears coming, and she didn't know why. All the hands touching her, Todd on one side, Mrs. Maggy on the other, pressing the flat of her palm to Elise's cheek like a mother checking for fever. Elise began to cry, quietly at first, and then gulping sobs that robbed her of breath. And the brothers and sisters cried with her, praying and laughing, dancing and swaying, until they were all in the throes of a joyous weeping and calling out. Her arms and legs felt paralyzed, like she might never move them again, her neck too weak to hold up her head. Elise felt her lips moving, the words forming.

"Jesus," she whispered. "Jesus."

The preacher raised his arms. "Say it louder! Praise the Lord!"

There was a shout, and Mrs. Maggy was bouncing like a pogo stick, her large breasts bobbing from waist to neck. The piano beat out a steady rhythm. Elise took one step, and then another, and soon she, too, was dancing.

Afterward, as they hugged her and said they'd see her at prayer meeting come Tuesday, Elise realized she'd never felt so happy. They loved her so easily, these people. They saw her as one of their own. She wished she had known them all along.

She gathered her coat and looked for Todd, who was talking to his mother and father. When they motioned her over, she went willingly. Mr. Maggy's tie was loose at his neck, his face sheened with sweat.

"Have you ever been baptized, Elise?"

Elise could only remember the dunkings Manny had given her while teaching her to swim in the river. "I don't think so."

"Complete immersion. None of this sprinkling with water." The preacher smiled, and his cheeks dimpled. He turned when a boy came running back into the church, flushed with excitement.

"It's raining so hard!" the boy hollered. "The river is flooding, and it's going to take out the bridge!"

They all moved to the door to see the sheets of water coming down, the snowbanks sunk into muddy puddles.

"We'll need an ark to get home," Mrs. Maggy chirped.

Todd took Elise's hand, pulled her back. "Is Manny coming to pick you up?"

"He should have been here by now."

"You might have to stay here for a while." He squeezed her hand.

"Where's Noah when we need him," Mr. Maggy joked. He grew more serious as he examined the rich stream of mud funneling past the doorway.

A large man with a red moustache stepped in from outside, coat and hat covered in plastic. He swept his flashlight across their faces, then clicked it off.

"Sorry to say it, folks, but we've already evacuated most of this street. If you want to make a run for it, I recommend you do it now."

Elise looked at Todd, who looked at his mother, who looked at her husband.

"God's house is our haven." Mr. Maggy shook the sheriff's hand. "There's room for you, too, if you need the rest."

The sheriff snorted. "There's not going to be any rest tonight." He motioned toward the door. "I've got sandbags in the trunk. Might want to grab a few."

While Todd helped his father unload the sheriff's car, Mrs. Maggy took two candles, handed one to Elise, and motioned that she should follow her upstairs. The room was big and open, used as a nursery and for Sunday School. Bright red fire engines and plastic blocks scattered the floor. A beanbag chair, a child-size picnic table, and several small chairs lined one wall. On another, behind what looked to be a kind of snack counter, someone had taped a life-size drawing of Jesus, his long hair colored brown, his robe various shades of blue, the wounds of his hands and feet crayoned a cheerful pink.

"There's napping pads and covers in the closet," Mrs. Maggy said. "Let's get us some pallets made, and then we'll see what the kitchen holds."

Elise followed orders as Mrs. Maggy shook Cheerios from the blankets. "Stick the men over there." She nodded toward the wall closest to the bathroom. "Us girls will bed down behind the counter. Little more private."

Elise set her candle on the counter and layered the pads evenly, smoothed the blankets printed with cartoon spaceships and oogly-eyed frogs. She trailed Mrs. Maggy back down to the kitchen and followed instructions: "Get that rat cheese out of the fridge. Dills too. Everything in there's going to waste."

When Todd and his father came in from sandbagging the doorway, they were black with mud. "Get those dirty clothes off, now," Mrs. Maggy said, menacing with the cheese knife. "Don't want to be dirtying God's house. There's some choir robes in the closet."

When Todd and Mr. Maggy returned barefoot in their golden gowns, Elise covered her mouth and laughed. The preacher did a little jig and pulled his wife into a quick spin so that his hair fell forward in a spit and the hem of his garment fanned out, revealing a pair of knobby knees.

"Watch your skirt!" Mrs. Maggy gasped and fanned herself back to the table, candlelight fluttering in her wake.

Todd stood in his robe, a little embarrassed, his pale collarbone cut by the yoke's corded piping. Elise felt a sudden tremor in her chest, a desire to touch his skin just below the ear, to kiss him there.

"Food's on," Mrs. Maggy called and directed them to join hands around the table. Reverend Maggy offered a prayer of thanks for the cheese and pickles and even for the rain, then squeezed Elise's fingers in his own. "And thank you, Lord, for bringing Sister Elise to us today. Another soul has found her way to Jesus. Your will, dear Lord. Your sweet will."

They ate the cheese and drank grape Kool-Aid. The rain hit the windows so hard they thought it might be hail. They talked about the flood and remembered Noah and all the animals two by two.

"There's always a feeling of peace after a big rain," said the minister. He wiped back the strings of hair that had fallen across his forehead. "God's rainbow is his covenant. He had to wipe us out once, but he promised he'd never do it again, at least not until after the Rapture. He could come for us right now. Like a stranger in the night. This could be our last supper."

Elise felt the preacher's words settle into a space she didn't know she had inside of her. She'd heard him tell of the Second Coming, all the sinners left behind to face untold torment. Blood to the horse's bridle. A lake of fire.

"We're headed up to bed," Mrs. Maggy said. "You two snuff all them candles when you come. Wouldn't wait too long. That river keeps rising, you'll want to be on higher ground."

Todd and Elise cleared the table, wondering aloud if the river had made the road, if the bridge would hold.

"I wonder what it's like at Omega," Elise said.

"River won't reach that high." Todd took her hand. "Come on," he said. "Let's go play some music." They moved to the sanctuary and lit a few more candles. Todd patted the bench beside him. "Let's play 'Chopsticks.' " He bumped her shoulder, crossed his hands over to play the next octave higher, and Elise felt the heat come into her ears. He smelled clean, like fresh alfalfa. His hair had dried into wispy curls.

"Todd? You two coming up?" Mrs. Maggy's voice boomed down the stairway.

Elise slid to the opposite end of the short bench, her heart racing so hard she thought she might faint.

"I was teaching Elise some gospel. That okay?" Todd looked at Elise and winked.

"Keep it low. Your daddy's asleep."

"Yes, ma'am."

They waited for the steps to move overhead, for the sound of Mrs. Maggy's body settling onto the floor. The din of the preacher's snoring rattled with the rain against the single pane of stained glass, a depiction of Jesus on the cross, the thorns around his head elongated into golden spikes.

"We better play something," he said. "Or they'll suspect."

Elise felt as though she were not hearing him but reading his lips, which she wanted to taste again.

"Play 'Für Elise,' " she whispered.

"I don't know that one. Is it in the hymnal?"

"It's Beethoven. Let me show you."

Elise leaned in and struck the first few notes in a hushed tone.

"Here," he said. "The piano can play itself." He pulled a few levers that set the paper scroll in motion, "Shall We Gather at the River" plinking out in a toney ramble. They kissed, pressed together so hard that Elise felt her vertebrae pop. She could have been held harder. She wanted to be bent, to break open, let this moment into her heart. She ran her hand up Todd's leg, felt the hardness beneath his robe. He unzipped from his neck and let the satin folds fall open. She'd read the *Cosmopolitan* magazines at the library—"Ten Ways to Dress for Sex" and "Twenty Ways to Please Your Man"—but she'd never known this thing she now held in her hand, its pulse matching her own.

She remembered the magazines' instructions, lowered her face. He smelled clean there too. She laid her lips against the smooth skin, tasted salt.

"Oh, Lord," he said.

When his body went stiff, she thought she had hurt him, but he grabbed her hair, pressed her face closer. She gagged and the fluid ran down her chin and onto the robe.

"I'm sorry," she said. She wondered if it would take the color right out of the cloth.

"No," he said. "It's good." He reached for the box of Kleenex on top of the piano just as the scroll ended. "Play something," he insisted, and Elise found the first notes of Schubert's "Ave Maria." Her lips felt raw and swollen. Todd wiped at the dark stain across his lap. "I need a new robe. Keep playing."

The rainbow hues had already begun to flood Elise's vision. Schubert's sonata was as golden as the rays of Christ's crown. She hadn't realized how loud she was playing until Todd pinched her shoulder.

"Let's go," he said, smoothing the pleats of his fresh robe. "They'll hear that's not church music."

"But it is," she said. "It's a prayer."

"Not our kind of prayer." He moved toward the stairs. "I'll go up first."

She sat in the silence, nothing but the steady beat of rain on the roof. She snuffed all the candles, waited for her eyes to adjust before feeling her way up the stairs.

Mrs. Maggy lay still as Elise took off her shoes and slipped beneath the short blankets. The plank of the floor was a comfort, something solid to ground herself against. She was almost asleep when she heard Mrs. Maggy ask if she wanted a drink of water.

"What?"

"Do you want a drink of water?"

"No, thank you."

"I need one, and I think you best have one too."

Mrs. Maggy groaned herself to a stand. "Come on, girl."

Elise followed her down through the sanctuary and into the kitchen, where the sudden beam of a flashlight made her wince. Mrs. Maggy was in her slip, rolls of flesh bunched beneath her armpits. Elise took the paper cup Mrs. Maggy offered and drank it in one swallow.

"You needed that, didn't you?" The woman brought a candle and sat down across the table. She had threaded her hair into a loose braid. Strands of gray sprang from the twist like wire.

"I didn't think I was thirsty, but I guess I was."

The joy that Elise had seen earlier in the woman's face was gone. Her skin hung sallow around her mouth, and there was a pinch of anger between her eyebrows.

"Maybe you need another glass of pure water."

"I'm fine. Thank you."

Mrs. Maggy laid her palms flat against the rough table. "No, you're not fine. You might have been a few hours ago, but you sure ain't now."

Elise dropped her eyes from the woman's gaze.

"What kind of music was that you were playing?"

"It's a prayer. To the Virgin Mary."

"We don't worship idols in this church. We pray to Jesus."

Elise felt her face grow red. "It's just music."

"Todd says you have visions to that music. That's the Devil's work." Mrs. Maggy ran a finger underneath the strap of her slip where her bra had dug a deep furrow, then pointed that finger at Elise. "We welcomed you into this church. You knelt at that altar and asked Jesus into your heart. You either mean to join us in Heaven, or you're wanting to burn in Hell."

Elsie licked her lips and kept her eyes down.

"And I'll tell you another thing." Mrs. Maggy's eyes hardened. "You keep that stinking mouth off my boy, you hear?" She stood up from the table and took their cups. "You smell like the Devil's own cuttlefish."

Elise sat for a long time, listening to the heavy steps up the stairs. Mrs. Maggy was right: she had done what she wanted, never stopping to consider her sin. And in God's house. She thought about her mother, watching, listening, and buried her face in her hands.

When she uncovered her eyes, she saw the trickle of water slip beneath the door like a long, liquid tongue. She watched it snake its way along the kitchen floor, a stain that spread to the table even as she watched, flickering like fire in the candlelight.

She took the stairs two at a time. She had to tell them that the flood was coming. She bit her lip as she ran, and the taste of blood was the promise that it wasn't too late. That she might still be saved.

Chapter Fifteen

Deracotte walked from the barn to the house and slipped the fishing rod through the Volkswagen's window and into the backseat, noting the river below him, the roll of current, new cutbanks carved by the flood. The water was still too high, too cold for hatches, but he'd weighted the line and stocked his fly box with nymphs. It wasn't the catching of the fish that was most important; it was his new commitment to share this love with Elise.

He'd spent the past twenty-four hours in a transitory fugue. Sitting in his chair, studying the far hillside and the deep fissures left by the rains, it had come to Deracotte that some part of his own land had been washed away. He'd begun shuffling through books, looking for a pamphlet he'd once possessed detailing the consequence of soil reduction via erosion. How could it not be fate that, in his quizzical search for the text describing the properties of property, he had come across, instead, three volumes by Tolstoy: *A Confession*, *What I Believe*, and *What Then Must We Do?* Inside each cover, he found the date of acquisition (only weeks after they'd met—had she taken a class in Russian literature?), and Helen's name inscribed lightly in pencil.

Deracotte had stayed there on the floor, captured first by Helen's ghostly hand and then by the pages themselves—the pages that set him to *thinking* again, put him into a state he'd so diligently avoided. He hadn't rested at all but read the thin volumes straight through, forgetting even to smoke, mesmerized by the clarity with which Tolstoy's confessions reflected his own state of mind: "My life came to a standstill. . . . The truth was that life is meaningless. And it was then that I, a man favoured by fortune, hid a cord from myself lest I should hang myself. . . . To feel myself to be good was more important and necessary than for two and two to be four." Only through living a simple life close to the earth did Tolstoy regain some sense of purpose. He gave up all his worldly possessions and took up a pauper's existence, far better than the emotional poverty to which he'd been married. Everything that Deracotte had once believed with youthful passion came rushing back—like waking from a night of dreamless sleep into a sun-stricken room, the air electric and demanding.

But then the cleft of longing in his sacrum had grown into a chasmal yen. Deracotte had tried to smoke away his body's need for the Dilaudid, but the cords of his neck muscles twanged; every nerve in his body was a ganglion fray. He'd made himself believe he could withstand the withdrawal, and then, when that belief failed, he convinced himself that he could better appreciate his new state of grace in a more sedate state of consciousness. But the drug had washed away the tension that had given rise to his epiphany; trancing toward bliss, he'd had to remind himself of his commitment to Elise.

The kitchen was still warm from the previous night's fire. He leaned his ear against Elise's door and listened. He knocked, then inched the door open. In the dusky room, he couldn't make out her face, tell if she was awake or still sleeping.

"Elise," he whispered, then a little louder. "Elise."

He moved closer and sat on the edge of her bed. It had been too long since he'd touched her cheek, and he wanted to do so now, but he feared that such intimacy might threaten the fragile truce that had held between them for the past several weeks. He touched two fingers to her arm. "Elise."

She rolled to her back, blinking. "What are you doing?" she asked. Her hair had come loose of its braid, and he resisted the urge to push it from her face. Her breath smelled sweet, thick and jammy.

"I'm going fishing, and I want you to come with me."

"Fishing?" She rested her arm against her forehead.

"I want to teach you," he said. "I've never done that."

Elise looked to the window and then to the clock on her bedstand. "It's so early."

"That's when the fishing is best. I'll fix you breakfast while you get dressed. Wear something warm."

He whisked half a dozen eggs into the skillet, buttered the toast. By the time Elise came into the kitchen, he'd poured orange juice and coffee for each of them.

"I'm not really hungry," she said. She wore several overly large sweaters, a long skirt, ridiculous for fishing, but he wouldn't say so.

"You need to eat. We might be at the river for several hours."

She shrugged, took a sip of coffee. "Maybe just some toast. No butter."

Deracotte considered the scramble of eggs. His own appetite had left him. Mornings were always hardest.

"Maybe I'll just have toast as well. We'll leave the eggs for Dog."

They ate in silence, Elise still rubbing the sleep from her eyes. Deracotte felt a certain urgency to get to the river, to get his mind off the drug, to remind himself of his mission. He gathered their dishes and left them in the sink.

"You'll want a coat, I think."

Elise pulled Manny's barn jacket from its hook. The grass was chill with dew, the Volkswagen's windows nearly frosted. Deracotte shivered and levered the heaters. Elise sat hunched beside him. Ever since Allegro's death, she'd seemed sullen and withdrawn. Maybe it was to be expected. A phase she was going through. A temporary depression. He'd need to practice patience with this, as well.

He turned right before crossing the bridge and parked several yards from Home Beach. Elise stared straight ahead, arms crossed.

"I'll carry the rod," he said. "We'll practice from shore today. Next time, when it's warmer, we'll bring waders." He stepped out, felt the give of ground still soft with spring thaw.

"I'm not fishing here."

Deracotte stood with his door still open, bent at the waist. "What do you mean?"

"Not *here.*" She looked at him with what he could only read as disgust.

He straightened and looked out over the beach, the river where Helen had drowned. He laid the rod against the car and slid behind the wheel. "I'm sorry. I should have thought of that."

Elise dropped her head, and he thought she might be crying.

"We'll go somewhere else. There's another good spot just up the road."

"I just want to go home."

Deracotte let his shoulders drop. "I'm sorry, Elise. Please. Will you help me?"

"I don't want to go fishing."

"We don't have to fish. We can just sit here and talk."

Elise looked out her window and bunched Manny's jacket tighter against her chest. She seemed tired and pale, as though she'd been sick. Had he missed the signs of some infection? The quiver in his own chest made him remember the cold lake wind blowing through the thinness of his coat as a boy, when he'd longed for layers of wool and down, the luxury of warmth. He looked toward the river, took a deep breath.

"Tell me about the church you've been attending. Is it Catholic? Presbyterian?" Deracotte thought of the church buildings in Fife and realized he had seldom taken account of their denomination.

"Pilgrim Holiness."

Deracotte had expected Methodist, perhaps even Lutheran. "Is that like the Brethrens? Quakers?"

Elise looked at him. "Quakers?"

"There was a Quaker church in New Haven. The Friends Church. I went there once. They don't talk during their meetings."

"Holiness talks." Elise sat up straighter and seemed to relax. "We speak in tongues."

Tongues. Deracotte raised his chin and studied Elise more carefully. "Do you mean glossolalia?"

"The tongues of angels." Elise wiped back the loose strands of hair and turned a little toward him. Her face had taken on new color. "We pray for the sick, and they're healed. I've danced in the Spirit. Miracles happen all the time."

Charismatics. Fundamentalists. It all came back—the loud praying, the crying out, the exhortations against sin, the promise of Hell. The preacher's damnation of his mother's soul.

"It's Pentecostal, then."

Elise nodded, eager now. "Have you been?"

"It was my mother's faith. For a while, anyway."

"But not yours?"

"Never mine."

"You should come with me." Elise leaned closer. "We could go together."

Deracotte rolled down his window, the chill gone, his body flushed with sweat—the first minor signs of withdrawal. Maybe he would take a sedative when they got home. Something to tide him over, get him through the worst of it.

"I'm not inclined toward that kind of belief," he said. "I'm surprised that you are."

Elise drew back, the eagerness gone from her face. "I've asked Jesus into my heart. I'm born again. I don't want to burn in Hell."

"Is that what they've told you? That you'll burn in Hell?"

"I will. And you will too, if you don't believe. The Bible says."

Deracotte let his head fall forward. "That's not true. You can't believe that."

The set that came into Elise's eyes. The willfulness. Like Helen. Just like her.

"I *do* believe."

The river filled Deracotte's vision. The previous night's epiphany seemed years ago, a memory of someone else's life. He could step out now, take his rod, let Elise find her own way. The cold water would help numb the soreness of his spine, soothe the burning in his stomach.

"Let's go fishing," he said.

"I want to go home."

"Let's go fishing."

Elise looked at him, her mouth arched with disappointment. "Fishing won't save you," she said. "Nothing but God."

He breathed in slowly, turned his face away to hide his anger. He listened to her door open, close. The slide of her feet through the heavy grass, then the rush of the river.

He watched her cut to the path that bisected the ridge. A shortcut compared to walking the road, but long and steep. He wanted to warn her about snakes, tell her what he'd learned: they would be dull with cold, seeking warmth. He would tell her to watch for rocks just catching the morning sun, to keep her eyes down, her feet close on the trail. But even to follow her weave upward made his head hurt. He wasn't sure his legs were strong enough to follow. Maybe it was better this way. Maybe they were both better off alone.

He waited until she was out of sight before taking the rod to the river. No waders, no boots, but he stepped in anyway, stopping to let the cold settle the ache. He nipped the weighted nymph from the tippet, replaced it with a Pale Morning Dun. The season was too early for such a presentation, the overhanging alders just greening, the slow runs free of feed. He cast, mended his line to dead-drift, noted the wake of his fly, cast again. His fingers trembled against the reel, and he grasped the cork handle tighter, cast again. The current rocked his hips, shushed the beat of his heart. He imagined Elise climbing to the house. Manny would be there. He'd make her breakfast. They'd talk about things that Deracotte couldn't—the details of the day, the plans for tomorrow. Maybe Manny would attend church with her.

The fly tipped into a dimple, and Deracotte raised the rod, felt the weight immediate and tensing. He worked with the fish and the water, giving line, retrieving. By the time he released the big cutthroat, its gills pulsing red, he was damp with sweat, the chill grown to a full-body shiver. A rising wind huffed up the canyon and knotted his line. Rain pocked the shallows. He couldn't feel the rocks beneath his feet, and he stumped toward shore on dead man's legs. The Volkswagen's weak heater was never enough, and he drove the hill home in a white-fisted clench.

A hot shower. Soup. Coffee dosed with whiskey to keep his mind quiet, his hands still, his need at bay for one more hour.

He pulled into the dirt driveway rutted to mud and saw that Manny's pickup was gone. He felt a spark of gratitude: a trail of smoke from the chimney. He left the rod in the car and slopped to the porch. He should toe off his boots, which weighed heavy as anvils, shed his soaked clothes, but both seemed an impossible effort. He rested his shoulder against the doorjamb, tried to work the knots from his laces, but his fingers throbbed and failed. Whatever Tolstoy's misery, it could never have matched this.

I just need to get warm, he thought. Things will be easier then. He opened the door and stepped into the kitchen, where Elise sat at the empty table, still wearing her many sweaters, her muddy skirt. Her hands were folded, her eyes closed, her mouth moving around words he couldn't hear. He remembered his mother just so, tears streaming down her face as she silently pleaded that his father would come home.

"I'm going to take a shower," Deracotte said. He raised his voice. "Maybe you could make us a sandwich." He wasn't really hungry, but it would give her something to do, get her eyes open, her hands busy.

Elise turned her head slowly toward him, as though she hadn't heard him come in.

"I'm praying," she said. "I'm praying that Jesus will save you."

"Don't," he said. The hardness in his voice felt good. "I don't need you to pray for me."

Pity. That's what he saw in Elise's face. Pity and sorrow, as though he was already lost.

He didn't wait to leave his boots but slogged through the kitchen and into the bathroom. He locked the door but left the light off. He didn't need to see himself, his desperate face. He stepped into the shower fully clothed. The water stung, and he turned it hotter until the steam rose and the mud bled down the drain, then lay beneath its spray, finally warm, wrapped in wet cotton like a second skin. He drifted, memories of the late-summer days he had spent with Helen, the hours they'd napped in the tent, Helen waking him to make love, the slide of her against him, sweat and salt. What kind of fidelity had kept him chaste for so many years, still married to a dead woman? The thought of a strange body against his filled him not with desire but dread. Helen had left him ruined, and maybe that had earned him its own kind of salvation, his life an ongoing penance.

When the water ran cool, he stood. He knew he should leave his clothes in the tub, but he'd grown accustomed to the heaviness draping his shoulders like a monk's robe, the anchor of his legs. He stepped into the hallway and looked toward the dim kitchen, expecting to see Elise still there, stubborn in prayer. Maybe he could talk to her about Tolstoy. Maybe it was middle ground for both of them. But instead of her form at the table, he saw her body on the floor.

That moment between the stopping of his heart and the lifting of his feet, the long time it took him to reach her, to kneel, to roll her over, to turn her face toward him. To see her eyes closed, her lips lightly parted. To place his ear so close that he could feel the softest respirations. To touch her eyelids and have them open. To pull her to him so tightly that she moaned and he felt the water wick from his skin and into the rough weave of her sweaters. She blinked slowly, as though waking from a dream.

He could not imagine what had happened. Had she fainted? He noted the symmetrical dilation of her pupils, felt the steady pulse at her throat.

"Are you dizzy?" he asked. "Did you fall?"

She rolled her head against his arm. "I'm waiting," she said.

"Waiting? What do you mean?"

"I'm waiting for God," she said, "to tell me what to do."

And then Deracotte understood. She was praying, prostrating herself before God on the floor of the kitchen. What space the fear had filled in him emptied, replaced by an anger so intense that he felt his hands tighten around her shoulders. He stood and pulled her up after him. She wouldn't meet his eyes.

"I've got a demon," she said. "Reverend Maggy saw it in a dream. That's why I see colors when I hear music."

Deracotte stood stunned. "You know that's not true. None of this is true." He wanted to shake her back into sense, slap the awful calm from her face. He dropped his arms to keep his hands from gripping her tighter. It was all he could do to breathe.

On the table was her Bible, its pages open. He clapped it shut and held it in his fist. "You go to your room and stay there. Don't come out until I tell you to."

She held out her hand. "I want my Bible."

Deracotte stepped to the woodstove, opened the door, and pitched the Bible in. He heard the sharp intake of her breath.

He moved toward her, wanting to make her understand, but she turned and was running out the door before he could reach her, running as though what she feared most in the world was not the demon or even the Devil, but him.

Chapter Sixteen

It was Elise's voice that brought Manny running from his pickup. Not a call for help, but a near scream: *Daddy!* Three times she cried it, as though she were calling him back from the dead. But, Jesus God, he had not expected to see Deracotte dragging the girl across the yard as she twisted to get away, her skirt muddied and torn.

Manny didn't know that the words had left his mouth until Deracotte stopped and turned his way. And so he said it again. "Let her go, Thomas."

And Deracotte did. He let the girl go.

Manny relaxed the clutch of his fists. He hadn't thought beyond the words, but he knew, now, that he'd been ready to strike, to take Deracotte to the ground.

Elise ran weeping toward the barn, and he wanted to follow her, to make sure she was all right. But Deracotte had turned to face him, his eyes a jolt of gray-white, and Manny knew that this must be settled, somehow, between them. The dog stayed at his heel, tense, ready. Manny feared that, even wrecked with age, she would attack Deracotte, close the distance between them before he could stop her.

Deracotte held up both clenched hands, pounded them once against his thighs, then opened his fingers across his knees, and began sinking as though his shoulders were a yoke cast in iron, his spine soft lead. Manny lunged to catch him, and both of them went down, Deracotte making little *unh-unh* sounds, like an animal dying or in the throes of birth.

Dog, sensing mercy, licked their hands. Deracotte was crying, though it sounded more like a series of coughs, each sob like a jab to the breastbone, expelling puffs of air. Manny smelled the sourness of Deracotte's clothes, the clabbered breath, the hair grown long at the collar, but what could he say? Such observation might shame them both, drive them more firmly into the silence that had settled between them.

"Here." He nudged Deracotte upright. "Let's get in the house. Get warm." He stood and pulled Deracotte up after him. He tried not to be too tender, though Deracotte was rain-wet and trembling. They trundled together across the yard and through the door. Manny led Deracotte to a kitchen chair, took his jacket, and hung it along with his own on pegs behind the stove. He filled the coffeepot and put out a plate of fig bars. He was sure Elise had gone to his apartment. He would let things settle, give her some time.

He brought the coffee and whiskey and sat at the table with Deracotte. They'd made a mess of the floor. Weeks since the flood, and he was still dozing the mud, moving it from one ditch to another, from mound to mound, like shoveling sand. He pushed the cookies closer to Deracotte before taking one for himself. He wondered if Deracotte was clearheaded enough for the whiskey to help.

Deracotte wiped back several thin strands of hair, his hand shaking. "I'm not fit for this," he said. "Not for any of it."

Manny took his time chewing, poured a little whiskey to cool his coffee, which he needed sooner rather than later.

Deracotte pulled a cigarette from its pack and rested both arms on the table. “I came in, and she was lying facedown on the floor, arms out like she was dead.” He drank his coffee in a single draw and poured straight whiskey. “They told her that the Devil is in her eyes.” Deracotte leaned back in his chair. “And she believes it.”

“There’s been a lot of stuff that she’s believed,” Manny said. “She’ll get over it.”

Another pour of whiskey. Deracotte’s mouth worked around the liquid as though he were eating glass. Manny would talk to Elise, convince her of the lies that they were telling her. Make her laugh, just as he had when she was little, shooing the monsters from beneath her bed, the ghosts from her closets, bringing another night-light, convincing her that she was safe.

“Maybe the best thing is to let it ride for a while. Wait and see how things go.” Manny picked up the mugs and moved to the sink. The scant shot would make him more sleepy than relaxed, and he wished he hadn’t drunk it. He’d needed to get through the day’s work. He hoped his boots had dried some.

“I’ve already told her,” Deracotte said. “She’s not to leave the house.” He rose, reached for his jacket, and slammed out the door.

Manny wasn’t sure where Deracotte was headed. Maybe to the river. Right now, he didn’t care. He rinsed the mugs and placed them in the drainer, then pulled on his boots and coat and stepped outside, Dog limping beside him. The Volkswagen was gone. He noted the slough of mud, rock, and debris that still bermed the barn’s north side. The rush of rain and snowmelt down the draw had nearly wiped the barn off its piers. If Dewey and Stubb hadn’t done such a sound job of anchoring, it would all be gone, and he realized how much he missed their sturdy presence. He climbed the narrow stairs and knocked lightly before opening his own door. Elise was lying on the couch, covered with what had once been Allegro’s saddle blanket. He had washed it, offered it to her as remembrance, but she had shaken her head. Since that time, it had draped the back of his worn sofa, gone from utility to décor.

Dog wanted to nuzzle and lick Elise, but Manny pointed to the floor and she sat, the stub of her tail beating a phantom rhythm. Manny thought that the dog loved Elise almost as much as him, and he was glad. The girl was something of an orphan, and he understood how the church might fill that need for family—all those brothers and sisters caring so dearly for your soul.

Manny folded a piece of bread around a swathe of peanut butter and heated milk for hot chocolate, mixing it the way she liked, a dash of cinnamon on top, then sat down across from her, noting the quick rise and fall of her breathing.

"Here's some cocoa. And a sandwich. Get you through until dinner."

"I'm not hungry," she said, her voice muffled, childlike.

Manny set the plate and mug on the old bench that served as a resting place for his books and for his heels when he was reading.

"Well, here it is anyway. Eat what you want." He waited. He needed to get the tractor unrigged and put away. Animals fed. But he couldn't imagine leaving her sad and alone beneath the old wool blanket, its stripes shrunken and bleeding into one another because he had failed to remember what some mother most surely had taught him: never wash wool in hot water. He thought of the scratchy remnant of his father's horse blanket that he had carried from house to house, how each good woman in succession had attempted to wrest it from his hands, sure it harbored fleas. How he'd bawled and fought until they'd given up but kept their eye on it as though it were a snappish cur. He couldn't recall when he last had it in his possession. How could he have held on to something so fiercely and not remember letting it go?

The dog lay down, drowsy with warmth. Maybe he'd let his boots dry for a few minutes, then get to it. He sat in the chair closest to the window and dozed. When he heard Elise stir, he watched through half-closed eyes as she fed Dog the sandwich, then set the mug on the floor to be lapped clean. He could have questioned her actions but didn't because he was seeing something he hadn't noted before: the pallor of her skin, the joints of her elbows swollen against the thinness of her arms. The sunken hollow at her neck.

Beneath the sweaters, the tangled skirt, she was nothing but a clatter of bones. It had happened so fast. How could he have missed such a dwindling?

When she rose and took the empty plate and cup to the sink, Manny pretended a yawn.

"That tasted good," Elise said. "Thanks."

Manny smiled because he didn't know what else to do.

"I guess I'll go home now."

"Okay."

"I don't think I'll be hungry for dinner. Maybe I'll just go to bed."

"Okay."

She looked out the window, the moon rising over Angel Ridge. "Do you think we'll ever find her?"

Manny wondered what answer he should give other than the one that was true.

"No," he said. "We'll never find her."

He waited until her steps had left the stairway, then watched from the window as she walked to the house, her skirts catching the wind coming up off the river. He pulled the blanket to his lap and wondered at the disappearance of that girl he'd taken to the fair only months before, sassy in her showy clothes, smoking with the bravado of a barmaid. He felt a sudden and knowing sadness that somehow he had failed. Like Deracotte, he wasn't fit for any of it.

He would put the tractor away, feed the animals. He'd clean the mud from the kitchen. And while he was doing these things, he would plan dinner. Something Elise would smell and be unable to resist. Fried chicken. Mashed potatoes and gravy. Carrots cooked in butter and brown sugar. He wished Allegro were still with them. He wished for his father's giant horses that had carried him so carefully across the land. He wished for Helen, for things to be like they were before.

"Come," he said to Dog. "We got work to do." They went out into the almost dark, stopping long enough to note the car lights following the river's curve. In a few more hours, the temperature would drop and the roads become sheer with ice. He wished he could warn those distant travelers, tell them of the dangers ahead.

He fired up the tractor and steered toward the barn. Already, he could hear the old cow *mawing* for feed. The hens were down to four, the rest gone to raccoons and an overly lustful rooster, who killed with his splendid ardor, then was himself carried off in the soft muzzle of a fox. The goat pens were empty, the horse stall given over to spiders and pack rats. It was a diminishment he believed he could live with, a reduction that intensified the care of what was left, although there were times when, lying in bed, he felt the immense emptiness of the barn below him.

By the time Thomas returned home, Manny would have the food on the table. Maybe a pecan pie. Maybe a shot of whiskey after dinner, when it was right. He might put on some quiet music that would have pleased Helen and would prove to Elise that the Devil was not in her. Maybe he'd go to the church with her. Maybe they would shift their gaze toward him, divine all the demons that he harbored.

The cow grunted as he pitched the hay and threw the chickens their scratch. "Come, Dog," he said, and headed toward the house, where light illuminated the kitchen. Through the window, he could see Elise at the table, her head bowed. He saw her stand, raise her arms, and begin to sway. He thought he could hear the singsong repetition of her praise. She looked like a crazy woman, her hair matted, her skirt torn.

She brought the tips of her fingers to her eyes, then raised her hands. Two times she did this, as though her eyes were twin mouths, her fingers ferrying kisses to Heaven. And as she brought her fingers down for the third time, he saw the look on her face change, no longer peaceful in prayer but angry, like the face of an enraged child. She shook her head, cupped her ears as though trying to keep the sound of the world at bay. And then she brought her fingers to her face and began clawing as though she meant to blind herself.

Manny ran to the door and reached the table as the chair skittered from beneath her. He grabbed her wrists, pulled her hands away, Dog barking wildly beside him. Elise was screaming, thrashing. Manny straddled her thin body and pinned her to the floor. She was wrenching her head, back and forth, and all he could see were the scratches along her cheeks, the dark spatter of her lashes.

He held her there until she had exhausted herself. She was crying, and the thought of the salt in the wounds made him groan. He rolled her into his lap, felt how small she'd become, and clasped her wet face to his chest. He heard the car turning in and saw the headlights cut across the window.

"Hurry," he whispered, swaddling the girl in her rags, rocking, rocking, humming a lullaby that came from some heart once held close to his own.

Chapter Seventeen

The lawn stretched down the hill to the road, and the road circled the complex of low-roofed buildings before leading back to Fife. Beneath each oak, maple, elm, was a bench, and on each bench was a brass plate etched with names of families who had donated to the Clearwater Hospital Foundation. Green knuckles of daffodils punched up through the thawing earth. Morning and evening, deer browsed the budding leaves of mulberry and laurel. Elise watched them from the meal room, where she would stay until she had eaten some part of what they placed in front of her.

After breakfast, lunch, dinner, the aides ran gloved fingers along her gums, under her tongue. They weighed her, weighed her clothes, weighed her food, weighed her again, and then her clothes again, whose seams were inspected for pennies she might have sewn into the hem. They watched her urinate, defecate. They charted the length of time it took her to brush her teeth and cautioned her to spit only once. Even her saliva was enough to tip the scales.

The psychiatrist who came from Folgate on Wednesdays said it was temporary dementia brought on by anorexia that had caused her to hurt herself. Pastor Maggy came as her spiritual advisor and insisted it was Satan. She didn't know what to believe, which way was right, and so she prayed, she took her medicine. She read the Bible, she wrote in the journal the counselor said she should keep.

She didn't tell the counselor about the night of the rain, the music she had played with Todd beside her, the water flooding the floor. She'd run upstairs to warn Todd and his parents, but they were already bunched together, whispering. It was she who had brought the sin into God's house, Mrs. Maggy told her, and now they would all be punished. Her memories came to her like a dream: their injunction that she purge herself with fasting and prayer. Finally, when starving herself had not erased the color of music, she took the Bible they had given her and let it fall open, just as the preacher had done, to the book of Mark: "And if thine eye offend thee, pluck it out . . ."

"Starving yourself will not cure you," the psychiatrist said. "Seeing colors when you hear music is a condition known as synesthesia. It's not uncommon." Why, then, she wondered, had fasting brought such peace? The first few days, she'd craved everything: oatmeal, hamburger buns, black plums. But then the congregation had prayed over her, and the hunger had gone away: she felt she could live forever without food. Was it a sin that she had lied to Manny, telling him she'd eaten when she hadn't, flushing soup down the toilet, the empty bowl evidence of her appetite? She gave her sandwiches to Dog, left the crust. The more complex her deception, the more satisfied she felt. An omelet might take an hour of preparation—chopping the ham, grating the cheese, keeping the heat low enough not to scorch—and then the whole of it thrown to the chickens, who fell upon the eggs with carnivorous delight.

She wanted to get better, to go back home to Dog and Manny,

to see Todd again. When called to the meal room, she marched forward, reciting from the Song of Solomon: "He brought me to the banqueting house, and his banner over me was love." A chant that did not vary in tone as she slid into her chair. "Honey and milk are under thy tongue." A kiss of sweet tea. "Apples, pomegranates, cinnamon, spiced wine." A slice, a seed, dark juice. "Let my beloved come into his garden, and eat his pleasant fruits." Still, no matter how hard she tried, she couldn't swallow more than a few bites without her stomach knotting. She did what the counselor suggested to keep her mind off the food and engaged the other patients in dinner conversation.

"What is the name of your horse?" she asked Belinda, a blond-haired rodeo queen who was relieved of her duties when the toilet backed up in the royalty RV: bags of corn chips and packages of Oreos, the Hershey bars she'd secreted in her boot duffel—everything she ingested and regurgitated while standing in the closet-like bathroom with her hand ready to flush. Even with the few pounds she'd gained, Belinda looked hollow, her skin nearly translucent over the shell of her forehead, the scallops of her cheeks. After each bite, she lowered her fork, pressed her lips together, and breathed through her nose for a count of ten. Elise counted with her, exhaled in unison.

Elise asked Rodney, round-bellied and balding: "Which stone was your favorite?" He had collected them, first as a hobby, then as an obsession, the garnets and tourmaline giving way to chunks of dull granite, buckets of pebbles hauled in off the river that filled his bedroom and spilled into his kitchen. And then came the grass and ferns potted in loose soil. An introduction of butterflies. Night crawlers lifted from the dewy lawn. Two rubber boas and a clutch of spider eggs that erupted and spread to the corners of every room. A dozen starlings trapped and released. Ladybugs and bats, squirrels and a small maple dug from the neighbor's lot. An electronic sprinkler system. Finally, the floor had collapsed, producing a pleasing landscape of arroyos in the basement. "A biosphere,"

Rodney insisted. "A perfect creation, don't you see?" But a favorite stone? He had none. All rocks were equal in his eyes.

Each evening after dinner, Elise read a chapter of *Pilgrim's Progress* to Sarah, a plump thirty-five-year-old given to filling her orifices with spoons, candles, candy canes—anything she might pilfer and privy away. Sarah thought that Pilgrim wore a buckled hat and shoes—that he was questing not for salvation but for turkeys. Elise had tried at first to dissuade such interpretation but had finally given up, allowing Sarah to weave the story of Faithful and Hopeful and the Celestial City into a tale filled with Indians and muskets and maize.

In the last hour before bed, Elise would pull on her coat and walk Mr. Lambert out to the patio for his nightly look at the stars. Moderately tall and handsome, he appeared sane in every way, clean, courteous, and intelligent. Only his stance seemed a bit off. He tilted to the left, chin tucked, as though he were being reined into a tight circle. He needed a steadying hand at his elbow, which Elise offered, and as they pointed and named the constellations, he would smoke a single pipe of tobacco. White moustache and neatly combed hair—Elise thought he looked like a British gentleman. But when she had asked where his family was from, if, perhaps, he'd been raised in England, the corners of his mouth had drooped, and he'd begun rolling his lower lip. No, he'd said, not *England*. Surely she could see he was from Nazareth. His shoulders slumped forward, the pipe fell from his hand, and he began braying like a donkey.

"Ah, Christ," Sarah said, "he's Mary's ass again," and she hurried to tell the attendant.

The preacher had told Elise that it would help if she were baptized, that it would wash away her sins. The staff couldn't argue against such religious expression, and so the preacher and his wife had come, and, along with the aide, convened in the tub room, once used for hydrotherapy, now vacant except for the porcelain tub itself, long and solid as a crypt, surrounded by nothing but gray tile.

Elise, dressed in a white hospital gown, stepped over the high rim and sat with her legs extended, cold water to her waist.

"Why," Pastor Maggy had asked, "are we gathered here today?"

"So that I might be washed in the Blood of the Lamb," Elise answered.

"Then I baptize you in the name of the Father, the Son, and the Holy Ghost," and he had taken her head in his hands and tipped her back until the water covered her face.

Sister Maggy shouted and danced a tight step between the tub and the wall. The minister beamed and was proud in a way her father had never been. Since then, it had become part of her free-time ritual to bring the water to the edge of overflowing, ease herself into the tub, and slide beneath the surface. At first, the aide had bellowed her name, jerked her up by her hair. "I won't let myself drown," Elise had promised. "Watch, and see."

So they'd watched her, and each time she resurfaced, she smiled and told them how peaceful it felt, how *therapeutic,* until they'd left off their vigil. Sometimes she wished that the preacher had held her down a while longer—long enough for her to listen more carefully to the rattle of pipes, the spark of electricity in the walls, drowning out the languid music piped into every room that made her woozy with ennui. Such truer sound the water carried, and she'd felt like a tuning fork tapped against the porcelain rim, set humming.

Elise was in the bath, water filling her ears, when they brought the new patient into the hospital: the heaviest doors unlatching, the vacuum of air. The commotion in front of the nurses' station. She bobbed up, slid back under, listened harder, and thought she could hear his music: a bass pulse, a rampant tambourine.

She dressed and walked out into the hallway, where she saw Sarah passing information to Belinda, her description like a police report: young white male, five feet eleven, 170 pounds. Green eyes. Brown hair. Missing little finger on right hand.

Dinner was grilled cheese and tomato soup, squares of lemon sponge cake for dessert. The larded air, smoky and sweet, settled on

Elise's tongue. There was a whisper, like moths' wings against a screen. Sarah reached across the table and snatched Elise's spoon, then slipped it beneath her shirt.

"Everyone," the counselor announced, slapping the meat of her palms together. "This is Lucas." She pointed to the empty place next to Sarah. He pulled out the chair, never taking his eyes off the food.

Elise wondered at his stillness. Only when the sandwich was at his mouth did he look up. He seemed to consider their watchfulness for a moment, then continued eating. When he tipped the bowl, a streamer of red soup ran down his chin.

"He's *bleed*ing," Sarah screamed and covered her face with both hands. The purloined spoon clattered to the floor. When Lucas leaned down to pick it up, Elise saw the stub of his finger—a nubbin of bone cowled in flesh, a twitching half-joint, tender and raw.

Mr. Lambert ground his molars around a lettuce leaf and motioned toward the spoon. "I wouldn't touch that if I were you," he said. "It might be soiled."

Elise began to explain to Lucas, then stopped. It wouldn't be generous to speak of Sarah's illness so bluntly. But Lucas was waiting, as were the others, to see what she would say. Sarah leaned a little his way and eyed his fork.

"Mind your utensils," Mr. Lambert cautioned.

"*Sarah,*" Elise said, a little too loudly. She lowered her voice. "Why don't you tell us about your new picture of Daisy." Daisy was the Guernsey Sarah had been raising as a 4-H project before the first emergency room visit, the gynecological examination that produced one and a half place settings of silverware. Sarah's parents sent holiday photos of the heifer: Daisy, muzzle painted with bloodied fangs, cape tied at the bulge of her enormous neck; Daisy with reindeer antlers, nose rouged with lipstick; Daisy wearing fuzzy cow slippers, a birthday hat, and a placard reading "Happy MOO-day!"

Sarah squealed, "Oh! She's so cute!" and proceeded with an

animated description of Daisy's Easter costume: rabbit ears, a snout of whiskers, tail banded into a tuft.

Elise nodded encouragement, even as she kept Lucas at the corner of her vision. As he ate, he surveyed the room, his gaze moving from left to right, ceiling to floor, as though he were reading the pages of a book. People were invisible, ghosts he could see right through.

Was he dangerous? Demented? Disturbed? Perhaps only depressed. In her short time at Clearwater, Elise had learned that not all illness requires the flesh, only the steady rain of impulse and compulsion. The severed finger might have been an accident—or a ritualized amputation. She wished she could see more of him, but he was finished with his meal and being guided into the closed room next door for examination, evaluation, observation, interrogation. The residents called it the *-Tion Room.* It had taken Elise some time to realize the spelling, to not hear it as *shun room* and believe it justly named. The blinds tight against the windows, the locked door, the way no sound entered or escaped: you could lose your soul in there, feel it sucked out and into the air grate above the supervisor's desk.

Elise tidied the day room and helped Mr. Lambert find his glasses and slippers, then sat next to Sarah on the couch and picked up their reading where they had left off: Pilgrim questioning Hopeful about the good of his soul. Elise smelled the sourness of Sarah's hair and felt Sarah's fingers plucking at the back of her arm—little pinches not quite hard enough to hurt. Like a cat weaned too early, kneading for milk.

"Do you remember," Elise asked Sarah, "that we're with Hopeful now?"

Sarah nodded and burrowed a little closer. Elise fought the impulse to scoot away from the press of soft flesh, the pinching. She remembered the way Allegro would shift her weight against Manny when he lifted a hoof to shoe. How Manny would good-naturedly bark, "Get off me, you lazy heifer!" and elbow the horse in the ribs.

Elise resisted the urge to do the same to Sarah. She focused on the dialogue between Hopeful and Christian: " 'One day,' said Hopeful, 'I was very sad, I think sadder than at any one time in my life. And as I was then looking for nothing but hell, and the everlasting damnation of my soul, suddenly, as I thought, I saw the Lord Jesus looking down from heaven upon me, and saying, "Believe on the Lord Jesus Christ, and thou shalt be saved." Then I said, "But, Lord, what is believing?" And then I saw from that saying, "He that cometh to me shall never hunger, and he that believeth on me shall never thirst." ' "

"I'm hungry," Sarah said.

"Sarah, we just had supper."

"I'm thirsty." Sarah laid her head on Elise's shoulder and began sucking her thumb. Elise smelled Sarah's spit and the bacon-grease odor of her hair. Sarah's pinches were beginning to sting.

"Why are you doing that, Sarah? Stop."

"I'm sorry, I'm sorry, I'm sorry." Sarah turned her face into the back of the couch and curled the knobs of her knees to her chest. "Sorry, sorry, sorry."

"Sarah, don't. They'll take you to bed."

"Sorry!" Sarah sucked her thumb harder and began pinching the inside of her own arm—savage twists of skin that turned immediately blue.

"Someone needs to quiet that child," Mr. Lambert said and went back to reading his evening news.

Elise heard the -Tion Room door opening. She turned to watch as they moved Lucas down the hall. When the attendant stopped to key the lock of the empty sleeping room, Lucas looked toward the commotion. Elise was sure that he couldn't see her other than as one of *them,* her hair loosely gathered, her plain face. But he *did* see her, he looked right at her, and lifted his chin just a little before turning his whole self to face her, as though swung toward some magnetic core.

Elise knew that she should look away, but she couldn't. She was fixed on the dark green swirl of his eyes, the heavy lines of his eyebrows, the too long curl of hair over each ear. The way his shirt had pulled down to expose the pale collarbone. The absence of the finger's last joint, though, for a moment, she was sure she could see it there, whole again.

The attendant touched his shoulder and turned him toward his room. Before they entered, Lucas whispered something, and they both peered at her. As the aide pressed Lucas through the door, Elise saw the small resistance, the way Lucas let his shoulder cave against the pressure. The way he never quit looking at her and the slight nod before the door closed, as though in quiet acknowledgment of some charter, some silent acquiescence she had not known she was giving. Like with Todd at the piano.

Her fingers slipped from the pages and moved to her cheek. She touched the red welts where the scratches were still healing. She felt a hot panic rise in her belly, a cloud of acid in her throat. The bile pooled in her mouth, and she leaned forward, let it spill out.

"Yuck," Sarah said. "Yuck, yuck." She pulled the book from Elise's hands. The slap of it on the floor startled them all. "Corn and potatoes and pumpkin pie." Sarah stood and began clapping her hands. "Cornandpotatoesandpumpkinpie! Cornandpotatoesandpumpkinpie!" She marched around the chairs, her voice growing louder with each chorus.

Elise closed her eyes tight, but still she could see it: a crimson swoon, a rage of orange and yellow. Like flames licking beneath her lids, hot tongues swirling her ears.

She might have been screaming for Sarah to stop. She might have been crying, or praying. She didn't feel the hard tile or the kicks as Sarah stomped around and over her. She didn't know that the aide had separated the circle. She didn't feel the needle or know that moment when her body let go its coil and she lay, finally, limp and whimpering.

Later, when she awakened in the dark of her room, her wrists and ankles were swaddled in fleeced cuffs; her neck and back and the calves of her legs ached as though she had lifted some great weight.

From somewhere came a moan, a night cry of terror or longing. Her breasts rose and fell against the rough sheet. Her stomach grumbled its emptiness. There was the brush of something outside her window, the huff of sweet breath—the deer browsing the laurel, their teeth taking the tenderest of leaves.

Chapter Eighteen

Lucas Jainchill did not think he was beautiful. Not the way his grandmother had said he was. The high forehead she held when he convulsed with fever, the thick brows she smoothed, the full lower lip—he didn't see them at all as he passed the mirror on his way to the meal room. First one there, which meant it was his duty to start the coffee. As the water heated and began to perk, he drank five of the miniature creamers. He was hungry for whatever might be on the menu: Cream of Wheat or waffles—he didn't care. Just bring it, he thought.

He sat at the table and remembered his grandmother's sourdough pancakes, thick with huckleberries in late summer. He had loved her small farm tucked in the hills outside of town, the yeasty flesh of her arms wrapping his head. In the absence of his grandfather, who had gone to the store for cigarettes and never come back, Lucas fed the chickens, collected the eggs, learned to milk with his ear pressed to the cow's warm flank. At night they sat on the porch, listening to the radio, dunking corn bread in coffee. And when his father came for him, momentarily sober or not, Lucas clung to the woman, even as she hushed him and pushed him forward.

He sometimes wondered why she didn't keep him there, knowing, as she did, what his life was made of: the school counselors' reports, the foster homes that lasted a month, maybe two, and then the cycle repeating. His father would move them from one small town to the next, sometimes squatting in empty trailers or abandoned garages. A new school, a little more time before things got bad again. But those moments with his grandmother were both the sweetest and the worst: the only time he felt joy was on the drive to her farm; his greatest despair was when his father returned. Maybe his grandmother believed the punishment for his wanting to stay would be greater than what she had already borne witness to those nights when she bathed him in the old tub, its four talons gripping orbs of cast iron. She'd touched each bruise without comment, cleansed him with soft rags. He never cried out, not even when the iodine bit his skin.

He was glad his grandmother hadn't been there for his sixteenth birthday, when he had stood over his father with a tire iron raised in his left hand because his right one was useless, slammed in the car door as punishment for some grievance. Lucas had fully intended to do what he did, murder his father, and he didn't hesitate to tell everyone who asked: the police who cuffed him as he gasped with new pain, the amputated finger still pulsing; the doctor who had photographed his scars, and the psychiatrist who had tested and determined that he was marginally fit to stand trial as an adult; the judge who read his file and looked upon him with such pity that Lucas had wanted to kill him too. Lucky, his court-appointed attorney had said, that the judge was a man with a large heart. Instead of being locked away for first-degree murder, he'd been sentenced to two years in minimum-security with work release, to be followed by a period of psychiatric reevaluation. His relief came less from the merciful punishment than from the absence of his father. Prison had seemed like a paradise.

"You ain't hungry, are you?" It was Ed, the one they called the bull cook, five feet nothing and thick as a barrel. He'd been in charge of feeding a hundred lumberjacks steaks and potatoes during the days of the logging camps, but now he'd been reduced to this: soft eggs and custard. Lucas wondered how the man could stand it.

"I'm ready for whatever you're fixing." Lucas grinned. "Shit-on-a-shingle, I'm there."

Ed waved his spatula. "You wish. Maybe I can sneak you some bacon before it gets mashed. Don't get your hopes up."

Lucas watched him disappear back into the kitchen, then smelled that the coffee was ready. He drank the first cup standing and felt it scald his gullet. The second cup he dosed with sugar and another five creamers. What he really wanted was a platter of soft scones with clotted cream, eggs Benedict smothered in hollandaise. It was an appetite he had developed during his work release in Seattle. His caseworker had found him a kitchen job at Rossellini's, where he'd watched and listened and learned how to roux and braise even as he bussed the dishes and mopped the floors. He'd longed to wear the crisp white shirts and creased chinos of the waiters, to drape the linen across his arm as he opened the wine—a deft tilt and turn of the bottle at the end of each pour. Instead, he had perfected the efficiency of collection and disposal and learned to load the dishwasher in such a synchronized manner—wineglasses to the left, water goblets to the right, plates soldiering up the middle—that he had earned the Good Employee certificate four months in a row. A premium parking space had come with the honor—just a few feet away from the door—but he had no car to fill it. He might have offered the space to the pretty hostess who sometimes shared her cigarettes with him but chose instead to stand straddle-legged in the space for several minutes after each shift, looking up into the drizzle of another Seattle night.

When Mr. Lambert walked into the meal room, Lucas nodded and made his way to the table. He'd been on the ward for over a week and still hadn't spoken to anyone but the staff. He watched as the old man, back as straight as a spar pole, filled his cup with hot water, added a tea bag, and tapped out a single packet of sugar. And then it was Belinda and Sarah, leaned together and tittering. Elise followed, pale and timid, her arms folded as though she were cold. She sat down across from him at the far end of the table and kept her eyes lowered.

Lucas wondered if she knew how pretty she was: long dark hair, eyes the color of smoke. When he'd asked what she was in for, the aide had shaken her head. "Thinks she's possessed or something. Won't eat."

While in detention, Lucas had witnessed all manner of disease: inmates who tore out their hair one strand at a time; hand-washers whose knuckles were cratered with ulcers; one man who couldn't look at anything—windowpanes, floodlights, the bars of his cell—without counting and dividing by three. But he'd never seen a man who would not eat what was placed in front of him. Forgoing food was an act of defiance or of piety, and few of the prisoners had the stomach for either.

"Soup's on," Ed called, and the patients lined up with their trays for French toast and applesauce. Lucas forked three slices and then added another before pouring extra syrup. He watched Elise take a single piece—no butter or syrup, just egged bread, which she stared at as though it were an indecipherable text. He wanted to encourage her, but he feared she might startle or fall apart like she had his first night there.

The toast was soggy but not bad. Lucas went back for seconds and more applesauce and washed it down with black coffee followed by orange juice. He didn't mind that the others followed him with their eyes but never said a word. In prison, he'd learned that there were two kinds of silence, and this wasn't the bad kind.

After breakfast came Group, then free time, then lunch, then art therapy, then consultation with his caseworker, then dinner, then recreation, which meant soap operas, board games, or reading. Finally, it was little different from where he'd been before. While imprisoned, he'd watched an entire season of *Days of Our Lives* while tattooed men sighed and fussed beside him. He'd raced Queen Frostine through Candy Land and traded the Reading Railroad for Park Place. He'd read his way through the library, including the children's editions of Shakespeare and King Arthur. It kept his mind on pages instead of months. Unlike other inmates, he had never had the desire to keep count. It would be over when it was over.

Lucas moved into the day room and pulled a chair into the circle. Group was his least favorite activity, but he had discovered that as long as he stayed attentive and pleasant and nodded his head every few minutes, the leader, a forty-something woman named Beth with thick, curly hair who dressed in gauzy smocks and heavy sandals, would leave him alone. He half listened as each resident was asked to recite a "thought for the day." It seemed to him that, more than anything, Group served as a kind of communal confession: Sarah quickly offered that she had lusted after someone's silverware; Belinda detailed the dream she'd had of stealing two bags of marshmallows. Mr. Lambert said he missed Rodney, who had been moved to State Hospital South, where he could be closer to his parents, and abruptly committed suicide. The elderly man laid out his plans for a tribute to his friend: starting today, his art therapy would be to paint a canvas of Rodney's ideal world, full of plant life and animals. He held out a sketch of a landscape worthy of Hieronymus Bosch: lizards with giant heads feeding on cactus, a butterfly with a camel in its talons, and, at the center, a handsome haloed donkey. Lucas was surprised. The art was quite good.

When it was Elise's turn to talk, she looked out at the group with eyes so weary, Lucas felt the impulse to break his silence and comfort her. Her wrist bones looked swollen. She picked at the knee of her pants.

"I guess all I have to say is the same," she said. "I don't know what's wrong with me."

"Elise." Beth leaned forward, her hair falling close to her face. "You know that there is nothing *wrong* with you. You have a condition called synesthesia, which means you see color when you hear music. You have an eating disorder called anorexia nervosa. But nothing is *wrong.*"

"Yeah, Elise," Sarah chimed in. "Nothing's wrong with you."

Lucas could tell that Elise wasn't convinced, and neither was he. He watched her fingers play over the hem of her shirt. Long and limber, he thought. A pianist. There was more that he had picked up by listening: her father was the local physician; her mother was dead. She'd once had a horse named Allegro. Mixed in was the story of some church that had convinced her she was demon-possessed.

When Group was dismissed, Lucas watched Elise make her way to the tub room, as she did every day at this time. Part of her ritual, he thought. Time alone, which he understood the need for. He found his chair in the corner and thumbed through the magazines, each one perused so thoroughly that its pages were dog-eared and torn. He chose *Ladies' Home Journal* for the recipes—simple food, comfort food, food that his grandmother might have cooked. There was something about the perfection of rice pudding that caused everything to make sense.

But he couldn't concentrate on the measure of milk, the dash of salt. All he could think about was Elise in the tub room. It wasn't just that she was beautiful; it was the pinch of her face, the thinness of her arms. More than anything, he wanted to feed her.

He waited until the aide slipped outside for her smoke break, having already noted that her fifteen minutes never lasted less than thirty, then made his way down the hall. He leaned his ear against the door and listened. Nothing but the shush of water. He thought about the days he had remaining before he was free. He thought about ways he might make a mess of that. He thought about Elise, alone and hungry. He turned the knob, and the latch clicked open. No patient was allowed to lock anything.

Maybe she didn't know he was there; maybe she heard him and

didn't care. He walked around in front of her and stopped. Her hair moved in the current around her shoulders. Her face floated like a pale moon on the water's surface, eyes closed as though she were awash in some celestial music. He left her there and stepped back into the hallway, his hand shaking as he pulled the door shut. This, he thought, is not like prison. Not at all.

The next day, he planned more carefully and waited. It was a maneuver a drill sergeant might have admired, calibrated to the seconds of the aide's break. It was Elise's hair that he wanted to touch, feral with whatever spirit was left in her, and she let him. The third day, he moved to her shoulder, the nub of his emancipated finger resting lightly on her collarbone. The fourth day, his journey to the tub room was interrupted by Beth, who reminded him that he hadn't completed his evaluations. That evening at supper, Elise met his eyes for the first time, and he realized she was wondering if he had betrayed her.

The fifth day, he knelt beside the tub, took off his shirt, laid his arms atop the water, and let them float there so that she could see the muster of proud flesh where the cigarette had twisted, the rumple of bones unmended. He tilted his head so that she might witness the lumpish fact of his jaw, the cauliflower flourish of his ear. Each day after was a presentation of pain: his spine bared so that she might count the knotted fists of fracture; the V where his father had pressed the iron; the ragged rash that spread down his side, the gravel he'd been dragged through still pebbling his ribs. He took her palm and pressed it to the socket of his eye so that she might feel the chipped bone like the delicate ruin of a teacup. Without speaking, he was saying: Come see the persistence of me.

Monday, day eight, the aide smoking, the patients engrossed in some soap opera, he stepped in to find Elise waiting, wrapped in a white towel, the institution's initials inking one corner. When she let the towel slide down, he brought his fingers to touch the paper-smooth skin of her stomach, the unmarked tablet of her back. He wanted to tell her how beautiful she was, how whole, but all he could do was kiss her and give himself over to his own hunger.

There on the cold tile floor, he made love to her as easily as he could. There were other women he had known before—a ninth grader named Clarisse who had surprised him with her offer beneath the bleachers; the waitress at the restaurant in Seattle, in the backseat of her car, in his parking space—but he had never been in love. Elise held to him as though fearing that some part of her might escape, as though the blood that spilled from her were some soul-letting, and he her high priest of purgation.

He might have been ashamed if not for the calm that took up residence in her eyes, her smile that was the first he had seen. They talked for a moment then and met in the days after—a Monday here, a Thursday there, but never on weekends, the aide a non-smoker who strolled the halls in her Dr. Scholl's and checked each room with the thoroughness of a security guard. If the other patients suspected, they never let on, enthralled as they were by the television drama in front of them, lovers disappearing, children fathered by mysterious men, a secret wife found floating near a millionaire's yacht.

In the minutes of their shared solitude, Lucas heard Elise recite the accusations of the church. Simply by listening, he was allowing her to make sense of her life, allowing her own intelligence to kick in. No psychoanalysis. No prognostication. A raised eyebrow and a smile were enough to indicate the ridiculousness of her trial, just as a touch to his wounded finger was her way of letting him know that she could accept the absurd horror of his past.

Lucas watched with a certain kind of pride as, over the next few weeks, Elise beat him to the meal room, tentative at first, smelling each dip of salad dressing, flicking her tongue into her bowl of stew. Soon, she was quick to grab the heaviest slice of pound cake, the most generous ladle of corn pudding. She added cream to her coffee, chocolate to her milk, sugar to her cereal. The aides left off their examinations of her mouth and clothing. The psychiatrist thought biweekly sessions would suffice. If Lucas had thought her lovely before, the new color in her cheeks made it difficult for him not to track her every move. During Group, he kept his eyes averted, fearful they might be found out. Who could miss the look that might pass between them? At night, Lucas could hear the music floating from her room, a lusty string quartet turned down low.

He gleaned everything he could from the ward's dictionaries and encyclopedias concerning synesthesia. "Synesthesia is generally hereditary," one source noted, "and is located in the cerebral cortex of the brain—a cognitive constellation." He discovered the names of several famous synesthetes, including the novelist Nabokov. In the tub room, he recited to Elise all that he had learned.

"My father could have told me," she said. "I wonder if my mother had it?" Elise stirred the bathwater.

"Maybe your father would know."

"No one knows anything," she said. "It's like she never really existed at all."

Sometimes, they only talked, every second tamped tight with bits of personal data, dreams from the night before, questions about what came next. Other times, they did nothing but touch, as though Braille were the only language worth speaking. As focused as Lucas was on counting the seconds of their meetings, he had forgotten to count the days. Now time mattered. How many months had he been at Clearwater? How long did he have left to be with her?

It was only when he noticed Elise once again hovering over her food that he became suspicious. The fact that she was gaining weight was no surprise, but the pallid complexion had returned, and she'd lost her taste for Ed's wildly popular huckleberry cobbler. In the tub room, when he asked her how long since her last period, she began crying.

"What will happen?" she asked. "What will they do?"

Lucas wasn't sure he knew how to answer. They could tell the supervisor, make a request for a minister to marry them, but Elise was seventeen and would need her father to give his permission.

"He won't," Elise said. "I know he won't."

And so they told no one. The psychiatrist interpreted the morning sickness as bulimic relapse and extended Elise's treatment plan until September 1. She traded clothes with Sarah, her shape lost in the billowing smocks and loose pants. It seemed that in a world defined by peculiarity, no one noticed Elise's common condition.

The night before her release, the last August heat blooming against the windows, Elise pushed her food around on her plate, taking small bites whenever the aide looked her way. Lucas worried that she would sabotage her own liberation, and what good would that do either of them? One more month, and he'd be released, free to find her.

When Elise moved from the table to the couch to read, he noticed that Mr. Lambert was setting up the Monopoly game, an evening ritual that the elderly man undertook with great fanfare, counting the money into neat stacks, ordering the property cards into rows delineated by value. It was a solo activity, one in which Mr. Lambert did grave battle with himself, but tonight Lucas decided to join him.

Lucas looked over the miniature playing pieces. "I'll be the cannon," he said, but Mr. Lambert shook his head.

"Nay. I am the cannon."

"The top hat then."

"Nay. I am the top hat."

"Battleship?"

"Nay. I am the battleship."

Lucas glanced around the room at the other patients, who were absorbed in an episode of *M*A*S*H*. "Okay, Mr. Lambert. What should I be?"

"The thimble is yours, if you desire. It's a woman's trifle."

"The iron isn't?"

"Great damage can be done with an iron."

"Tell me about it." Lucas kept Elise at the corner of his eye as Mr. Lambert tapped the Community Chest and Chance cards into smart alignment and counted out the pastel currency.

"A total bank of fifteen thousand, one hundred and forty dollars. One thousand five hundred to each player. No loans. No Free

Parking jackpot. No bonus for landing directly on GO. No income tax on weekends and after four p.m. because the office is closed."

"Whose rules are those?"

Mr. Lambert looked at him with cool blue eyes. "I beg your pardon?"

"Never mind. I'm in." When it was his turn, Lucas rolled the dice and moved his thimble to Vermont Avenue. "I'll buy it," he said.

"I'm sorry. It's not for sale." Mr. Lambert steepled his fingers and leaned back in his chair.

Lucas was tempted to stand up and walk away, but he feared it might be the last he'd see of Elise. "Okay, Mr. Lambert. What advice do you have for me?"

"Get your guns and be out of town by sundown."

"May I donate my wealth back to the bank?"

"That would be most wise."

Lucas shuffled his money across the table, which caused Mr. Lambert's lower lip to roll down in dismay. He waited for the braying to begin, but the old gentleman seemed to recover his human instincts and began carefully smoothing the bills, shaking his head over such carelessness.

"The Reading and the Pennsylvania have fallen on hard times," Mr. Lambert noted. "Uncle Pennybags is not pleased with the state of the nation."

Lucas looked at Elise and lifted his chin as he stood. "I think I'm headed to bed. This venture has worn me out."

"Empty your pockets," Mr. Lambert said.

"I don't have any pockets." Lucas was dressed in the loose drawstring pants doled out by the institution.

"Show me your mouth."

Lucas leaned forward and stretched his mouth wide.

"Good night, then."

Lucas nodded and made his way to the hall. The night aide was in the kitchen, eating the last of the cobbler, reading a magazine. He let himself into the tub room without turning on the light and waited. When the door cracked, he leaned away until he was sure it was Elise who had followed him. He pulled her in and kissed her forehead.

"I don't want to go," she said. "I want to stay here with you."

"Just one more month. It will go by fast. You've got to eat."

"I've just been so sad."

"We're going to be okay." He held her fingers to his mouth and kissed each one and felt the wetness of her face. "Remember that this is a good thing."

She trailed her hands down his chest before slipping back through the door. He waited another two minutes before following her. His room was cool, the thermostat set lower at night, and he was glad. He'd always loved sleeping outside, no tent, no tarp, only the stars and moon above him, the black clouded sky. He'd watched lightning storms from the roof of his grandmother's house, lying on his back, heat radiating off the asphalt shingles. He would trace the bats as they reconnoitered for moths. Even then, he'd preferred the leaded afternoons of winter to the smoky sharpness of fall, the overcast days of spring to the open heat of summer.

This season was almost over, the cusp tipping between one solstice and the next. He was glad that August was done. Long before he understood calendars, he knew the month of dog-day afternoons and dangerous nights. He remembered the windows nailed closed so that he couldn't escape while his father slept. He thought he might suffocate those nights, but he dared not lever a sash or unbolt the door. The best he could hope for was that a woman would stagger home with his father, someone else to take the heat for a while. Sometimes, at dawn, when their noise had stopped, he would sneak to the kitchen, climb into the sink, and tap the window open just enough for a draft of cool morning air. He hadn't yet realized that he could run; he hadn't yet learned the lesson of being found. For that moment, crouching amid a ruin of soured dishes, the sun still a mild glow in the eastern sky, he was happy.

Lucas lay between the stiff sheets and waited for the aide to complete her check before beginning to compile the grocery list of what he would need for the next evening's imagined meal. It was a mental exercise that he had formulated in prison, one that demanded his full concentration, counting lamb shanks better than counting sheep. Sometimes it would take him hours to work his way through five courses, and he most often fell asleep before completing the complex hors d'oeuvres. If he made it through his pantry list, he could begin the actual preparation: washing and chopping the vegetables, clarifying the butter, whisking the roux. And then there was the wine to be paired with each serving, dessert.

Soon, he thought, he'd make it real. He'd whispered to Elise the dishes he would prepare for her: partridges wrapped in pancetta, terrine of dove, its sauce of currant sherry. Wild mushrooms in vermouth, jugged hare with juniper berries, fiddlehead ferns, prosciutto and figs, a pitcher of gingered cream. She often hummed to his recitation, as though the words carried some melody, a song of sustenance and love, savory, sweet.

He opened his eyes to the dark and imagined her lying in bed with his child growing inside of her. Why Elise? Why in this place? Why now? Maybe he should thank his father for paving this road for him—the path that had led him back to this small town along the banks of this river, a place he hardly remembered but which held some remembered part of him.

Chapter Nineteen

Wild turkeys preened and gandered across the manicured lawn as Manny parked at the farthest end of the lot that separated Clearwater from the high school. The short walk would give him time for a smoke.

The first of September, and the air smelled of sweet grass. The riverbanks still bore scars of the flood, a brackish hide that blistered and curled atop the tumbled rocks. Hard to remember the town as one big swamp, dotted with islands of dry ground that people hopscotched across to keep their feet dry. Even now, where the creeks met the river, debris lay strewn as though carried and deposited by a tornado rather than water. The one-hundred-year flood, they were calling it. Manny knew he'd not live to see another and was glad.

He was tempted to say it was simple laziness, another sloughing off of responsibility that had necessitated his presence at Clearwater, but he knew it was more than that. Ever since they had hauled Elise to Fife for treatment, he'd watched Deracotte sitting at the window, staring off into the distance like a mooncalf, filling the house with smoke—almost enough to make Manny want to give up the habit himself. Deracotte had taken a vacation from his work, closed up his office for a few days, then weeks. How much of it was grief, how much self-pity, how much the drugs kept hidden as though still secret? When Manny had announced that he was leaving for Clearwater, Deracotte had looked at him curiously, as though he were a piece of furniture just given the power of speech, then nodded before turning his gaze back to the window. Manny had wanted to grab him by the shoulders, shake him until the cigarette fell from his mouth and his teeth rattled. But what right did he have? Everything he owned could be loaded into the bed of his pickup and hauled away in a single load. And to where? He wasn't even sure that his old shack still stood. He could never abandon Elise. He knew that he owed Helen this, at least.

Manny stepped through the outer door of the building, then through another door that had to be unlocked by someone behind a window meshed with wire. He sensed a certain wariness in the way the woman supervisor looked over the forms. Even though he couldn't see out without raising the blinds, he felt that he was being watched. He pinched the crease of his jeans, slapped the dust from his cuffs. He heard a key in the lock and stood as the aide brought Elise in. She'd gained weight, but she still seemed sad and kept her arms crossed as though trying to shield herself.

The supervisor shuffled papers and tipped her head toward Elise. "I'm sure she's eager to get home."

"So am I." Manny waited for Elise to rise, but she remained in her chair. He glanced at the supervisor, who smiled encouragingly. There was a moment when he believed that there might be some kind of struggle. He had a sudden vision of the supervisor in her skirt and heels helping him wrestle Elise out the door.

"Dog's in the pickup," he said.

Elise looked at him for the first time, and he saw the way her lips trembled, like she wanted to tell him something. He hadn't thought this would be so hard. The times he'd visited, she'd stayed quiet, and he believed his presence caused her more pain than comfort. Still, he'd imagined her suitcase packed, ready to get the hell out of Dodge. But maybe that was because he could only imagine himself in her place, waiting to break out.

"Come on. I'll buy you an ice cream at the Ox."

Elise pushed herself upright. Beige knit pants, a smock-like blouse covered with ladybugs, white tennis shoes—Manny thought she looked like she'd just come from a game of bingo. Maybe they'd make another stop at Duggy's Department Store. At least get her back into a pair of jeans.

He followed her toward the door, slowing his pace to match hers, even though the need to bolt was eating at him like termites in his hip sockets. She looked down the hallway and waved to the few patients in the day room. One woman curled into the corner of the couch and began bawling loudly, her round shoulders and large breasts pinched by the fabric of her T-shirt, her buttocks dimpled beneath too tight pants. Manny thought she looked like a child grown too big for her clothes. They stepped out into sunlight as the woman's voice rose to a wail.

"Friend of yours?" Manny opened the passenger door and waited while Elise roughed up Dog, who squealed and yipped like a pup.

"Sort of." Elise's voice was softer, as though it came from somewhere deeper inside. She pulled herself into the pickup and shook the dog hair from her hand.

"Needs a good brushing. Maybe we can do that when we get home." He knocked the gearshift into neutral, turned the key, and rolled down his window.

They parked in front of the café and walked to the department store, where Manny bought Elise jeans and a snap-button blouse that she'd touched, then turned away from. As they walked back to the café, Manny thought that all she needed—had ever really needed—was a warm day in town with nothing more to do than buy a few clothes and have an ice cream.

He checked his watch and saw it was close to dinnertime. "How about a burger before dessert?" His mouth watered at the thought of salty fries dipped in ketchup.

A waitress with long dark hair and short legs handed them menus. Manny wondered why he'd never seen her before, then remembered how long it had been since he'd lingered in town. After Helen's death, there were too many questions never asked but held in the eyes of the townspeople, who knew such a story was never simple. They knew the woman was dead. They knew the doctor remained in the little house on the hill. They knew that his daughter had been kept at home until being committed to Clearwater. They knew that Manny had chosen to stay on. What they didn't know was why, and that question, left unanswered for so many years, had made him a stranger to them.

He watched Elise study the menu. When she closed it and covered her face, he reached across the table and touched her arm.

"We can wait until we get home," he said. "I can cook you something."

The waitress moved toward them, but he held up his hand and laid a dollar on the table for her trouble. He held Elise's elbow until they reached the sidewalk.

"I think I need to lie down," Elise said. She smelled like hot lemonade.

Manny looked across the street to the pharmacy, where he knew Dr. K hunkered in his dusky apartment, doctoring his own ailments with whiskey. The druggist had let the store go without ever closing. The door remain unlocked, the shelves mostly empty, the windowsills littered with dead bugs. Only cats roamed the aisles, keeping an infestation of mice at bay.

"Let's go see Dr. K," he said. He wasn't sure what condition they'd find the old man in, but it might give Elise a place to rest.

He told Dog to stay, then led Elise around to the alley and up the stairs to the door, sun-dulled to brown. He knocked lightly, then harder, heard the druggist cough and call them in. Manny led Elise to the couch and moved aside the stacks of old newspapers.

"Who's this?" Dr. K adjusted his glasses and turned on a small light by his chair.

"Deracotte's daughter. Feels kind of rough."

Dr. K pulled himself up and hobbled to the sofa. He knelt, the effort etching his face, and studied Elise in the pallid light. He felt her forehead and touched the glands of her neck.

Manny turned his head as Dr. K examined Elise and watched the window until he heard Dr. K groan himself to a stand. Elise had rolled to her side and looked as though she were sleeping, as though the old man's hands had exuded sedation.

"Don't ever let anyone lie to you," Dr. K said. "The golden years suck."

"I believe you."

"Doesn't matter if you believe me. You'll find out soon enough." He coughed, then settled heavily into his chair and raised one foot atop a small hassock. "Better break out that whiskey you brought me."

Manny stood with his hands on his hips. "Guess I left it in the truck."

"Better get it, then."

The liquor store was only a few blocks away. Manny closed the door behind him and clattered down the steps, his dress boots slick with disuse. By the time he got back with the whiskey—a pricey pint of Maker's Mark for good measure, who knew what trials lay ahead—Dr. K had fallen asleep in his chair. Both he and Elise snored softly, and Manny thought that the apartment was like a cave, insulated against sound, shadowy and damp, fit for hibernation. He poured himself a shot and stood at the sink to drink it, hoping it might settle him a bit. Deracotte would be wondering where they were. Or maybe not. There was a lot that Deracotte preferred not thinking about.

Elise stirred, rubbed her eyes, and looked at him, then smiled. "I'm really glad it's you," she said.

Manny opened the refrigerator. Butter, milk, eggs, bacon, a few apples, half a loaf of banana bread wrapped in foil.

"Scrambled eggs?"

Elise wrinkled her nose.

"How about banana bread with butter. Apple on the side?"

"Yeah."

Manny cut the loaf into six slabs, smeared them thick with butter, then set the bread beneath the oven's broiler to warm. He sectioned the apple, poured two glasses of milk, then filled a shot glass with bourbon and set it beside Dr. K's chair, along with a third of the food. He and Elise sat on the sofa and ate their share of bread and apple and drank the milk. It was better than anything they could have had at the café, Manny thought. Almost as good as Dr. K's pie.

Elise ate with a kind of curiosity, smelling, taking a bite, pulling her head back to study the food. "Things don't taste like they used to," she said and wiped her fingers down her pant legs. Manny remembered the new clothes. It might be good if she changed before heading home.

The old man coughed himself awake, wiped his mouth, and slid one hand behind his head to look at them. "Still here, huh?" He picked up the shot glass, dipped one finger, and licked it clean. "Dickel?"

"Fooled you."

"Jack?"

Manny shook his head.

"Tell me it's not Ten High. I'm not that far gone, am I?" The old man moved the shot beneath his nose, lifted one eyebrow. "Hell, I'm just going to drink it." He emptied the glass. "Now I'd say it's Maker's."

"That's *good,*" Manny said. He looked at Elise and winked. "He's still got it."

"What I got is empty." Dr. K worked himself to the edge of the chair, hung his hands between his knees to catch his breath, and motioned to their plates. "Is that going to be enough for you?"

"Plenty for me. How about you, Elise?"

"I'm fine," she said. She wasn't looking at him or at Dr. K but at the room, its webbed corners, its floor cluttered with newspapers and old magazines. "It's so *quiet* in here."

"Got to like an upstairs alley," said Dr. K. "Only thing I ever hear is cats fighting. Or something."

Manny rose and started for the kitchen. "Another round, then we've got to head on home."

Dr. K held his glass as Manny poured, then watched Manny pour a short shot for himself. "That all you're having?"

"Deracotte is probably wondering where we are." He cast his eyes toward Elise, who was examining the pile of catalogs fallen against the wall.

Dr. K sipped, then set the glass on the table and folded his fingers together. "How are you feeling, young lady?"

"I think I'm better."

"Good." Dr. K looked up at Manny. "How old is she?"

"I'll be eighteen." Elise straightened and pushed back against the sofa.

"Well, that's old enough, in some ways." Dr. K sighed and lifted his gouty foot back to its stool. He seemed suddenly exhausted, maybe from too much whiskey, or not enough. He leaned forward, his paunch settling atop his thighs.

"Now," Dr. K said. "Let's talk about what comes next."

"Home," Manny said. He wanted to stay positive. "I'm thinking we need to start looking for another horse. A filly to break."

Dr. K looked at Manny for a long beat, then snorted. "You don't know, do you?"

"Know what?"

The pharmacist shook his head. "Here's the thing, Manny. She's pregnant."

Manny stood still, as though the words might not find him. He looked at Elise. He could see it now—the thickness through the middle, the way she sat. How blind could he be?

Dr. K pointed to the bottle of bourbon. "Bring that over here. Have some more yourself. Might be the best medicine we got."

"Whiskey isn't going to help."

"Not you, maybe."

Thin light seeped from the curtained windows. No matter the news, there were evening chores, and no one to do them but him. Manny imagined Deracotte sitting in his chair, smoking, watching the river. He imagined having to tell him about Elise.

"I don't want to go home," Elise said. "I don't know what he'll do."

Dr. K cut his eyes to Manny, then back to Elise. "Are you afraid he'll send you back to the hospital?"

"That wouldn't be so bad."

"What, then?" Dr. K studied Elise's face.

"He's going to be angry."

"I think any father would be. But he'll get over it."

Manny tried to imagine Deracotte's reaction. Part of him believed that Deracotte, doctor though he was, might never know if they didn't tell him. He poured himself another shot. He saw that this could take a while.

He watched Dr. K limp his way to the sofa and put his arm around Elise's shoulders. Manny thought that they resembled unlikely lovers, leaned against each other. What Dr. K offered was comfort, something Deracotte had been unable to provide and Manny hadn't always known how to give. Easier to see her where she was, Dr. K offering her the last of his apple. She took a bite between her teeth, chewed slowly, and opened her mouth for more.

Manny understood, then, that he would go home alone. Maybe he'd tell Deracotte that Elise wasn't ready to leave the institution. Or that Dr. K needed someone to take care of him. Maybe he wouldn't tell him anything at all.

He pulled the last twenty from his wallet, laid it on the table. The child that Elise carried he could not imagine into the world. Helen's grandchild. He remembered Elise's own birth, whose sounds still filled his dreams and raised him in a sweat from his bed, his hands fluttering amid the tousled sheets like netted birds.

When Dr. K lifted his chin, Manny nodded, stepped out, and closed the door quietly, descended the stairs, and, for the first time in years, thought of the black widow he'd named Buck. How long, he wondered, might a spider live in its closet of glass? He should have opened the jar, set her free. He could not imagine why he hadn't done just that. The shack, the long hours of darkness illuminated by nothing but candles and moonlight, even the spider—he missed it all. He missed that boy he once was and could never be again. That time when the only life that mattered was his own.

He let Dog ride next to him, but instead of hanging her head out the window as she once had, she collapsed down on the seat and slept. It was dusk by the time he got to the barn. If Deracotte wanted to know, he'd have to come and ask. Manny helped Dog to the ground, where she stood stiff, unwilling to walk. He carried her up the stairs to the apartment, where he laid her on his bed. She sighed and was asleep before he had a chance to take off his boots.

The barn held big and empty below him. He found his cigarettes, turned off the lights, and sat on the couch, thinking about how things might have been different, if he had been. What had Helen wanted from him that he had not given? He remembered that part of the story he had never told. How she had pressed herself against him, how at first he had thought he could still turn away and save them both. How he stood unbelieving as the current caught her, swept her away. He closed his eyes and smoked in the dark, husband to nothing but air.

It had been a long time since he'd thought of the bones. He turned on the lights and walked to the closet. He always felt the same impulse—to arrange them like a puzzle—and he laid the skull fragments out on the table, then placed the arms and legs into some semblance of order. The pieces were so small, and he knew he had missed some when he had sifted the dirt.

The jawbone fit neatly into the palm of his hand, and he remembered Elise as a baby, hungry and mewling. He'd dip his finger in cream, amazed by the strength of her tug, her anger when she realized she'd been duped. He'd have fed her anything, then, to quiet the squalling until Helen returned and comforted them both.

Manny rose, turned off the lights, and sat on the bed next to

Dog. Another baby. Another raising up. The rabbit hutch needed mending. The pasture was too weedy for a pony. When Dog huffed in her sleep, he laid his hand on her sore hip, thinking some warmth might help. He thought of the mare's bones, gnawed by beetles, smoothed by the perc of water through stone. A horse's skull was a fine thing, the nose long and slender, the sockets set deep on the sides. Maybe he'd retrieve it someday. Maybe when the time came to put the dog down. Maybe he'd ask to be buried there too, although he didn't know who would be charged with that task.

Maybe this new child, he thought, and the dog settled deeper beneath his hand.

Chapter Twenty

Morning was an adagio: first, the weight of darkness thinning, the air softening in her lungs. Shades of gray, then brown tinged white, then yellow rising to fill the room with tattered light. Elise lay still to take in the torn arms of the sofa, the stained rugs, the piles of newspapers wilting atop mildewed magazines, the old radio, which had remained silent since her arrival, and she realized that this was some part of the calm: no music. It gave her room to breathe, to think, to see more clearly. From morning to night, Clearwater had been suffused with the placid ballads of sixties folk groups, lilting instrumentals, cowboys singing love songs for Indian maids.

In the kitchen, an orange cat balanced on the counter amid the scatter of dirty dishes.

"Kitty, kitty," she called quietly. "Kitty, kitty." She rubbed her thumb and finger together, and the tom's ears pricked forward. He jumped from the counter to the table, paused to lick along the edges of the butter dish, then leapt to the floor and padded to the couch.

She picked him up and rested him atop her stomach, where he worked his paws, milking the coarse blanket.

"Weaned too early, weren't you?" she whispered. The cat rolled to his back and began cleaning his chest with long, extravagant lolls of its tongue. Elise watched as he licked a slick of fur into a twist, which he then began suckling, his visceral contentment sending delicately tinted vibrations up through her own chest.

She moved the cat to the floor, where he stretched and began washing his face. The short hallway led to Dr. K's bedroom, the door still closed, and the bathroom. A toilet, a small sink, a metal shower. She sat, and the release of warm urine made her shudder.

Back on the sofa, she brought the blankets to her neck, snugged them tight. She was thinking about Lucas, wondering if he was eating breakfast, or reading. If he missed her as much as she missed him. Only four more weeks, she told herself. Just a little while longer.

After the breakdown with Sarah, she'd endured the extended sessions with the counselor. Yes, she agreed, she needed to mind her limits. Set firmer boundaries. Perhaps an extended period of therapeutic reinforcement *would* be a good idea. What she did not tell them was that she wanted to stay, that she had to see Lucas again.

At first, she'd watched as he sat quietly at the window, reading *TV Guide, Reader's Digest, Good Housekeeping, Watchtower*—anything. He caused no trouble but gave up nothing, not even in Group, when the counselor asked, "Do you have anything you want to add to this conversation, Mr. Jainchill?" The patients would lean forward expectantly, filling the silence with their constricted wheezing.

But something had passed between them—a half-glance, a current of recognition. It was more than a kiss she was after, more than what had happened in the church with Todd. And so she had waited, submerged to her ears in the bath, hoping he would find her, just as he did.

And her hunger then! The fast was over. She had tried to tell them, even as she spooned the mashed potatoes, took another bite of apricot puree. Look, she wanted to say. I'm drinking, drinking, drinking the thickened shake, watery rice cereal, salty broth. Bring on the barbecued ribs, the broccoli crowns, the new peas and potatoes seasoned with drippings. Leave me the butter. All of it. Vanilla pudding. Pandowdy. *Can't you see? I'm healed.*

But then this new sickness. She should have known, but she didn't care. Some part of her was glad to have made this baby in such a strange place, isolated, protected from the stranger world outside.

The cat mewled into the hallway. Elise heard Dr. K's cough, his shuffle from his bedroom, the bathroom door squeak shut. She folded her blankets, moved into the kitchen, found the coffee, and set it to brew. She placed the previous night's dishes in the sink and let them soak while she wiped the counter and stove. By the time Dr. K hobbled to the table, she had bacon popping in the skillet.

Dr. K groaned his way into a chair and rubbed his knees. "I'm going to have to have a cigarette." He ran a hand through his hair and patted his shirt pocket. "Guess I'll step outside."

Elise felt her mouth water as she turned the eggs. She added a thick welt of cream to her coffee and pinched a crisp end of bacon to tide her over until Dr. K returned. By the time he came back in, she had eaten two pieces of toast heavy with jam and more than her half of the bacon.

"Guess you're feeling better." Dr. K settled himself at the table. He broke the yolk of his eggs with his fork and hashed them onto his toast.

"Manny left us money for groceries," she said. "I was thinking I could bake a chicken for dinner. With lots of garlic. Do you want your bacon?"

Dr. K shook his head, and Elise ate the last two slices, savoring the salty fat.

"Maybe we should raise some chickens," she said. "Layers. Barred Rock are best." She wiped a triangle of toast around her plate, sopping the last of the yoke. "We could build a coop off the porch out back." She felt Dr. K watching her, but she couldn't stop. Maybe it was the food, she thought. The energy was ricocheting around inside her bones. She'd make a grocery list. She'd drop the old magazines at the library.

Dr. K leaned back in his chair, rubbed his neck, and squinted. "I'm not sure I'm ready for chickens."

"No roosters. We just want eggs."

"What about bacon? A cow and churn. How about an acre or two of wheat? Hell, maybe a whole damn farm."

Elise sat back and rested her hands in her lap. She felt the tears begin to well.

Dr. K snorted a laugh and patted the table between them. "That was good cooking. And if it's chickens we need to keep it coming, it's chickens we'll get." When Elise raised her eyes, she saw the mischief in his face. "Don't know what we'd feed them," he said. "Not much scrap left around here."

Elise smiled, got up, and ran fresh water in the sink. "Do you know what chickens like to eat more than anything?"

"Don't believe I do." He stripped the toothpick between his fingernails and slipped it into his shirt pocket.

"Each other. They're crazy about chicken skin. I've seen it. When Manny and I used to feed the hens. And you have to be careful about the chicks. They'll peck one another to death going after a spot of mud. They draw blood, and that makes them peck even more. They kill each other that way."

"I forget what a country girl you are." Dr. K stood and shuffled toward the bathroom, the effort enough to bring on another round of hacking.

"Chickens," Elise said to herself. "And maybe a horse." Manny would help her, she was sure. And then she remembered her father.

It took her a moment to picture him, and when she did, it was not a memory but an image from a photograph: her father with her mother at the edge of the river, the sun casting their faces into shadow, hands visoring their eyes so that they seemed caught in some gawky salute. But they were smiling and holding hands. She would sit on the floor and study the picture from different angles, in daylight and by the glow of the lamp. She counted their fingers entwined, the parallel planes of their hands raised against the glare. She noted the fit of her father's shirt across his straight shoulders, her mother's long hair and large eyes. What captured her most was the simple fact of their togetherness. The way they peered into the lens so intently, as though seeing some distant reflection of themselves. She had come to believe that what registered on their faces was a combination of amusement and pleasure—two emotions she could not remember her father ever possessing.

By the time she heard the bathroom door open, she had dried the dishes, stacked them in the shelves, and begun scouring the sink. Dr. K turned the corner and stood frozen as though startled to see her there.

"Jesus," he wheezed. "I forgot." He sank into his chair, blowing like a ten-mile horse.

"Are you okay?" Elise moved to his side, her hands gritty with cleanser.

"Hell, no, I'm not okay." He raised the recliner beneath his feet. "But I will be, after a fashion."

"I thought I'd go to the store."

Dr. K focused on her face. "Too bad you're not old enough to buy liquor."

She waited for him to say something more, to shake out the paper and begin reading, but he lay still, only his chest rising and falling. She hesitated, then borrowed a sweater that smelled of cigarettes and eucalyptus. She pocketed the money and list. The stairs pitched her forward and made her feel as though she might tumble head over heels to the bottom. She held to the rickety rail and hesitated at the sound of voices a block away. She hadn't thought about other people seeing her. For the last few hours, at least, it had seemed that she, Dr. K, and the cat had the town to themselves.

A few cars parked along Main. She hunched her shoulders and

kept her eyes down. When she lifted her head to check her progress, she saw the deteriorating sandbags still logging the buildings' foundations, the dried sludge of pine needles and garbage that clogged the gutters. Across the narrow canyon, she could make out the raw slide of rock and dirt where the hillsides had given way, huge chutes that had taken the tall trees and undergrowth with them.

She looked to the north hill, where Clearwater's lawn spread green across the hillside. They've finished breakfast, she thought. They're getting ready for Group. She gathered her sweater against the chill. Her breasts were tender. She craved plums and salt in dark chunks like Manny had laid out for the cow. She stopped to pick up a smooth oval stone, white and speckled as an egg, and put it on her tongue. It felt soft, not like she had imagined rock would be. She touched the hard roundness of her belly and imagined the baby growing there, suspended in its liquid air.

When she got to the liquor store, she spat out the rock. A bell rang as she stepped inside, and a woman with red hair piled on top of head turned and smiled. She'd looked younger from behind, dressed in tight Wranglers, a wide belt—more like a cowboy than an old woman, her face a pinch of deep wrinkles.

"Mornin', hon. Something I can help you find?"

"Maker's Mark?"

The woman laughed, a hoarse chortle that caught in her throat. "To your right, second shelf over."

Elise read her way from label to label. The cost surprised her, and she quickly calculated how much she'd have left for groceries. She chose the smallest bottle and carried it to the counter.

"That going to do it for you?" The woman rang up the whiskey. Her fingers were covered with thick silver rings.

"Yes, thank you." Elise reached for the brown paper bag, but the woman hesitated, and Elsie was sure she'd been found out. She thought of a lie she might tell, how she'd lost her driver's license, how her father was waiting in the car.

"You're the Deracotte girl, aren't you?"

Elise stood frozen, unsure how to answer.

"I knew your mother. She was the prettiest gal."

"That's been a long time ago," Elise said.

"Might seem so to you, but I can remember her clear as day."

Elise let her shoulders drop and clutched the bag. "I don't remember her at all."

The woman nodded. "My mother either. I was seven. Old enough to recall, but I don't. The smell of her sometimes. I've got no memory. Just all the sadness that came after."

At least sadness was something, Elise thought. She wished she felt that, at least. But all she had was emptiness. Her mother was nothing to her. Nothing at all.

"I'm going to have a baby," Elise said, startled to find that the words had left her mouth.

The woman smiled, a beautiful smile that lifted her face. "I see that," she said. "Babies are always good. Your mother would be happy. That's what she talked about, was you. Worried that you'd be hungry."

Elise felt the tears coming, and she wasn't sure why. She turned and stepped out into the warming light. She hadn't meant to think about her mother, hadn't thought to miss her, but now she did. She remembered how, as a child, she had rocked and called her own baby doll Elise. "Elise is hungry," she would say. "Let's feed Elise. Is the baby hungry?" The doll's face had become stained with jelly, and Manny had finally had to pull off the head to dislodge the moldering food that Elise had forced between the bowed lips. "You feed anything too much, you'll kill it sure as starvation," Manny had said, and it was a lesson she'd learned with the animals as well: too much scratch gorged the chickens' craws. Too much silage and the cow bloated and rolled. Too much green feed and Allegro would founder, the coffin bones pushing through the soft flesh, splaying the hooves.

By the time she had stopped at the grocery store and returned to the apartment, Dr. K had taken a shower, changed into a clean shirt, and sat reading the paper. She flashed the Maker's and then put it to the back of the cupboard.

"No need to make it so hard to find," he said.

"I'm just making room. If everything is in its place, there is more place for everything."

"Who fooled you with that bullshit?"

Elise remembered that he teased this way, and she shrugged her shoulder without turning around. She leaned down and stroked the cat's back, and he arched as though her palm were a magnet. She moved into the living room and sat on the couch.

"Can I talk to you?"

The pharmacist laid down his paper, clasped his hands across his chest, and closed his eyes. "Okay. I guess I'm ready."

"It's about a boy."

"Knew that already. Just get to it."

"He's the only one. Ever." Elise blushed with this admission.

Dr. K opened one eye and peered at her. "You know that doesn't matter. One is enough."

"I know." Elise folded her hands across her knees, then unfolded them and leaned back against the couch. "I just didn't want to think about it that way."

Dr. K opened both eyes. "I might need a drink." He rose and filled his whiskey glass.

Elise reached out and picked up the tomcat whiskering her ankles. "Have you ever been in love?"

Dr. K pulled out a cigarette and stuck it behind his ear. "Let's just keep this conversation about you."

"Lucas has been hurt really bad." She felt her smile falter. She didn't know how to begin to tell it all: the burns and scars, the broken bones. She hadn't realized how sad it made her feel. "That's his name. Lucas Jainchill."

"Lucas Jainchill." Dr. K turned his gaze toward the ceiling. "Let me think a minute."

The cat climbed into Elise's lap, lay down, and began licking his belly fur.

"I remember Lucas Jainchill. Grandmother raised him. Brought him in with a broken arm. Maybe twice. He went after his old man with a tire iron. Made the world a better place." Dr. K looked at her over his glasses. "What's he like? This Lucas."

Elise took a deep breath. "He's not crazy."

"Didn't say he was. What's he like? To you?"

Elise crossed her arms, lifted her shoulders, and smiled. "He makes me feel glad. Like everything's okay."

"That's probably all I need to hear, then. You can save the rest for later." He motioned toward the door. "Cigarette break."

"I'll come too. I like being outside."

They stepped onto the porch and looked out over town toward the river. Elise inhaled and caught the hint of honey in the air. She had missed the months of chokecherry blooming white along the roadside, the balsamroot unfurling its arrowed leaves. She always thought of spring as *loud,* the forsythia wanton in its crashing yellow, the greens vibrating with urgency. The shrill white petals of syringa, the ocean spray calling like sirens to the sailor bees, purple like a floral chant—violet, lupine, lavender, lilac. But fall was just around the corner, the noise muted with heat: the umbered leaves of ninebark, the fronds of fiddlehead fern baked to ash.

"He'll be out in four weeks," Elise said.

Dr. K raised his eyebrows. "Then what?"

Elise tipped her head. "We talked about staying around here. Maybe a little farm."

"No such thing as a little farm." Dr. K inhaled sharply and fell into a fit of coughing. Elise held her own ribs against the racket. He stubbed his cigarette and looked around the porch. "Not much here to hold chickens, but what there is, you can have," he said, and stepped back through the door.

Elise tried to imagine a coop built out over the alley, like a suspended dovecote. She peered down and saw a rangy tom peering back. She tried to imagine the next day, and the next, at home in the apartment with Dr. K and the cats and maybe some chickens. She heard the music starting. It was Vivaldi, the violins rising in a pale pink flush. She thought of her mother's hands, the way they must have played over the piano keys. She rested her stomach against the rail and felt the baby move inside her. She would tell her mother what Eppy had said, if she could: that babies were always a good thing. That they were fine now, even without her. That everyone was going to be fine.

Chapter Twenty-one

The muscles of Deracotte's legs jumped against the seat, and he took a deep breath to still the creeping hanker in his chest. He rolled down his window and shivered as the breeze caught the dampness at his collar. The periods between his need were getting shorter and shorter. Perhaps he should have told Manny that he had decided to drive into Fife and bring Elise home, asked him to come along, but this felt like something he wanted to do alone, without Manny's help.

Better, he'd told himself, to stay away while she healed. Whenever he thought of her, all he could see was the way her mouth had moved in prayer all the miles to Clearwater, her eyes bound with the gauze he had unrolled around her head. The wounds were superficial—he'd had the presence of mind to determine that, at least—and the ward nurse had done little more than wash the scratches and treat them with salve. Watching Elise being measured and weighed, he had been unable to resolve himself to the fact that she had transformed from a robust teenager into a waif in a matter of weeks, it seemed. He was sure he'd heard the nurse wrong when she announced Elise's weight. His first impulse had been to defend himself—to say that she had been born prematurely, was thin by nature—but he knew better. He'd missed the simplest signs of her illness. Once again the shame was his.

He turned onto Main and parked in front of the drugstore. The windows were opaque with dust. He knocked lightly against the glass, and then walked around the building and into the alley. A cat skittered down a set of stairs and into the shadows, and Deracotte looked up to see a woman, one hand holding to the rough rail. He startled as though he were seeing a ghost. The long dark braid over one shoulder, the large eyes—she looked just like Helen, he thought. Just like her. When Elise took a step back and stumbled, he moved forward quickly, wanting to steady her, but she turned and disappeared through the door.

Deracotte stood stricken. Perhaps Elise hadn't recognized him. Or maybe he had simply surprised her. He climbed the stairs, sidestepped the coffee can full of cigarette butts, and knocked. The rustle of papers, a groan. When the door opened, it was the druggist, bent forward at the waist. He eyed Deracotte through a pair of finger-smudged glasses set low on his nose as he struggled to catch his breath, each inhalation a liquid burble.

"I'm here for Elise." Deracotte felt strangely shy, like some unexpected suitor come to call. "I'm her father," he added, as though this were information the man didn't already possess.

The druggist cleared his throat, a rusty gear breaking loose. He fumbled for his handkerchief and coughed it full of sputum. Deracotte couldn't stifle the spontaneity of his diagnosis: advanced emphysema, perhaps cancer. It would kill him.

The druggist shook his head. "She's not here," he said.

"But I just saw her."

"She's gone."

Deracotte saw the couch and the neatly folded pile of bedding. "I don't believe you."

The old man waved the paper between them and hobbled to his chair, where he collapsed, the newspaper tenting his lap. He pushed himself back in the recliner and laid both hands across his chest, pummeling gently, as though he might drub air into his toiling lungs.

Deracotte stepped in and surveyed the rooms of the apartment—the narrow twin bed and pasteboard dresser, the tidy kitchen. He resisted the impulse to check the cupboard beneath the sink, as though Elise might tuck herself away in such a small space, as she had when she was a child. He and Manny had searched and called for her past dark, fearing the river, only to have her sneak out of the cupboard and into bed, where they found her sleeping. Deracotte had gone to his chair to smoke away his fear and anger, his sense of betrayal: why would she hide herself away from him?

The tremor in his hands had spread to his chest. He reminded himself that when they got home, he could have a dose if he needed it. In the hallway, he spied the narrow door. A closet, he thought, but when he turned the knob, a draft of air passed into the room, bringing with it the smell of cat urine.

Deracotte glanced back at the druggist, who seemed unaware of his discovery. He searched the wall for a switch but found none and felt his way down the stairway until he saw the pale light through the drugstore's windows. The shelves were empty except for a few lidded jars and an abandoned counting tray. The old cash register was powdered with dust, its drawer yawing open. In one corner, he found a bottle of blue tincture and remembered how his grandmother had once painted the inside of his mouth with the stinging antiseptic though it was no help for the lesions that had cratered his palate. And, here, a bottle of Mercurochrome, its only transformative properties contained in its color: iridescent green, then bloodred when water was added, the supposed cure often more damaging than the injury—the mercury itself was poison. In the corner, behind the shadowed display of crutches and canes, he saw some movement. A cat, he thought, but then the curve of a shoulder, the tremor of a body trying too hard to hold still.

"Elise, it's me. I'm here to take you home." He moved forward slowly, holding out his hand. When he saw the shadow rise and straighten, he stopped. She was taller than he remembered, her face fuller. She wiped some invisible distraction from her throat and tucked a wayward strand of hair behind one ear.

"Where's Manny?" she asked.

Deracotte felt the muscles bunch at the base of his skull. He reminded himself to be patient. He blinked the sweat from his eyes and saw what he had not noted before: the rounded shoulders, the mound of her stomach. He stared without apprehension, taking in what he couldn't believe but knew to be true: Elise was pregnant. He felt the blood boil to his face, his teeth clench into a rictus grin.

Elise bolted past him and thumped up the stairs. He stood for a long minute, attempting to understand what was happening. The more he tried to think and remember, the harder it became. His stomach ached. Sweat dripped from his forehead; his shirt was soaked through. He took hold of the railing and worked his way up the steps. They were waiting for him, Elise half hidden behind the old man's chair, watching him as she might a rabid dog. They were acting as though he were some kind of monster.

Dr. K motioned to the sofa. "Sit down. Let's talk."

"Someone needs to tell me what's going on here."

"Nothing is going on," Dr. K said. "But there are things that need to be worked out before Elise can go with you. Let's sit."

"You're not telling me what I can do with my daughter." Deracotte stepped forward, his fists bunched. "Not you, not Manny. No one. She's mine."

The old man pulled himself forward to the edge of his chair. "We can work this out if you'll just calm down."

It was all Deracotte could do not to topple the druggist where he sat, throw him from his chair, and wring his awful neck.

"You calm down, or I'm calling the sheriff."

The sheriff. Deracotte felt the hot marks at the crease of his arms. The cold grip in his gut. Maybe he should go home, come back later, when he was sure he was ready. But Elise had her hands on the druggist's shoulder as though he were the one who was her father. Deracotte shuddered and felt a violent rise in his stomach.

"You're sick," the druggist said. "Let me help you."

Deracotte turned, wiped his mouth with his sleeve, gave a choked laugh. "Do you really think that you're a *doctor*?" Elise watched him, wide-eyed. When he reached for her arm, she jerked away.

"None of that now." The pharmacist pushed himself from the chair and shambled forward. "Let's just sit and talk this out."

Deracotte felt the pain knotting his stomach. He needed to get home. He stumbled outside, held to the railing, steadied himself down the stairway. A few people stopped on the sidewalk to watch as he pulled open the car's passenger door and slumped inside. The chill shook his spine and made his teeth chatter. He closed his eyes and dropped his head. He didn't want to see them watching. And then he heard the other door open.

"I can drive," Elise said.

She turned the key, shifted into first, killed the engine, started it again. They lurched away from the curb, through town, and onto the highway. The muscles in Deracotte's back spasmed, and he grimaced. He felt a whimper rising in his throat.

He wasn't sure he knew when they left the road and crossed the bridge at Omega. The last mile up the hill was an impossible distance. When Elise stopped the car in the driveway, he tried to keep himself from running for the house, for the vial and needle tucked beneath his mattress. Once inside, he didn't stop to wash his hands or sterilize his skin. He didn't care. He cried aloud as the Dilaudid entered his blood and he collapsed to the bed.

Evening light came gray through the window by the time he roused himself. The sound he heard was rain hitting the glass. He peered at his watch: how many hours had gone by? He was more careful now as he tipped the vial and administered the drug. There was the bitter taste of chalk in his mouth. He lay back on his bed, waiting for the drift, for everything to slow and soften. It wasn't until he heard Manny and Elise talking in the kitchen that he allowed himself the question: Who? Who was the father?

He tried to think back. There was the boy at the church, the preacher's son. Or could it have been someone at the institution? The pharmacist was an impossible consideration.

And then he thought of Manny.

He stared blind into the weak light, a weight on his chest pressing the air from his lungs. Manny. Always there, always with Elise, just as he'd been with Helen. Alone with Helen the day that she died.

Deracotte pushed himself upright. Had he been so stupid, struck senseless by his own misery? The harder he tried to think, the harder the truth came to him. A fool. Always a fool to believe in anything at all.

Bile pooled beneath his tongue. He spat into a handkerchief and took several deep breaths. He needed to remain calm, to make this right. He stood, dizzy with blood rush, and willed himself to straighten, to practice the stance of a righteous man. He opened the door of his bedroom and stepped into the kitchen. Meat sizzled in a cast-iron skillet. Manny and Elise sat at the table, leaned toward each other as though they'd been whispering secrets.

"I'm hungry," Deracotte said because it was the only thing he knew to say.

Manny and Elise looked at each other. Manny rose from his seat and moved to the stove.

"I'll help," Elise said.

Deracotte sat and watched them working together. Easy. Familiar. Just like with Helen. He waited for his anger to propel him forward, to give him the will to tear the man down, but he felt welded to his chair. He looked at the clock, tried to remember how long between doses. There was some memory of rising, of seeing a ring of light in the mirror. Had he injected himself and forgotten? Overdose, he thought, but the word brought with it no emotion.

What he felt instead of fear was a bitter, ironic awareness. They were each of them absurd. Ludicrous. Ridiculous.

Deracotte clasped his fingers behind his head. His tongue was thick, and he realized he might be smiling.

"May I ask who the father is?"

Manny pulled plates from the cupboard. "You want bread?"

"I want to know who the father is." Deracotte yawned in spite of himself.

"Elise will have to be the one to tell you that. It's not my business."

"Maybe it's your bastard."

Elise spun around, surprise widening her eyes. But it was the change in Manny that Deracotte found most interesting. He stood with a plate in each hand, his face flushing crimson. It dawned on Deracotte that he had never seen Manny truly angry. He felt a mild curiosity about what might happen next.

Manny turned and carefully laid the dishes on the counter. He stood at the window for a moment before shifting his gaze back to Deracotte.

"Tomorrow, you're going to Dr. K's."

Deracotte snorted. He wanted to laugh, to bend forward and laugh until his stomach hurt. Until he cried.

Manny's jaw tightened. "Get help or this place is done. There's nothing left."

"This is my house." Deracotte lifted his chin. "You're nothing but a bum."

Manny was across the room before Deracotte could brace himself. He felt the blow to his chest and fell backward, busting the table. Dog barked frantically at his knees. Deracotte looked up into Manny's eyes. When had the boy grown so tall?

"This time," Manny said, "you're going."

Elise stood with her arms crossed, crying. Deracotte felt panic burn the pit of his stomach. He pulled himself up, staggered to the bedroom. He waited until he was sure that Manny wouldn't follow, then lay on his bed. He just needed to rest, to gather his strength. He opened his eyes and focused on the rain-splattered window. A small brown bat hung trembling on the screen, its mouth open, panting in an uncommon way. Deracotte rose to his elbows, but the bat was gone.

The house had gone silent. He licked his lips, tasted sweat and the bite of nicotine. He felt his hand along the nightstand, found the pack empty. Maybe there was one in the bureau, or fallen beneath the seat cushion. He remembered how, in the first months of his habit, he had stashed cigarettes in secret places so that Helen wouldn't know. Maybe he could find one. One was all he needed.

When he rose and stepped into the emptiness of the kitchen, he was surprised by its warmth. For a moment he couldn't recall the season. Was it summer, the house still holding the day's sun? Or was it winter, the woodstove radiating heat?

He searched the drawers, the shelves. Atop the refrigerator, he found the delicate cookie jar that Helen had hauled from Connecticut. Inside, a pack of Kools, a brand he had never smoked. He stood for a moment, turning the green and white package in his hand. He tapped out a cigarette, the tobacco dry as dust. And then he remembered their first meeting, the book Helen held in one hand, the menthol in the other.

He stood at the sink and peered out into the dark, felt the panic coming back into his chest. All he needed was a smoke.

Mud slopped his shoes as he made his way across the yard. Even in the damp cool of midnight, he felt the sweat beading, mixing with the rain. The stairs leading up to Manny's apartment caused his heart to race, and he stood for a moment before knocking, working to catch his breath, blinking against the light when Manny opened the door.

"I need a cigarette."

He might have turned away from the look on Manny's face, but he held his ground. It was a small thing that he needed.

Manny reached for his jacket and pulled out a pack of Marlboros. "Take them," he said. He hesitated as though gauging the depth of his own mercy. "Might want to come on in. Dry off."

Deracotte stepped into the room. It was like a foreign land, everything strange to him. Red-tail feathers, beaver-peeled sticks, miniature nests of hummingbirds decorated the bookshelves. His eyes settled on the low table scattered with bones.

Manny followed his gaze. "I dug them up when Allegro died. Thought it was an animal carcass."

Deracotte closed his eyes and opened them again. It was as though the child were lying in repose, palms up and open, jaw slack in the way of newborns who have fallen into sleep. He moved to the table, touched the small skull. "The plates hadn't joined. You can see that now." He laid his hand over the sockets, the nose gap, covering the face completely. "He's mine. My son. I couldn't save him."

He could feel Manny watching him, disbelieving. But what did it matter? Helen was gone. Elise was lost to him. The boy was all that was real in the world.

He made a sling of his shirt, nested the bones. Manny stepped back to let him pass, out the door, into the dark. The bones felt both solid and weightless. When he reached the house, he laid them on the bed: tibia and femur, humeral, ulna. Pieces were missing, perhaps still buried beneath the hawthorn, perhaps strewn along the path he had followed, but the boy was there, mostly whole.

The rain had stopped, and he thought that if he listened hard enough, he might hear Elise, the easy breathing of her sleep. He could have let her go, given her up to Helen's family. Elise was all they would ever have, they said, to remind them of their youngest daughter. But what about him? Without some memory of Helen, what would his life be made of?

But wasn't he the one who had killed her? Brought her to this place he loved more than reason. Left her in the care of the hired hand and gone to the river, believing she would be waiting when he returned.

Physician, physician, he thought. Do no harm. He lay back on the bed, smoking, thinking about what came next, reaching every now and then to touch his son, who lay small and still beside him.

Chapter Twenty-two

Lucas stood in front of the mirror, tucking in his shirt, pressing the stiffness from his collar. The dull end of his shortened finger moved more delicately than its mates, like a newborn mouse testing the light. He considered the openness at his neck, the welt of flesh blooming at his collarbone like a pink carnation. He tucked his hair behind his ears, then brushed it forward. He'd asked the aide to trim it, and she'd taken a few desultory swipes with the blunt-nosed scissors: a straight line of shorter hair at cheek level marked the beginning and end of her efforts.

Maybe he shouldn't have been surprised when the psychiatrist called him into his office and announced his superior progress and early release, as though what he had been working toward were not liberation but a gold star on his report card. He wished they would have let him go two days sooner, let him walk out the door with Elise.

He collected his wallet, the ten dollars given to each inmate on release, and the ring of keys that was part of his personal belongings he didn't remember owning. What lock might they have opened? What ignition could they have turned? He felt their sharp teeth against his palm, the saliva collecting beneath his tongue as though their metallic coolness were being absorbed through his skin.

He hesitated at the door held open by the aide, nodded his thanks, and walked out into the warmth of the September afternoon. He wished he had a handkerchief—hadn't he had one once?—and dabbed his forehead with his sleeve. Indian summer, the maple leaves brightening toward maize. He looked out over the town and raised his nose as though the hot breeze might carry some scent of her. Easy enough to follow the road, a winding lope down to the streets of Fife.

He wasn't sure how long until lunch, but he knew he was hungry and remembered a café from his days with his grandmother, the Blue Ox, where she'd taken him for ice cream. He slid into a booth, pulled the plastic-coated menu from its slot. It was the kind of place where you could get breakfast for dinner, and he liked that. The waitress, a middle-aged woman with a streaked blond ponytail, stood so close he could feel the warmth of her thighs against his shoulder.

"Steak and eggs, please, rare, over easy. Hash browns. Biscuits and gravy on the side."

He could sense her watching him, wondering. He wasn't the first release she'd seen come through. He picked up the newspaper, turned to the classifieds. He would need a job, some way to make a living until they decided what to do. The waitress returned, balancing the plates on her wrists, leaned back at the waist like a hod carrier.

"Anything else?"

"I'm good," he said.

"I bet you are." She smiled with one side of her mouth. "My name's Julie. I'll be back in a minute to check."

He pricked the eggs before peppering the gravy black. It was after the longest nights, at the end of drunken runs that sometimes lasted for days, that his father would collapse, sleep for hours, then rise into a kind of gentleness that frightened Lucas more than his rage. Those mornings, he was awakened not by the sound of his father snoring but by the smell of bacon, the spit of fat in the skillet, the hum of some old gospel song. For breakfast those mornings, always, there was gravy. Redeye gravy stained with ham drippings and spiced with coffee grounds. White gravy thick with flour; brown gravy made rich with Floral Bouquet. Bacon gravy, sausage gravy, turkey gravy—any bone would do, any carcass stripped, simmered, the broth set to cool, the fat rising to be skimmed. And when there was no meat to be fried or boiled or browned, lard was enough, sluicing the skillet, a few spoons of flour, salt, and then the milk poured in. White bread and hamburger gravy made a meal. Potatoes and gravy. Biscuits and gravy. Sometimes nothing but gravy on the plate his father set before him, a spoon instead of a fork.

Julie worked her way to his table, refilling coffee mugs along the way, bantering with the regulars.

"Guess I'm ready for my tab," Lucas said.

"Come on back for dessert," she said. "We've got five kinds of pie."

"Might do that." He started to stand, but she held her ground.

"You like this booth?"

"Sure."

"I'll save it for you." She patted the batting as though it were a pillow.

Outside, he took a deep breath, smelled the wind off the river, more dust than water, and felt a yearning for the coastal mist he had come to love, the entire city shrouded in a soft haze. It had made him feel invisible, as though he were cloaked, protected. Here, he felt raw and exposed, and he knew why. It was the place that kept his hardest memories. Even as the corrections van had carried him from Seattle back to Fife, he had felt the moisture leaching from his eyes, his throat gone dry. He thought of Elise, the baths she loved. He had believed from the beginning that he could make her hungry again.

The sun crested the western ridge. He'd need daylight to find her, enough hours to walk the highway if he had to. He turned toward the river, followed the sidewalk south until it spilled out into a run of gravel, then sand, and was surprised to find himself alone. How could the whole of Fife not be here, wading the pools of cool water?

A hundred yards downriver, he saw a shack, listing toward town as though striving to rejoin its kin. He knocked, though the latch was undone, the seams of the doorframe warped and splayed. Inside, a single bed, a mattress shredded by mice. The windows were strewn with the intricate skulls of birds, their beaks as white and chalky as cuttlebones. Beer cans were scattered about the floor. A mildewed magazine splayed open showed the soured skin of a centerfold. Lucas recognized the signs: boys came to the abandoned shanty to drink and talk of what they'd do to women once they had them, left the remnants of their carousing and dreams behind.

On a round of pine next to the bed, Lucas found the bottles stoppered with candle stubs and several library books, their covers warped. He blew at the dust and regretted it immediately; the small gust set up a swirl of detritus. He found a broom, its straw worn down to nubbins, and began sweeping—first the ceiling, and then the rough walls. He moved the bones from the window to the narrow table and swept the casements, and then the floor. He flipped the mattress and swept its better side free of spider eggs. When he'd finished, he laid his wallet and keys on the window, stripped off his clothes, and stepped to the river. The cold water made him shudder, but he stayed submerged and let the current float him up until his skin prickled. He waded to shore, stood with his legs apart and arms held out to let the warm air dry him. Here was something that Seattle would never allow, and he smiled to himself. He scrubbed his clothes free of grit and laid them along the rocks.

Fir branches peeled easily from the nearby trees, and he spread them across the mattress, then lay spread-eagle in the cool of the shack, smelling the cleanness of evergreen. He listened to the sounds he remembered from his boyhood: ravens calling across the canyon; the winnowing of a snipe. He picked up one of the books, *The Great Gatsby,* read the first few paragraphs: ". . . just remember that all the people in this world haven't had the advantages that you've had." It was good advice, he decided, and he closed his eyes to hear the wind in the great trees above him, the *tick tick* of pine needles falling like rain. A sign, he thought. Tomorrow, he'd find Elise.

He awoke in the dark and lay still to listen. Voices from the path leading to town. The sound of boys, laughing and jousting toward the cabin.

Lucas slid from the bed, wishing he'd brought his clothes inside, grabbed a branch of fir and held it over his crotch just as the door kicked open and a flashlight cut the dark, illuminating his face.

The three boys yelped in unison. One ran straight up the path before turning to see who followed. The tallest held his ground, stepped forward with the flashlight.

"What are you doing here?" His voice was pitched low, and Lucas thought he must be the oldest.

"I was trying to sleep."

The two other boys crept in behind the tallest and peered around his shoulders. "Hey, man," one said. "You're not supposed to be here."

Lucas shrugged. They were about fourteen, he guessed. Maybe fifteen.

The leader ran the light along the floor and the bed. "What did you do with our stuff?"

"Out back with the rest of the garbage."

There was a malicious whisper between them, and then the light was back on his face.

"This is our place." The oldest moved forward a step. "You get the hell out." His two companions hissed their agreement.

Lucas thought of all that he had in his possession—the keys, the change from dinner—nothing with which he might barter or defend. Even the broom was out of reach, tucked tidily into the distant corner. He dropped the bough and stood exposed. The flashlight made a quick dip down.

"Is that what you're here to see?"

The two friends snickered, but the oldest stood silent. He clicked off the flashlight. "You'd best get out of here," he said.

Lucas thought he could probably make a charge and scare them away, but then there he'd be, no way to know if they were circling back, plotting revenge. He knew better than to underestimate such boys.

"Listen," he said, "I just need somewhere to sleep tonight. Tomorrow I'm gone, and it's all yours."

"Get out of here."

"I'll need my clothes."

"Throw them in the river," the oldest ordered.

"Now wait," Lucas said. "Let's make some kind of deal."

"What deal?"

"You tell me."

"Man," the third boy said, "we could use some more stuff."

"Shut up." The leader stepped forward. "Some beer. Another magazine. Swisher Sweets."

"I don't have any money," Lucas lied.

"I got five bucks," the youngest said.

"Give him his clothes but keep his shoes."

It was the last thing he should be doing, Lucas thought as he stepped gingerly through the weeds toward town. He could simply leave and not go back. He could try to find the sheriff. But what would he tell him? That he'd left the mental institution and was squatting along the river? That he'd been blackmailed by a troop of local boys?

He stepped into the gas station, found his way to the beer cooler, grabbed a twelve-pack of Schlitz, then nodded to the rack of stag magazines behind the counter. "A pack of Swisher Sweets and the worst one of those you've got."

"Big night, huh?" The man was older, one arm limp at the shoulder, his hands palsied.

"Guess so." Lucas paid, then stepped back out into the dark, felt a jab in his heel, and cursed softly. Puncture weed. By the time he reached the shack, he was gritty with sweat. Candle stubs flickered. The room smelled different, warm and earthy.

The tallest boy moved from the corner, took the bag, threw the magazine to the boys on the bed before popping a beer.

"Are you a bum?"

"I'm just moving through, that's all."

"You from the nuthouse?"

"Sure. I just need my shoes."

"Come on," the boy said. "Tell us some stuff." He held a beer out to Lucas. "My name's Cody."

Lucas hesitated. It had been easy enough to empty the slag of his father's whiskey, to finish the half cans of Buckhorn he found abandoned in the yard. It had been a long time. He nodded, took the beer.

Cody puffed his cigar. "Why were you in Clearwater?"

The other two were watching now, seduced from the magazine's pages. Lucas needed his shoes, but there was something else. The beer and centerfolds such mild pleasures. The boyhood he'd never had.

"I'll take a Swisher." He pulled in a mouthful of smoke while they waited, their attention fully on him now.

"I was sixteen. I killed my father."

The boys on the bed looked from Lucas to Cody.

"Why?" Cody asked.

"He beat my mother, then me. Took my finger off with the car door."

"Fucker," Cody said, and then they all were quiet.

"I should have hopped the train instead." It had been his dream, one he had planned night after night, listening to the train's whistle at the edge of town. His raw feet prickled against the rough-hewn planks. He lowered himself to the floor, crossed his legs, and leaned his head back against the wall. Sometimes he felt so old, like his bones were bent with age. Cody was looking out the small window, and Lucas could see the shadows settle into his face. Who knew what secret miseries the boy carried? What hate he husbanded against whom? It sometimes seemed to Lucas that every man's life was defined by violence done and received. He lipped the cigar and pointed toward the window. "That train is always there. Remember that."

Cody looked at Lucas, his eyes half-lidded. He drained his beer, crushed the can in his fist.

"Yeah," he said. "I will."

Chapter Twenty-three

The river at night, swollen with the first cooling rains. Home Beach a thin slip of light between the darkness of the water and the flow of basalt that fingered out before him.

Deracotte stood on the strip of sand and considered the temper of the wind. He looked out over the reach and remembered the current there, how he would cast upstream and allow the fly to drift before it settled into the stillness of the eddy. How many trout had risen to that lie?

He knelt at the water's edge and let the sling of his shirt fall open. The bones clicked against each other as they dropped to the sand. He lifted each one and peered at its singularity in the moonlight. He traced the coronal suture undone, the fontanelle that would never close, then arranged the bones before him like an unkindled fire. If it were solstice, he might warm his hands over them like the pagan he was, partake in that ritual purgation. Bone fire. Bonfire. A pyre. The Vikings piled the wood on a ship and set the boat adrift, the fire already blazing. Why couldn't he do the same?

Because he had no matches, no lighter, no fuel. Lying in his room with the bones, lilting in and out of sleep, he had awakened to the moon knocking against his window. He understood with a racking clarity that the morning would bring a battle he wasn't yet willing to face. There was no plan, just a desire to run, to get away. Intent upon gaining the river, he'd left his jacket, the cigarettes, everything but the bones behind. He shivered with the thinness of his shirt, the mist settling around him like a dewy mantle. He was in that place between intoxication and the first throes of withdrawal—a sweet time free of need, a period of grace he craved nearly as much as he did the drug itself.

How many autumns had he witnessed in this place? When he looked in the mirror, he saw the lines at his mouth, the paunch of his belly. The first few years after Helen's death, he had thought he could still be something without her, but he'd been wrong. Having Helen taken away was like having the sphere of his cerebellum split in half: he could no longer define himself against who he was; he'd lost all sense of who he might yet be.

Deracotte took a deep breath and yawned, an involuntary response. His skin prickled. The moon crested, nearly full, and all the stars around it disappeared. He felt the heat screeve from his body like a heaven-bidden soul. He lifted his head and listened. What had he heard over the chatter of his own teeth? He stood and looked toward the bridge: a beam of light cauterized the dark as the locomotive slowed for the crossing. He held his ground as the train ratcheted by, regaining speed as it stoked toward Folgate. He was about to retake his seat in the sand when a movement caught his eye from across the track. A heron, perhaps, rattled from its rookery by the engine. Or maybe a raccoon. But the shadow was tall and upright. Deracotte waited as it approached, and he discerned in the cast of the moon that it was a man, who stepped toward him with a smooth, even gait. As he drew closer, Deracotte saw that it was Manny.

"Pretty moon," Manny said. "Nearly full."

Deracotte glanced upward. He hadn't thought to notice.

Manny stepped quietly across the tracks, walked to the edge of the water, and studied the gilded current. "Haven't been night fishing for a long time." He kicked free a loose twist of driftwood. "No reason why this won't burn." He gathered several more pieces and used his hands to dig a shallow well in the sand before pulling a bundle from his pocket. "Steel wool," he said. "And flint. Never need much else." He built a wigwam of wood, tucked the wool inside, struck three times. The spark glowed in the draft of his breath and tindered into flame.

The fire threw their shadows long across the beach. Deracotte stood in the new light and felt the river and copse fall away. All the world was made of nothing more or less than the simple blaze. Manny pilfered his pockets and produced a skein of fishing line wrapped around a cardboard spool. He tipped the nearby rocks until he found a centipede, leggy and squirming. He stabbed it onto the hook and trailed the bait in the water, letting the current pull the line taut.

"We'll give it a minute." He looped the line around one finger, the cardboard anchored in his palm. "Maybe a trout, maybe a crawdad. Something worth eating, either way." He squatted at the fire and looked up at Deracotte.

Deracotte remembered the bones. He knelt and sifted the sand with his fingers and tucked them into the wrap of his shirttail. When he moved to the fire, Manny nodded.

They faced each other across the modest blaze. It was just enough to cast off the chill, and Deracotte thought he could live just this way. Who ever truly needed more? The line ticked in Manny's hand, and he disappeared into the dark, came back with a foot-long chiselmouth—a bottom-feeder that Deracotte had never deigned to eat. He watched as Manny gutted the fish, then scraped the scales with the blade of his knife and washed the fish clean. From an inner pocket of his jacket, he pulled a neat square of foil, which he unfolded and unfolded, then wrapped the fish carefully, pinching the ends, and lay the packet near the embers. They sat in silence until the fish steamed. Manny lifted the foil and set it on a flat rock before plying it open and cutting loose the skin. He speared a fillet on the tip of his knife and held it out to Deracotte. It tasted of the river: mud and moss, frog eggs and lichen fronds. It was clean and not gritty and fed something in Deracotte that no man-made fare could touch.

When they'd finished, Manny scooped a fistful of sand to dust between his hands. Deracotte pushed himself to a stand, the bones held close.

"We could sleep here tonight, if you want," Manny said. "There's no reason not to. Weather's still warm enough. Might be good for both of us."

Deracotte felt the words catch in his throat, as though he'd been days without water. Now that he was up, the trembling had begun, and he felt the muscles in his thighs bunch and spasm. "I need to get home," he said.

Manny leaned forward and peered up at Deracotte. "It's never going to get better, Thomas. Not this way. You know that."

Deracotte knew he'd waited too long. He felt an urge to run to the river, to cool the sear in his spine. The taste of the fish was in his mouth, and it was nothing like it had been before, the flesh gone putrid in his belly. He grimaced, felt his body bend double.

"I think you'd better sit," Manny said. "Let me get you some good water. There's a spring just the other side of the tracks." He stood and touched Deracotte's shoulder. "You just sit now. Let me bring the water."

Deracotte slumped to the sand. If he waited much longer, he might not make it up the hill. To shortcut would take him through bramble and the dens of snakes. He needed to stay to the road.

Manny returned with a tin and held it to Deracotte's lips. "Just a little," he said.

The water was the coldest he had ever tasted, and he wanted more, but Manny pulled the drink away, then moved back to his place at the fire and studied Deracotte's face.

"Tell me again about the bones."

Deracotte remembered the hammock of cloth twisted in his hand. What reason was there not to tell it all?

"My son." Deracotte laid one hand over the bones. "Helen was pregnant with twins. I didn't know. I should have, but I didn't." He shook his head. The sickness was on him, and the muscles of his face jumped. His scalp was being eaten from the inside out, weevils boring his skull. "I delivered Elise, and then this boy. He was too small. He was alive, but I couldn't save him. Not here. Not in this place."

Manny waited, silent beside the fire.

"I buried the body beneath the hawthorn. How many years ago?"

"Almost eighteen," Manny said. "I'm sorry, Thomas. I didn't know."

"No one did. Only Helen."

"What was his name?"

Deracotte hadn't realized that he had his eyes closed, and when he opened them, the sky was bright with starlight.

"Coleman. Coleman Thelonious." He had never spoken the words aloud, and he shuddered with their softness in his mouth.

Manny reached into his pocket, pulled out a small metal whistle. "My father gave this to me before my mother died. I always thought I would give it to my own son." He laid it gently atop the bones. "You need to bury him, Thomas."

"I buried him once. It wasn't enough." Deracotte felt the tears spill down his cheeks. It was the pain that racked his shins, the ache in his gut. It was Manny and the bones and the river crooning by.

Manny rose to face him. "Let me, then."

Deracotte closed his eyes, felt the sway of vertigo. Manny caught his arm.

"Thomas, look at me. There is something I have to tell you. You need to listen."

"No," Deracotte said. "Please. Just let me go home."

Manny held him for a moment longer, then released his arm.

The fire licked the thin breeze, casting their shadows across the water.

"All right," Manny said. He looked to the river for a moment before pulling a handkerchief from his pocket. He held it flat as Deracotte transferred the bones. They seemed smaller now, little more than a handful, as though they were disappearing, his touch enough to erode them away.

Manny rolled the bundle, nested it against his chest. "Can you make it up the hill by yourself?"

"I can." This last time. Just this one last time. He turned from the river and found the tracks that led him to the road. His shoes, full of sand, rubbed his heels. He stepped out of them, kept walking until he reached the house, the kitchen, the smell of something warm and sweet, the pie he found still cooling on the counter. He ate it in handfuls, like a bear pawing for honey, the pecans browned and nutty, the crust flaking his mouth. He looked out the window to where the moon spilled its silver and listened to the train whistle in the distance. He looked at the empty pie tin, then turned toward the bedroom. What waited for him would take away the longing. It was all that he wanted, all that he needed, all that he would ever have.

Chapter Twenty-four

Elise had awakened during the night and listened as her father left the house. She'd risen, checked the driveway, but there was the Volkswagen and Manny's pickup. She hadn't known what to do but wait and, while waiting, make the pie. She'd thought she might sit until her father returned, but the cramp in her back made her long for her bed. She hadn't heard him come back in but woke to find the pie, its center gone.

In the light of day, she was glad she hadn't waited up, hadn't seen him come into the kitchen, ragged and morose. If, only months before, she had feared the way he had taken hold of her and dragged her across the yard, she now feared the deadness of his eyes. "He's sick," Manny had told her. "It's the drugs. Half the time, he doesn't even know what he's doing."

The single car key hung behind the door. She scribbled a quick note and left it on the counter, then called Dog and stepped out into the cool morning air. She'd spend the morning along the river, let Manny take care of her father, take him to Dr. K for help.

She cracked the Volkswagen's window as she accelerated onto the highway, Dog panting happily beside her. She didn't want to go to Home Beach, where her mother had drowned. There was another place she remembered, up and over Angel Ridge, where Manny had taken her when she was a girl. He'd discovered it while walking the railroad tracks: a small crescent of sand where a spring opened its mouth to the river. They'd spent hours doing nothing but sitting at the water's edge, looking for arrowheads. They'd found several nearly whole, made of obsidian, agate, jasper, and flint. Elise had taken them home, put them in a jam jar filled with water, and placed it on her windowsill, where it caught the light. She remembered how long that afternoon had lasted, as though the sun had held in the sky just for them. She remembered how she had heard a soft whistle and turned to see a doe the color of cream watching them from the forest's edge. She wanted that magic again.

"White Doe," Elise said aloud, recalling the name she and Manny had agreed on for their secret place. She was happy with the sound of it in her mouth. It was quiet there, secluded, and she felt the need for solitude. She longed for the calm of the water, the current to float her up, rock her, comfort the ache that had settled into her hips. She was ready for it to be done, to have the baby in her arms instead of her belly. To once again be able to mount a horse and guide it through the air in a flying change.

"Six more weeks," she said to Dog. "Not so long." Lucas would be with her by then.

The rain had washed all the dust from the air, the September heat ticking away the moisture. She drove slowly down the county road, considering each path that might lead to the water, trying to remember the way Manny had taken her. Over the years, she was sure that they had visited every beach along this stretch of river, and she could have driven directly to any number of them, but this one was special. No empty beer cans, no wads of toilet paper in the bushes. Just clean sand and cool water. All to herself.

Ragweed grew rampant, choking the ditches. A single poplar and crumbling chimney were all that was left of a former homestead. She watched the berm for some sign that a road might exist, stopped, drove on. In the middle of a dense grove of black locust, she saw twin ruts grown over with loosestrife and mullein.

"I bet this is it," she said to Dog. Cottonwood and pine rose close on either side, blocking the sun. Elise pointed the car downhill, trying to keep the tires centered. It was steeper than she had expected, the ruts washed deep by runoff. When the car caught and shuddered, she stopped.

"Maybe we'd better not," she said. Dog panted and peered into the gloom with her milky eyes. I should have just gone to Home Beach, Elise thought. Why do I always have to do things the hard way?

She shifted into reverse, but the tires skittered atop the rain-slicked duff and the car died. She sat for a moment and considered: maybe the easiest thing to do was to go on down. Surely there would be room to turn the little car around once they reached the floodplain.

"Hang on," she said, but when Elise released the clutch, the dog pitched forward against the dash and whimpered.

"I'm sorry," Elise said. "Just a little farther. We'll get to the river and be glad." She imagined her arrival back at Omega, the Volkswagen leaking oil, the paint etched down to metal.

She followed the path to the bramble, which seemed like something she could punch her way through, but as she pushed on, cringing as the thorns screed along the sides, she felt as though they were being swallowed, the canes closing in behind her, over her. She gunned the engine, gave it more gas, but the tires spun wet against the skinned vines and crushed berries. Forward, reverse, forward, reverse. The smell of clutch and rubber smoked the air. Elise realized that, even in the cool, she was sweating, her breath coming hard and quick. The ache in her back had spread down her legs.

"Okay," she said to Dog. "Let's think about this." She turned off the key and sat in the sudden silence. So quiet, only the rasp of sawbugs, the low chuckle of quail. The bramble pressed in around her, covering the windshield, leafing into her open window. She reached for one of the berries, but it was as hard and white as a pebble. She wished she had thought to bring water, even food. She remembered the breakfast she'd skipped in her hurry to get away. She couldn't tell how much light was in the sky. She couldn't see the sky at all.

She pulled the handle and shouldered the door, but it held solid as a wall. She pushed harder and gained an inch or two of space against the tight weave of canes. She hadn't considered this, how the bramble might act like a net.

"Great," she said to the dog. "Now what do we do?" She leaned across and thumbed open the glove box. A few papers, an old map, and in the back, her father's razor.

"Okay," she said. "This might work." She chose a cane that looked tender and sliced the razor through. "Okay," she said again, but the next cane was as tough and fibrous as rope. She worked the sharp blade like a saw, her hands slick with sap. By the time she'd cut through three vines, she was exhausted. All the cool air was gone.

"I've got to rest," she said to Dog. "And then we'll try some more." She laid her head back and closed her eyes. She imagined she tasted the jam that Manny made each summer, the blackberries stewed with sugar and poured into jars that ticked and popped as they sealed.

Dog rose and licked her ear, but Elise brushed her away. She rubbed her stomach, felt the tightness and then a gripping pain. False labor, she thought. Dr. K had told her she might feel it. But when the pain came again, she knew.

Chapter Twenty-five

Lucas lay in the sagging bed, half blind in the light, and thought he heard rain. He slipped on his shoes, stepped outside, and lifted his face to the warm mist, felt the wet beneath his bare feet, enough to convince him that it hadn't been a dream.

After the boys had finished the beer, they'd stashed the magazine beneath the mattress, and he'd promised he'd leave it there. His life's first night of freedom, and he'd slept hard, forgetting the stains and mouse pellets. Already it was past noon, and he regretted the time lost. He wanted to find Elise. He'd thought to ask the boys if they knew her, then changed his mind. He wanted to shield her from the bawdy bragging and lewd photos of the night before.

He turned toward the door and stopped. An old dog stood just outside the threshold, wet and matted. Lucas knelt and touched her carefully. She trembled beneath his hands but stayed still. Deep scratches furrowed her nose; one ear was torn at its tip. He wondered if she had tangled with a raccoon. He stroked her neck, worried that there was some damage he couldn't see—internal bleeding or the staves of her rib cage fractured. When he touched her hip, she whimpered.

"Just hang on," he said. He gathered her up, stepped out into the breaking sun, and began walking toward town, softening his steps so as not to cause her more pain. He remembered the sun-bleached Rexall sign, the ghost of a mortar and pestle stenciled on the glass. Maybe someone there would know what to do.

The dog had gone limp in his arms, her head rolling over his shoulder. He tapped the door with the toe of his shoe, waited, then thumped again, a little louder, and heard a growling cough from above. He looked up to see a man waving him toward the alley.

"Come around back if there's something you've got to have."

Lucas made his way to the alley and up the stairs. When the door opened, Lucas saw an old man, hunched and wheezing, who pulled out his glasses and attempted to straighten.

"Is that Dog?" He pointed to the couch. "Put her down over there."

Lucas rolled the dog from his arms onto the sofa and smoothed the thick ruff. The man bent beside him, smelling of hot wool and Ben-Gay. He lifted the dog's eyelids, checked her gums, then moved his hands along her ribs before testing each leg. He sighed and worked his way to his recliner.

"There's no getting over old age." He pushed back his recliner, folded his hands across his chest. "I'm Dr. K. Who are you?"

"Lucas. Lucas Jainchill."

"Is that right?" The druggist tipped his head forward and studied Lucas with new interest.

"I'm in town looking for work."

"Is *that* what you're looking for?" Dr. K grunted and moved his hands behind his head. "You don't know where you are, do you?"

"You mean Fife?"

"No. I mean *here.*" The old man jerked forward and began

coughing, a hard, racking croup. "Jesus Christ. This is a hard way to go." He motioned to the narrow hallway. "There's a blanket on my bed. Get her warm while I think."

Lucas stepped into the small room and found the blanket. As he shook it loose from its fold, he heard something fall to the floor. He picked it up and turned it toward the light of the window. The silver barrette Elise had worn in her hair.

He walked into the living room, the blanket clasped against his chest, the barrette held out in his hand.

Dr. K nodded, his face flushed. "She's gone back home. Just yesterday." He rubbed his legs. "This is Manny's dog. Someone needs to get over there and let him know."

Manny. The one Elise had spoken of with such fondness, who had visited her at the hospital when her father didn't come.

"I don't have a car," Lucas said.

"Ask the liquor store lady if you can borrow hers. Just around the corner. Tell her I sent you."

Lucas ran down the stairs and across the street. What rain had pooled along the roadway was nearly gone, and the sudden sun felt hot on his neck. The door buzzed as he entered the flat-roofed building. He remembered waiting outside in the car for his father, the ride home with the bottle rolling on the seat between them.

A thin woman with red hair turned and nodded. Lucas hesitated. The woman moved closer and looked at him with such scrutiny that he felt himself blush. She smelled like cigarettes and baby powder.

"I'm Lucas Jainchill. I lived here a long time ago."

"Not so long." The woman's eyes softened. "I remember you, Lucas. And your grandma. Hers was a real nice funeral."

Lucas felt a familiar regret. He'd never seen his grandmother again after the trial, her death from a perforated ulcer sudden and unannounced.

The woman reached out and squeezed his arm. Her fingers were heavy with silver. "I'm just glad the bastard's dead."

When Lucas explained that he was looking for Elise and that Dr. K had sent him to borrow a car, she reached under the counter, pulled out a key chain in the shape of a martini glass, and pointed to a green Buick parked out front.

"I'll have it back as soon as I can." Lucas felt like he should say more, but she was waving him out the door.

"Two bridges down. Right across the river and up the hill, then left. Big barn. You'll see it."

Lucas settled behind the wheel, rolled down the window to release the heat. On the fifth try, the engine caught, and he revved it into a smooth chatter and punched the car onto the highway. He noted the first bridge he came to and counted the miles to the second. The Buick rattled across and lugged down on the hill. He shifted into low, kept his eyes on the ridge until he saw the barn, a small house. He parked, got out. Two men stood beside an old Ford pickup. Lucas was aware that he was a stranger at least. Maybe worse.

The younger man stepped toward him. "Something we can do for you?"

"I'm looking for Manny."

Manny cast a glance back to the pickup, where the older man stood smoking, as though he were waiting for a bus. "That's me."

"Dr. K sent me. Your dog showed up hurt."

"Where?"

"Just outside of town. There's a shack by the tracks."

The older man walked over, hunched as though the warming day were turning cold. The gray eyes, narrow face—Elise's father, Lucas thought. He smelled odd, like some distillation of sweat and road tar.

Lucas held out his hand. "Sir, I'm Lucas Jainchill."

Deracotte stood for a long moment, blinking as though trying to focus. "Lucas Jainchill," he repeated, his voice hoarse. "Years ago. Your grandmother brought you to my office." He reached up to touch his shoulder, as though he were making the sign of the cross. "Complete subluxation."

Lucas tried to remember, but there had been too many times. Even now, one shoulder hung lower than the other, permanently stretched from its socket.

"Elise had Dog with her," Manny said. "We need to make sure she's okay." He looked toward the highway, then back at Lucas. "She left a note where she was going. I should have gone after her. There's no way that car was going to make it."

Lucas saw the weariness and regret in Manny's eyes, like he'd been up all night wrestling with some demon. The dog, the pharmacist, the barrette—it had been easy enough to believe he was being led by fate to some fairy-tale rendezvous with Elise. Now, he felt the first kick of doubt in his gut.

"We'd better take the pickup," Manny said. "It's a rough road down to that place."

Lucas climbed in beside Deracotte, and they jostled together as they crossed the bridge back to the highway. The asphalt provided a few miles of smooth travel until they came to Angel Ridge. Lucas held to the dash as they chattered across the wooden floor bolted with steel. The pickup ruddered right, and he hung his head out the window, peered into the blue of the current, heard the pentimento chorus of water over stone, and felt the blade of his fear cut deeper.

"There," Manny said and pointed to the rye crushed down, the broken stalks of mullein. He worked the gearshift into low. The pickup jerked into the ruts and stalled. "Too wet," he said. "Better walk it. Thomas, you stay here. Lucas, let's go see."

The locust grove was like nothing Lucas had seen before, a canopy of tall trees, undergrowth so thick he wished for a machete. A hiding place, if you needed one, and he thought of all the secret places he'd found as a boy: beneath the porch, where he lay against the cool earth slatted with sun; in the dry culvert confettied with leaves, its emptiness echoing his heart; the lathe-and-cardboard shipping crate he had found behind the saw shop and sealed himself into, breathing the residual odor of new rubber and packing grease.

"She's here somewhere," Manny said, and pointed to the tire tracks.

How far down did the road take them before Lucas saw the car nudged into the bramble like some animal burrowing toward its den, mottled with pine moss that had drifted from the trees, its coppery sheen rich against the verdant green of mountain fern and vine maple? He hesitated, looked at Manny through the stippled darkness, cupped his mouth and called, "Elise!" They both waited but heard nothing, only the echo reverberating back. The birds had fled from the noise of their invasion.

"See if you can get in there," Manny said. "I'll try to get the pickup down far enough to work the winch."

Lucas felt his way to the car's side. Thorns pierced the back of his shirt, caught the skin of his shoulder blades, beaded his ears with blood. He bent his head and closed his eyes, working his way deeper into the tangle. It was a shallow pain, one he could absorb, not like the throbbing ache of fracture or the searing hurt of a severed finger. Some part of him believed that this was what he had been made for, his hide tanned to armor for Elise.

In the deep dark of the bramble, he ran his hands along the back window and traced his way to the door, vines tacked to his back like hydras. He pressed himself against the car's smooth surface and felt the wet pulp of berries beneath his feet. His fingers found the window open, a space where the dog must have pushed through. The air from the car came to him heavy and warm, spiked with the scent of marigolds. He couldn't see inside but thought he might hear breathing. He braced himself against the bramble's coils, gripped the door handle, and pulled, but the canes held tight.

Lucas worked his way out and wiped the blood from his eyes. Manny was unwinding the winch from the pickup's bumper, dragging the heavy hook toward the car. Lucas took the cable and felt the hydraulics tense and give. He knelt, reached for the Volkswagen's rear axle, and secured the lead.

"Stand back," Manny warned. "You don't want to be close if that cable snaps."

The winch wound up, rasping into a high-pitched whine as the cable drew taut. The pickup bucked against the torque, and Lucas feared it wouldn't be enough to pull the car free. He wanted to grab the cable himself, throw his weight to the line like some ancient sailor hauling his ship from the sea. The pickup slipped forward a foot, and then another. The sound of the winch cut deeper. Lucas looked to Manny, who never moved his eyes from the Volkswagen but stood stone-faced, unflinching as the hulk of the pickup crept, stuttered, hopped, and then dug in.

The sound of metal railing against metal, the creak of resistance giving way. Lucas felt his heart lurch as the Volkswagen tore from the bramble in a whip of vines. He waited until Manny eased the winch, then ran to the car and jerked open the door. In the dim light, he saw Elise pale and unmoving, her eyes closed, her dress saturated with blood. He touched her throat and felt the pulse, faint as a bird's heart.

"Elise," he said, and she opened her eyes enough so that he knew she saw him.

"I'm so thirsty," she whispered.

And then Manny was there, pushing him aside. "Get Thomas."

Lucas ran back to the pickup. The man sat as though paralyzed, focused on that point where the headlights failed against the darkness of the bramble.

"Come on," Lucas said.

Deracotte shook his head. "I can't."

The only man Lucas had ever hit in his life was his father. He wanted to hit this man now. Beat him to the ground with his fists. He gritted his teeth.

"Get out," he said, and he pulled Deracotte after him, dragged him stumbling toward the car.

Deracotte stood, shoulders slumped, and stared weakly at his daughter, then dropped his head into his hands. "She's going to die," he said.

"No." Manny gripped the man's head in his hands like a faith healer and raised his face. "She's not going to die. You're going to help her."

Deracotte closed his eyes, and then opened them again. "I miss Helen," he said.

"I know you do, Thomas," Manny said. He rested his hands on Deracotte's shoulders, rocked him gently. "I know."

"Please," Lucas said. "Tell me what to do."

Deracotte turned his gaze on Lucas, and then looked back at Manny. He seemed lost in some decision, as though there were other options he might consider, some better way. He lifted his shoulders, looked to where the canopy laced the sky, and took a deep, quavering breath.

"Get her out of the car." He lowered his eyes, moved his hand as though smoothing the ground. "Here," he said.

Lucas kicked away rocks, stripped off his shirt, spread it flat, and Manny did the same. They lifted Elise as gently as they could, guiding her head, her arms, their bare chests smeared with blood. They carried her carefully as Deracotte watched, solemn as a churchman, and laid her down. Lucas sat cross-legged and rested her head in his lap, stroking her face, smoothing her hair. Manny knelt at her side and held one of her hands in his.

Deracotte stood at her feet, arms straight as though weighted, his entire body shaking. He lowered himself slowly and sat back on his heels, steadying his hands atop his thighs.

"Tell her she's got to push," he said, his voice soft, nearly a whisper.

"You've got to help us, Elise," Manny said, his voice louder, sure. "You're strong. You can do this. Do you hear me?"

Lucas felt the slight nod of her head against his legs.

"Elise," Manny said. "You're going to help us, now. Push."

Elise moaned deep in her throat, but her body remained

lax. Lucas leaned his head forward, pressed his mouth close to her ear.

"Please, Elise. Push."

She opened her eyes. The words rasped in her throat. "I'm so thirsty."

"I know." Lucas pressed his palm against her cheek. "But you've got to work real hard now. Push." He made a loud grunting noise. "Come on." He grunted again and felt the muscles in Elise's neck tense. "Again. Come on." Manny joined in, and they groaned in unison.

Lucas raised Elise's head a little higher. "Come on, little baby, come on."

Elise pulled in her elbows and tensed forward. Her voice rose and their voices rose with it.

"One more," Deracotte said. His voice was louder now. "One more."

Lucas braced Elise's shoulders against his bare chest.

"Now, Elise. Right now." He took a deep breath and started low, an open chant rising from his throat. And then Manny, and then Deracotte, the men's voices echoing through the bramble.

Deracotte lifted his hands and the child was there, a glistening shadow in the last light. The silence was a roar that washed over them as they waited. Deracotte swabbed the throat with his finger, then leaned forward and breathed a light whisper into the small body. The tiny chest inflated, once, twice. And then a thin slip of sound, a mewl that grew into a rhythmic bray. Each wail pulled the air from Lucas's lungs, filled his veins with electricity. He rested his hand against Elise's forehead, and her eyes opened slowly, as though from a kiss.

"A girl," Deracotte said. He moved the baby to Elise's stomach, sat back on his heels, hid his face, and wept.

Lucas touched his daughter's skin and felt its warmth. Her face was bunched in an ecstatic scream of hunger. He moved her to Elise's breast, and she buried her nose, snuffling, latching on.

When he pressed his finger to Elise's mouth, he felt her lips tense, relax, an exhalation, and then another. She moved one hand to her daughter's head.

"I'm sorry," she said. "I didn't mean to."

"It's okay," Lucas said. "Everything is okay now." He touched Elise's cheek. "Are you hungry?" he asked, and Elise nodded.

He began to tell her, then, of the wondrous meal he would prepare for her, once they were home.

Epilogue

Manny listens to the sound of the pickup descending toward the highway. He'd helped Lucas position Elise and the baby on the seat next to Deracotte, told them, "Go." They'd be in Fife soon. Dr. K would know what to do.

A harvest moon emerges from the cleft of the canyon, the color of flamenco, of gypsy skirts and sashes. It is a bloody moon, and gorgeous, loud with its place in the sky. It shows Manny the trees cutting the horizon, the track. It shows him the river, pink and meaty as the backstrap of salmon. He remembers the doe, almost white, and believes that if he looks hard enough, he might see her even now, another ghost in this place, another memory.

He squats at the water's edge, washes his face, his arms, his chest. Maybe tonight, he will dream. Like desire, in all the years since Helen's death, his dreams have left him, a curiosity he can't quite explain. Or maybe he's simply forgotten. Maybe the dreams go on without his awareness, a whole world that doesn't really need him at all.

But the wildness of his boyhood nightmares: the fire eating its way into his bedroom, giant birds nesting in his closet. He would welcome even those dreams now—some horror he might rise from and believe himself lucky to have escaped.

He wishes for the cigarettes he left in the pickup. As a boy, he had puffed on anything that fired: broom straw, rolled cardboard, the stubs of cigarettes he found flicked to the gutter. He'd outgrown such easy pickings and forgotten his yen for smoke, yet here it was, on him again, no longer a want but a need.

He closes his eyes and lets the music of the river buoy him, as it had when he was a child. Once, he'd been wading the shallows with his mother and, against her warning, had followed her out into the current. He remembers how his feet had let go, that moment when he believed he wasn't swimming at all but being carried against the breast of the water itself. His mother came after him with long, even strokes, pulled him to her, and swam them back to shore.

She kissed him then, kissed him and cried. He'd clung to her, afraid not for his own safety but for hers: her weeping had instilled in him the certain and terrifying awareness that she would die. And hadn't she? Even now, grown older than she ever was, especially now, he misses her.

And in that moment, he remembers Helen more clearly than he ever has. The beautiful young woman he'd spied through the drugstore window, her head thrown back in laughter. The tender woman he had met that first day in camp, when he'd come to trade labor for room and board. The woman whose scent had clung to the baby he held in his arms as they danced, who had kissed him. That woman, the one who had led him to the river as the snow settled around them, who had taken him inside her and then stepped into the water and been swept away.

The train's whistle drifts downriver. Manny rests his head in his hands as it passes, his breath catching in the engine's wake.

He wishes that his life made as much sense as the pistons powering the rockers that turned the wheels that pulled the load toward such sure destinations. He wishes he had held her for a moment longer, long enough to tell her all that she was, and, to him, everything.

Acknowledgments

With thanks to Robert Wrigley, my partner in invention, and our children, Philip, Jordan, and Jace. Thanks to my parents, Claudette and Oneil Barnes, for their constant belief in my work, and to Claire Davis, my sister in the faith. To my brother, Greg, who shares my love of the river, a special note of gratitude and a spot of envy: may I someday cast my line over the water with such patience and grace.

To my fellow Free Range Writers—Collin Hughes, Buddy Levy, Lisa Norris, and Jane Varley—thank you for twenty summers of hard reads and easy laughter. Buddy, here's to the hobo in all of us. To my two tall women, Jeanne Amie Clothiaux and Kelly Madonna Quinnett, another serving of venison at three a.m.

For their information, inspiration, support, and wisdom, thanks to Robert Coker Johnson, Keith Browning, and Rochelle Smith. To Kelly Blikre, Annie Lampman, Jerry Mathes, Larry Mayer, Andrew Millar, and Anesa Miller, my thanks for listening, learning, and believing. Thanks, as well, to Karen Fisher, who offered direction at the crossroads. Bryn Parker and her grandfather, Dr. George Parker, shared their insiders' view of the medical world—thank you.

Thanks to Judy Blunt for her observation of how solitude can turn to isolation, and to the University of Idaho's Department of English for allowing me time enough.

My gratitude to my agent, Sally Wofford-Girand, who enters my world with such ease and awareness, and to my editor, Jennifer Jackson: Jenny, here's to Okies, baseball, and the fathers who have given us our appreciation of both.

A chicken-basted dog biscuit to Opal, who sat at my feet and lent me her ears.

Note: Some of the references to synesthesia and the phrase "a cognitive constellation" can be found in Richard Cytowic's book *The Man Who Tasted Shapes.*